WILLA CATHER'S
SHORT FICTION

WILLA CATHER'S
SHORT FICTION

Marilyn Arnold

Ohio University Press
Athens, Ohio   London

Library of Congress Cataloging in Publication Data
Arnold, Marilyn, 1935 —
    Willa Cather's short fiction.

    Bibliography: p.
    1. Cather, Willa, 1873-1947—Criticism and interpretation. I. Title.
PS3505.A87Z56   1984   813'.52   83-13269
ISBN 0-8214-0721-X

CONTENTS

ACKNOWLEDGMENTS

I am indebted to numerous people who in various ways provided help and support in the preparation of this book. I offer thanks to colleagues and students who acted as sounding boards and made helpful suggestions, and to various typists who gave an extra measure of effort through several drafts of the manuscript. I owe particular thanks to department chairmen and deans at Brigham Young University who provided both financial and moral support along the way. Many libraries and librarians also gave generous help, notably the people associated with the Willa Cather Pioneer and Educational Foundation in Red Cloud, Nebraska. The archives in Red Cloud are now administered through the Nebraska State Historical Society. It is risky to begin naming names, but I must mention Mildred Bennett and the late Bernice Slote, two women who have come to symbolize the best in Cather scholarship. It was Mildred Bennett who, one long ago January, graciously interrupted her labors at restoring the old bank building (I believe she was laying tile) which would become the Cather Foundation headquarters. She gave me a personal tour of the Cather sites in Red Cloud, talked at length with me about Cather, and took me to visit Cather's lifelong friend (then in her nineties), Carrie Miner Sherwood (the Frances Harling of *My Ántonia*). It was Bernice Slote who on more than one occasion sat down with me and discussed my Cather writing projects, the first of which was a doctoral dissertation on the novels. Her suggestions were vital in the conception and construction of this particular book. I also give special thanks to my parents, who have always believed, in blessed defiance of reality, that their only daughter could do anything.

A few small parts of this book appeared in somewhat different form in *Research Studies,* and I wish to thank the editor of that journal for granting permission to include them here.

INTRODUCTION

Willa Cather is known best as a novelist, but it should be remembered that her novels were preceded by many years of productivity in short fiction. She was a short story writer of considerable skill, one for whom the story was a natural form of expression. She was entertaining younger brothers and sisters with oral tales long before she began writing for publication, and her novels are full of shorter tales set within the longer narratives. In spite of her ascendant reputation as a novelist, she has gained considerable recognition for a few stories known to almost everyone who reads American literature. "Neighbour Rosicky," for example, establishes her as a short story writer of great sympathy and talent. "The Sculptor's Funeral" and "Paul's Case" are also well-known and highly regarded. There are other stories of exceptional merit which are not so well-known—"Uncle Valentine," "Old Mrs. Harris," and "Before Breakfast," to name a few—mainly because Cather never gave permission for most of her stories to be anthologized. Certainly, these stories and others of similar quality rank alongside those of America's most revered writers of short fiction.

This book is designed to serve as an introduction to all of Willa Cather's short stories. The reader unfamiliar with most of the stories should find the discussions a useful overview of that significant body of Cather's work. The reader familiar with the stories will perhaps arrive at additional insights and new sources of appreciation. Some stories that have received little critical attention in the past are given full discussion, and the more familiar stories are given generous emphasis. Less important stories receive only brief comment.

The general chronological treatment preserves the natural linear design Cather created in writing the stories and gives the reader a sense of biographical continuity. One hazard of the choice for chronological design is that the discussion of most of the more important and more interesting stories is delayed until after chapter 1, and chapter 1 is, to some extent, a rather mechanical summary of Cather's early work. At any rate, the stories do not chart a step-by-step pattern of artistic growth throughout a lifetime of writing. What they show are the early efforts and rapid development of a very young writer working toward her essential methods and themes, and the final work of a practiced and polished author, with a broad range of excellences and mediocrities in between. Cather herself said in a letter to Sarah Orne Jewett (Houghton Library, Harvard University, Cambridge, Mass.) that her competence in story writing did not seem to increase with her experience. She said she was like a naked, shivering new-born baby every time. The first twenty-six stories have many high and low points, but by the time Cather published *The Troll Garden* in 1905 she was capable of writing some of the finest stories of her career.

There is profit in devoting particular study to the short stories, for they span the fifty years of Cather's writing life.[1] Her letters, of course, cover the same years and more, but a stipulation in her will forbids their publication in whole, or in part. Her first story, "Peter," was published in 1892 while she was still in college; her sixty-second and last known completed story, "The Best Years," was finished in 1945. (She was born in 1873 and died in 1947.) Willa Cather had been writing short stories for twenty years before her first novel, *Alexander's Bridge,* appeared in 1912. Her twelfth and last novel, *Sapphira and the Slave Girl,* was published in 1940. As Cather devoted more and more of her energies to the writing of novels, her short story output slowed or ceased altogether at times, but she never totally abandoned the form. The stories complement the novels and give additional range to Cather's fictional world.

For the first twenty years of her publishing career Cather was a professional journalist and teacher, and it was during those years that she produced most of her stories. While still a student at the University of Nebraska in Lincoln, she contributed to campus journals and to one or two commercial magazines. Beginning in the fall of 1893 she also wrote regular columns for two Lincoln newspapers, the *Nebraska State Journal* (hereafter cited as the *Journal*) and the *Courier,* a Lincoln weekly. These columns were largely criticism of professional dramatic and musical productions and commentaries on books, writers, and scenes about town. After college, she continued to work with magazines and newspapers, writing mainly articles and stories for popular consumption. Then she became an English teacher, still writing stories in her spare time. It was during this period that she produced *The Troll Garden* and a volume of poetry, *April Twilights* (1903). Shortly after *The Troll Garden* appeared, she left teaching to accept an editorial position with a well-known national magazine, *McClure's.* By the time she terminated her career as a professional journalist and began producing long fiction, she had published forty-six stories.

Later, Cather tended to speak disparagingly of her early work, fiction, nonfiction, and poetry alike. In an August 1913 interview published in the Philadelphia *Record* and bearing a New York dateline, she is quoted as having said of her early stories, "Those stories were so poor that they discouraged me." She did not think much of her early critical writing either. In an interview reported in the Lincoln *Daily Star*, October 1915, Cather speaks of her early newspaper writing experience as a "florid, exaggerated, foamy-at-the-mouth, adjective-spree period" which she had to get through before she could begin her real work, a period in which, like "every young writer," she had to "write whole books of extravagant language to get it out."[2] Cather apparently did not think much better of her poetry. An undated postcard from Albuquerque, New Mexico, to Elizabeth Sergeant expresses humorous regret that Sergeant had found and read a copy of *April Twilights*. When she collected her work for a Library Edition in the 1930s, Cather chose to virtually ignore most of her short stories, and she made every effort to keep them from being reprinted.

Edith Lewis, Cather's companion of many years as well as her literary executor, agrees with Cather's assessment of her early work, adding that the writing she did for newspapers and magazines only delayed the real writing. Sergeant disagrees, suggesting that Cather's years of newspaper and magazine work were useful preparation for the artist, and were by no means wasted.[3] While it is true that Cather's newspaper and magazine work sapped energy she might have channeled into lengthy pieces of fiction, she was nevertheless writing all the time; and she was writing fiction. In my estimation, Cather proved herself as an artist long before *O Pioneers!* appeared in 1913. Some of her very earliest stories have the earmarks of genius, and a good many of them before *O Pioneers!* are superb.

Like almost any young artist finding her way to her own methods and materials, Cather was influenced by writers whom she admired and enjoyed. We know that she read a great deal. Her early columns and reviews make frequent mention of writers like Kipling and Stevenson, whom she liked, as well as writers like Zola and Howells, whom she did not always like. In letters, essays, prefaces, and interviews she acknowledges that she went through a period when her work was somewhat imitative, particularly of a writer like Henry James. She indicates in the preface to her first novel, *Alexander's Bridge*, written ten years after the novel was first published, that in this book and in other early work she was using materials like those she admired in the work of others, and had not yet discovered how to convert "the material that is truly [her] own" into art. She credits Sarah Orne Jewett with advising her to turn to her "own country" for her fictional materials.[4] She herself wrote in the copy of *O Pioneers!* she gave to Carrie Miner Sherwood that when she wrote that novel she "walked off" on her "own feet" for the first time. She said, "In this one I hit the home pasture and found that I was Yance Sorgeson and not Henry James."[5] Further, in a letter to Witter Bynner she speaks of James's reaction to *The Troll Garden,* her first collection of stories.[6] Bynner had apparently called James's attention to the book, and James had responded to it with some comments that affirmed his literary philosophy to be highly compatible with Cather's. Still a young writer (the letter was probably written in 1906), Cather expresses pleasurable anxiety in the anticipation of a second letter from James regarding her work.

Important as the James influence is in some of Cather's early work, however, I continue to be impressed with just how nonimitative most of her work is. I am also impressed with the fact that, in spite of obvious relationships between the novels and short stories, the separate works do indeed have their separate lives. In fact, with a few notable exceptions, the novels seem more closely related to each other than to the stories. And often, the stories Cather produced at a certain period have little resemblance to the novels of that period. Some of the correspondences appear in works years apart. In a way, the short stories act as both bricks and mortar, substance and bonding agents, in Cather's work. They keep the city aspects of her life and character salient through the years when she was setting her novels mainly in the desert and prairie. And then, as she moved to other landscapes—Quebec and Virginia—in her novels, she kept the Nebraska experience visible through the short stories. The stories give her work continuity.

NOTES

1. Most of the stories published during Cather's first twenty years of writing are collected in Faulkner's *Willa Cather's Collected Short Fiction, 1892-1912*. The stories published from 1915 through 1929 that had not already been collected by Cather herself appear in Slote, ed., *Uncle Valentine and Other Stories: Willa Cather's Uncollected Short Fiction, 1915-1929*. Prior to the publication of these volumes, two other short volumes appeared: Bennett, ed., *Early Stories of Willa Cather;* and Kates, ed., *Five Stories: Willa Cather.* Cather herself prepared three collections, *The Troll Garden, Youth and the Bright Medusa,* and *Obscure Destinies.* A fourth, *The Old Beauty and Others,* was published posthumously.

2. These two interviews are reprinted in an appendix to Slote, *Kingdom of Art: Willa Cather's First Principles and Critical Statements, 1893-1896,* pp. 446–52.

3. Sergeant, *Willa Cather: A Memoir,* p. 3. Lewis *(Willa Cather Living,* p. 43), describes Cather's discouragement during the Pittsburgh years when he was spending her strength on journalism rather than art. Her correspondence with Sarah Orne Jewett also attests to this discouragement.

4. See Cather's preface to *Alexander's Bridge,* p. vi.

5. As Woodress *(Willa Cather: Her Life and Art,* p. 156) says, ". . .it was not actually her first hit in the home pasture. It was, however, her first home run." Slote *(The Kingdom of Art,* pp. 360–62) discusses Cather's early reading of James and reprints two columns in which Cather wrote about him.

6. The letter to Bynner, with whom Cather worked at *McClure's* for a time, is in the Houghton Library at Harvard.

ONE

Apprenticeship in Journalism: Beginnings through 1900

From 1892, when her first story appeared in print, until the end of 1900 Willa Cather published at least twenty-six short stories, and still others may yet be identified. During this period Cather was learning to write. A gifted young woman with immense potential, she learned by trying her hand at almost every kind of fiction imaginable—romance, realism, fantasy, mystery, parable, adventure, juvenilia, the occult—with mixed success. She employed every mode from the ironic to the sentimental; she experimented with drama and dialect; she used "down home" materials and exotic materials. Although many of the stories of this period are obviously apprentice work, at least two of them (both appearing in the spring of 1900), "Eric Hermannson's Soul" and "The Sentimentality of William Tavener," are outstanding accomplishments for a beginning writer, and several others show Cather's unmistakable genius for telling a tale. All of them have value for the Cather enthusiast.

I. THE COLLEGE STORIES

A. STORIES OF THE DIVIDE

Four out of Cather's first nine published short stories—the nine known stories from the Lincoln (and Red Cloud) years—are set on the Divide and show a grim picture of life there. Little in these stories predicts the idyllic views toward the land seen in some later novels and stories. Chronologically, the stories are "Peter" (first published in *The Mahogany Tree*, 31 May 1892), "Lou, the Prophet" (first published in the *Hesperian*, 14 October 1892), and "The Clemency of the Court" (first published in *Overland Monthly*, January 1896).[1]

1

So blunt is the portrayal of life on the Divide that two of Cather's protagonists, Serge Povolitchky ("The Clemency of the Court") and Canute Canuteson ("On the Divide"), and even to some extent "Lou, the Prophet," are literally elemental men, at the mercy of nature and other forces they only dimly understand. Surviving largely by instinct, these men live in an atmosphere that is almost frightening in its coarseness, violence, and frank depiction of the raw underside of human existence bereft of the cultural trappings we count on to cover our nakedness. Here on the Divide, elemental man confronts untamed nature, unmitigated evil, and terrifying violence in a daily battle for his very survival. The land is a relentless threat, a heavy sorrow that breaks the body and the spirit. Perhaps Cather was still too close to the Divide to be objective when she wrote these stories, too aware of its agony to show its promise, and too young not to exaggerate that agony. Her hyperbolic portrayal of immigrant life might have been a literary pose, for as James Woodress notes, Cather's personal letters of the same period indicate that she liked Nebraska from the beginning.[2]

The mellowing changes that occur in Cather's literary treatment of the Divide are familiar to any who have read her later work, but it is useful to compare the suicide of Peter Sadelack in "Peter" with essentially the same incident in My Ántonia.[3] Many details of the two accounts are the same, but Peter has none of the quiet refinement or the legendary quality of Ántonia's father. The mature novelist makes an appealingly heroic figure of the talented lost child of Europe whom the young storyteller had first conceived as a homesick and broken musician at the mercy of his oldest son's bullying. And although Peter is not a primitive, nearly everything about the early story is stark and bare. Stripped of all superfluity, the tale is in complete harmony with its setting where "there was nothing but sun, and grass, and sky."[4] The very style, with its rather short, mainly declarative sentences which often begin "He did," or "He had," or "He was," echoes the austerity of life on the Divide. By contrast, My Ántonia (1918) portrays the heartbreaking displacement suffered by a character like Mr. Shimerda who cannot adapt to the harsh prairie, but in the novel the counterthrust of finding home through union with the prairie land is equally strong.

The story's antagonist is Antone (he foreshadows Ambrosch in My Ántonia), who, like the landscape, is unfeeling in his cruelty and inhuman in his demands. He threatens to sell his father's beloved

violin and orders his father to violate his conscience by cutting timber on the Sabbath. It is this same Antone who, even though he is
"mean and untrustworthy," is adjudged repeatedly by the ironic narrator to be "a much better man than his father had ever been" (p.
542). What counted was that he was successful. Of his hapless father, "no one knew much, nor had any one a good word to say for
him" (p. 541). Even Peter admits that his son is a better man than
he. Out of homesickness for his own land and the things he loved
there, out of yearning to hear again the marvelous human voice of
the Frenchwoman (Sarah Bernhardt) he once heard on stage, out of
love for his violin and the Virgin Mary, and out of fear of "the Evil
One, and his son Antone" (p. 542), he "pulled off his old boot, held
the gun between his knees with the muzzle against his forehead,
and pressed the trigger with his toe" (p. 543).[5]

Again in "The Clemency of the Court" Cather uses the ironic
point of view, this time to portray society, government—whatever
constitutes "the State"—as a cold and loveless force, even more impersonal than the somber Nebraska plains. This story is Cather's
first venture into overt social criticism in her fiction, and in spite of
the narrator's overbearing irony, Cather manages to generate honest sympathy for her unfortunate protagonist. Uneducated, unloved,
orphaned as a baby, "by no will of his own or wish of his own, Serge
existed" (p. 516). Handed from one family to another, regarded more
as an animal than a human being, this ignorant, primitive orphan
believes that the State is a parent that will love him and care for
him. He feels a vague kinship with the plains that seem desolate
like himself, and likes to think of the State "as a woman with kind
eyes, dressed in white with a yellow light about her head, and a little child in her arms, like the picture of the virgin in the church" (p.
518). The only love he has ever known is centered in a little yellow
dog named Matushka, and when in a fit of anger his master cleaves
the dog's head with an axe, Serge reflexively splits the master's head
with the same axe. The idea of crime or sin never enters his mind;
his one thought is for the dog. He buries the dog and is straightway
hauled off to prison where he dons a convict's clothing, "the State's
badge of knighthood," his lawyer tells him. Clumsy at making barrel hoops, he is subjected to the torture and solitary confinement
from which he eventually dies.[6] The narrator concludes that thus
"this great mother, the State, took this wilful, restless child of hers
and put him to sleep in her bosom" (p. 522).

Canute Canuteson in "On the Divide," perhaps Cather's most striking portrait of elemental man, is a seven-foot caricature of Serge Povolitchky. Canute, like Serge, is terribly alone but stirred by deep longings for human affection. His shanty is roughly furnished with a bed "fully eight feet long" and a "chair and a bench of colossal proportions"; his shoes are "of almost incredible dimensions" (p. 493). Cather's description of Canute's desperate battle to survive may be the bleakest picture she ever painted of life on the Divide, worse even than the account of the Shimerdas' terrible privations during their first winter in Nebraska. Adopting the simplified but highly dramatic style of the oral storyteller, Cather describes Canute as "the wreck of ten winters on the Divide" where winter is feared "as a child fears night or as men in the North Seas fear the still dark cold of the polar twilight" (p. 495). Cather's monosyllabic technique augments the dry barrenness of the summers which are nearly as great a test of human endurance as the winters:

> Insanity and suicide are very common things on the Divide. They come on like an epidemic in the hot wind season. Those scorching dusty winds that blow up over the bluffs from Kansas seem to dry up the blood in men's veins as they do the sap in the corn leaves. Whenever the yellow scorch creeps down over the tender inside leaves about the ear, then the coroners prepare for active duty; for the oil of the country is burned out and it does not take long for the flame to eat up the wick. It causes no great sensation there when a Dane is found swinging to his own windmill tower, and most of the Poles after they have become too careless and discouraged to shave themselves keep their razors to cut their throats with. (P. 495)

Cather graphically depicts the plight of these men who "spent their youths fishing in the Northern seas," and now find themselves strapped to "hard work and coarse clothing and the loneliness of the plains" (p. 496). Canute's daily life is body-punishing labor modified only by the nightly ritual of drinking himself into oblivion with raw alcohol. "He drank alone and in solitude not for pleasure or good cheer, but to forget the awful loneliness and level of the Divide." Canute was "a man who knew no joy, a man who toiled in silence and bitterness," a man "mad from the eternal treachery of the plains" (pp. 496–97). In desperation one winter night, he walks the four miles to the home of his nearest neighbor and asks for the hand of Ole Yensen's spoiled and sassy daughter, Lena. She refuses, but he carries her bodily to his cabin in a driving snowstorm, then goes for the preacher. In the tenderly moving conclusion of the story, Lena cries out in fright at being alone in the cabin. Canute, who is huddled outside the cabin door after having taken the preacher home, answers her cry and offers to go for her mother or her father. She replies softly, "Canute—I'd rather have you" (p. 504). This miraculous answer to his heart's sorest need breaks the great man-beast into tears, and he falls sobbing in the snow at Lena's feet.

It is clear, however, that before love entered his life, Cather's primitive entertained a frightening conviction that the earth does indeed belong to the Devil. He hung snakeskins on the door and carved demons and serpents on his windowsills. In a gross version of the Dance of Death he depicted "men fighting with big serpents, and skeletons dancing together." The demons could be distinguished from the men because "the men were always grave and were either toiling or praying, while the devils were always smiling and dancing" (p. 494).

Although it is the work of a very young writer, "On the Divide" is convincing and moving, even powerful at times. The language of the opening paragraph testifies to the writer's skill:

> Near Rattlesnake Creek, on the side of the little draw, stood Canute's shanty. North, east, south, stretched the level Nebraska plain of long rust-red grass that undulated constantly in the wind. To the west the ground was broken and rough, and a narrow strip of timber wound along the turbid, muddy little stream that had scarcely ambition enough to crawl over its black bottom. If it had not been for the few stunted cottonwoods and elms that grew along its banks, Canute would have shot himself years ago. (P. 493)

In "On the Divide" and "Lou, the Prophet" Cather drops the angry, ironic narrative voice she had used in "Peter" and "The Clemency of the Court" and introduces instead a narrator who speaks as one who lives "in our country" (p. 540). As such, he would know only too well that loneliness and hardship can bring a person to the brink of insanity and sometimes even push him over. Lou is a young man driven to insanity by loneliness, deprivation, sorrow, and drought.

His sweetheart marries another, his mother dies, and his corn withers in the rainless summer heat. Under the strain of these disas-
ters, Lou's mind snaps, producing a vision that convinces him that
drought is a punishment for human sin. A group of small Danish
boys entrusted with herding their fathers' cattle become his disci-
ples, and when he finally disappears just a few steps ahead of the
pursuing law, the boys loyally believe he has been translated like
Enoch. Surely, Lou is an early conception of the full-blown character
of crazy Ivar in *O Pioneers!*

B. STORIES OF INTRIGUE

The other stories of Cather's Lincoln years seem less typically
Catherian, probably because the subjects, settings, and characters,
for the most part, do not reappear in her novels. Several early stories
feature Orientals, and still another is set in an unidentified eastern
land centuries ago. Cather's newspaper columns, too, give evidence
of her interest in eastern peoples and culture. An early *Hesperian*
story, "A Son of the Celestial" (15 January 1893), characterizes the
Chinese in America as people of "terrible antiquity," who, even "in
the new west, settled down and ate and drank and dressed as men
had done in the days of the flood" (p. 526). A later story, "The Conversion of Sum Loo" (1900), confirms that the Chinese remained of
interest to Cather as fictional subject matter.[7] The two stories are
different in plot and circumstance, but Cather quotes almost verba-
tim from "A Son of the Celestial" for filler material describing Sum
Chin's early life in "The Conversion of Sum Loo."

In "A Son of the Celestial," as in "The Clemency of the Court,"
Cather uses the ironic narrator to make a comment about a modern
institution. (Perhaps Cather fell naturally into an ironic stance in
her early fiction because she was using it so freely in her columns
and reviews.) This time it is not the State or its penal system she attacks, but higher education and its sometimes stuffy pedantry. The
tone of "The Conversion of Sum Loo" is lighter than that of "A Son of
the Celestial," however, for in the later story Cather enjoys a little
joke at the expense of Christians who had wrongly assumed that
their Oriental "convert" to Christianity was safely in their throng.

Another somewhat trifling, though exotically appealing, story
was published just a month earlier in the *Hesperian* (22 December
1892) under the title "A Tale of the White Pyramid." It describes a
daring deed performed by a young stranger, and cryptically suggests

a forbidden intrigue involving royalty. The beautiful youth, favored greatly by the king but not trusted by the king's people, leaps onto a slipping, tilting pyramid capstone as it is being lifted precariously into place. At great personal risk he restores its balance, saving the stone and a great many lives as well.

The three remaining published stories of Cather's Lincoln years are quite different again, though they too show her unabating interest in mystery and intrigue. "The Fear That Walks by Noonday" (*Sombrero*, 1894) is, surprisingly enough, a football story, while "A Night at Greenway Court" (first published in the *Nebraska Literary Magazine,* June 1896) and "The Elopement of Allen Poole" (*Hesperian,* 15 April 1893) deal with mystery among the historical gentry and love and death among the commoners. Supposedly prompted to write "The Fear That Walks by Noonday" by her young friend Dorothy Canfield,[8] Cather describes fullbacks and ninety-yard runs and punts as if sportswriting were her business. We soon learn, however, that ghosts, not touchdowns, are Cather's primary business, in this story and others. She began writing about ghosts in 1894 with the publication of this story, and she was still writing about them in 1900 in "The Affair at Grover Station," and again in 1915 when she published a rather Jamesian ghost story called "Consequences." In "The Fear That Walks by Noonday" the ghost of a football player fatally injured in a previous game returns to haunt his team's opponents in a rematch. Ghostly stage effects and incidents abound—icy winds, sudden punts materializing out of nowhere, impossible fumbles, a player collapsing with a seizure just a few yards short of a certain touchdown—attesting to the presence of "the twelfth man, who won the game" (p. 513). The story's protagonist, halfback Fred Horton, resembles the lonely outcasts in Cather's Nebraska stories of this period in the fact that he is a loner, an isolate. He "was awkward and shy among women, silent and morose among men," and he played football chiefly because it "made him seem like other men" (p. 510).

Still writing about loners and outcasts, Cather sets "A Night at Greenway Court" in colonial Virginia, the geographical, if not the emotional and social, territory of her childhood home. A good piece for a popular audience, the story is enhanced by its remote setting and by the noble figure of Lord Fairfax who dwells there in apparent exile. The name of Lord Fairfax appears also in Cather's last published novel, *Sapphira and the Slave Girl,* where he is identified as the patron of proud Sapphira's ancestor, Nathaniel Dodderidge. Fairfax, in the *Sapphira* account, owned millions of acres in Virginia which he deeded out to settlers for the laying out of towns. There is no suggestion in the novel, however, of the intrigue that surrounds the nobleman in this early story. The young narrator of Cather's story, like many others, wonders "why, in the prime of his manhood and success at court, Lord Fairfax had left home and country, friends, and all that men hold dear, renounced the gay society in which he had shone and his favorite pursuit of letters, and buried himself" in a wilderness home where "gentlemen who had left dark histories behind them" gathered, "where law was scarce more than a name" (pp. 486–87). One of those wilderness guests is a Frenchman, M. Maurepas, who, under the influence of too much ale, insults king, God, and Lord Fairfax. His final insult is to raise an eyebrow toward the woman in a portrait which hangs in Fairfax's house. In the ensuing duel, Maurepas is killed.

The story is packed with the standard elements of courtly intrigue—a mysterious lady, an oddly damaged portrait, a Frenchman who drinks and talks too much, a clergyman who takes more interest in a bowl of preserved cherries than in the soul's salvation, a viscount of questionable reputation, a near murder, and a duel at dawn—but it also pays homage to honor and loyalty. And Cather's applause when the narrator chooses to disgrace himself rather than disclose a "friend's secret" or imperil "a fair lady's honor" (p. 492) is probably only slightly ironic.

A somewhat earlier and less mysteriously complex story, "The Elopement of Allen Poole" is drawn directly from Cather's Virginia memories. Bernice Slote, who first identified the story as Cather's, notes that "the story contains nothing less than a capsule description and recreation of Willa Cather's Virginia home, paralleled in almost every detail by passages in *Sapphira and the Slave Girl.*"[9] It is a charming if sad story of two young lovers who, in true "Highwayman" fashion, are thwarted in their plans for elopement by the revenuers' guns. Allen Poole, who has always distilled his own liquor, and always evaded federal revenue agents, is spotted and shot the very night he was to claim his love, Nell. Fatally wounded, he stumbles his way over the countryside, falls against the chestnut tree in Nell's yard, and whistles "Nellie Bly," his prearranged signal. She comes to him in what was to have been her wedding dress, and cradles his head on her lap while he dies.

In telling this story Cather tries to represent phonetically the speech and flavor of the Back Creek/Timber Ridge area of Virginia. The dialogue is odd-sounding and somewhat distracting as this typical example illustrates: "See here, Nell, I hain't goin' to make yo' leave yo' folks, I hain't got no right to. Yo' kin come with me, or bide with 'em, jist as yo' choose, only fo' Gawd's sake tell me now, so if yo' won't have me I kin leave yo'."[10] In spite of the rather awkward rendering of dialogue, the young writer demonstrates that she can evoke a mood powerfully and draw a landscape with impressive skill: "Behind him were the sleepy pine woods, the slatey ground beneath them strewn red with slippery needles. . . . Down in the valley lay the fields of wheat and corn, and among them the creek wound between its willow-grown banks. Across it was the old, black, creaking foot-bridge which had neither props nor piles, but was swung from the arms of a great sycamore tree."[11] On the whole, "The Elopement of Allen Poole" and the other stories of Cather's college years provide a remarkably fine introduction to a young writer in whom a solid talent was manifest from the very beginning.

II. THE HOME MONTHLY STAFF STORIES

Probably on the strength of her reputation as a columnist for the *Journal,* and on the recommendation of friends, Cather was offered an editorial position with a Pittsburgh magazine, the *Home Monthly,* less than a year after she graduated from the university. In the time she worked for the *Home Monthly* (summer to summer, 1896–97), Cather published at least six short stories in that journal. Two were signed with pseudonyms, and very likely all six were written largely out of a practical need to fill space in a general magazine designed mainly for women and children.

A. TWO WESTERN STORIES

"Tommy, the Unsentimental" (August 1896), the first Cather story to appear in the *Home Monthly,* is a rather customary little piece about a capable woman who loses a man to a frilly woman. When panic starts a run on Mr. Jay Ellington Harper's little bank, Tommy (actually Theodosia) pedals her bicycle over twenty-five "rough, hilly" miles (p. 477) with enough cash to bail him out. The delicate Jessica, Tommy's friend and schoolmate from the East, the darling whom Harper adores, starts out too, for she must stand by her love in his hour of need. But predictably she wearies and falters by the way, and it is Tommy who saves him only to lose him to the one person more helpless than he.[12] We see emerging in this story the pattern of the strong female and the weaker male that appears in several of Cather's novels.

Still another story portraying a strong woman and a weak man, this time in a more serious treatment of the male-female love relationship, is the last story Cather published as an editor for *Home Monthly*. The setting for "A Resurrection" (April 1897) is Brownville, an actual town in southeastern Nebraska which Cather had featured in a lengthy article for the *Journal* three years earlier.[13] In spite of some high points in the descriptions of town and character, the piece is basically a sentimental love story, and it sags at times under the burden of popular romantic expectations. As she was to do in many later stories, Cather stresses the rare attributes of a woman bottled up by circumstances, fated to spend her life among people too dull to recognize her quality. Marjorie Pierson is "one of those women one sometimes sees, designed by nature in her more artistic moments, especially fashioned for all the fullness of life; for large experiences and the great world where a commanding personality is felt and valued, but condemned by circumstances to poverty, obscurity and all manner of pettiness." These are the "women who were made to rule, but who are doomed to serve" (p. 426). Cather obviously feels great sympathy for this woman, now past thirty, whose young life and womanly energies have been poured into the rearing of someone else's child.

As a young woman, Marjorie (Margie) had fallen in love with a river man, Martin Dempster, who jilted her to marry a wily little flirt of French extraction. When his wife drowns and his money runs out, Martin comes home in disgrace, allowing Margie to rear his child as her own. But with a turn in his fortunes Martin voices his long-repressed love for Margie. Stunned, she hesitates, but only a moment, for it is, after all, the eve of Easter; and Cather uses the resurrection motif for both its religious and personal implications. Margie, who thought all her romantic passions were asleep forever, feels them "throbbing again through the shrunken channels, waking a thousand undreamed-of possibilities of pleasure and pain" (p. 438). Both age and isolation are defeated through the resurrection of love.

B. Two Chicago Stories

"The Count of Crow's Nest," another *Home Monthly* staff story, was published serially in September and October of 1896. Stylistically respectable, it is decidedly more solid than the sentimental, completely formulaic "The Burglar's Christmas" that appeared in the December issue under the pseudonym "Elizabeth L. Seymour."[14] Both are city stories, set in Chicago, and both describe characters who have fallen from high station. The narrator of "The Count of Crow's Nest," Harold Buchanan, is a young man of supposedly great promise who so far has distinguished himself rather meagerly as an observer of life and a verbal champion of dignity and quality in life and art.[15] Buchanan lives in a less than elegant boardinghouse dubbed "the Crow's Nest" alongside a whole gallery of embittered and failing artists of questionable talent. But among them is one person who keeps himself aloof from the general spoilage, a dispossessed old nobleman, Count de Koch, who has in his possession many valuable private letters and documents of immense scandal potential among Europe's noble families. The old man lives in near poverty, by moral choice; he had nobly sold his property to pay off centuries-old family debts. His stout daughter, Helena, a coarse, loud singer in the best kitsch tradition, propositions Buchanan to get the papers from the old man, expose their contents in a book, and make a fortune for them all. Buchanan, of course, refuses, and she retaliates by stealing the papers. In the last climactic scene, the old man and Buchanan confront her and recover the papers before she and her accomplice can leave town.

The count's chief sorrow is his daughter's spiritual poverty and her estrangement from him and all that he values. As a second-generation child in the new land, she foreshadows Cather's later exploiters of the pioneer West, exemplifying the worst imaginable in blatant materialism and shabby art. A cousin to crass opportunists like Ivy Peters (*A Lost Lady*) and Bayliss Wheeler (*One of Ours*), she is beyond redemption. But the old man and Buchanan, outsiders both, have found something of value in this cold world—an answer to their loneliness in human loyalty, personal integrity, and intellectual companionship.

More than the customary popular magazine potboiler, "The Count of Crow's Nest" also reiterates fictionally what Cather was saying about art in her columns and reviews. Helena, who sings "floridly" but does not "have perception enough to know it" (p. 461), represents all that is vulgar in third-rate art. And when Buchanan complains about the quality of English writing, the Count gives a Catherian response: "Yes, you [English writers] look for the definite, whereas the domain of pure art is always the indefinite. You want the fact under the illusion, whereas the illusion is in itself the most wonderful of facts" (p. 453).[16]

Unlike "The Count of Crow's Nest," "The Burglar's Christmas" is clearly a seasonal piece in the popular mode, a sentimental, heart-warming story of a prodigal son's return home at Christmastime. Driven finally to the brink of starvation, William (last name un-known) slips into a plush mansion, intent on thieving, only to find that he has stumbled into the luxurious new home of his parents who have moved west in the hope of finding him. Cather's one seri-ous notion in the story describes the restorative capacity of love to reach out and embrace a lost child, one who was "shut off as com-pletely as though he were a creature of another species" (p. 558).

C. THREE CHILDREN'S STORIES

Although there is very little that distinguishes a piece like "The Burglar's Christmas," at least one of the two children's stories Cath-er wrote for the *Home Monthly* during her year there deserves high praise. "The Strategy of the Were-Wolf Dog" (December 1896) shows her genius for capturing the flavor of the oral tale in print. "The Princess Baladina—Her Adventure" (August 1896), on the other hand, is a rather plodding but sweet little tale. Woodress suggests that these are stories of the type that Cather used to invent for the delight of her younger brothers and sisters, and Elsie Cather's recol-lections substantiate the suggestion.[17] "The Princess Baladina," which appeared under the pseudonym Charles Douglass,[18] recounts the adventures of a little princess who goes in search of a wizard and a prince with the assistance of a respectful miller's boy who carries her on his donkey.[19] "The Strategy of the Were-Wolf Dog" is one of those "how will Santa ever deliver the toys now?" stories so popular with children at Christmastime. In it Cather captures the flavor of the faraway northland with considerable charm and stylistic ease. She describes in shivering detail this

> bleak, bitter Northland, where the frost is eternal and the snows never melt, . . . where the Heavens at night are made terribly

beautiful by the trembling flashes of the northern lights, and the green icebergs float in stately grandeur down the dark currents of the hungry polar sea. It is a desolate region, where there is no spring, and even in the short summers only a few stunted willows blossom and grow green along the rocky channels through which the melting snow water runs clear and cold. (P. 441)

The plot of the story is old, but wonderful, involving again the great White Bear that figured in so many of Cather's girlhood tales. The Bear is Santa's special helper, and Cather's narrator is a great admirer of the White Bear who he believes has been ignored in too many tales about Christmas. The Were-Wolf Dog is a reversal of the White Bear, as cruel as the Bear is gentle. The narrator's introduction of the Dog is a classic model of oral folk literature:

When all was quiet about the house, there stole from out the shadow of the wall a great dog, shaggy and monstrous to look upon. His hair was red, and his eyes were bright, like ominous fires. His teeth were long and projected from his mouth like tusks, and there was always a little foam about his lips as though he were raging with some inward fury. He carried his tail between his legs, for he was as cowardly as he was vicious. (P. 443)

On this particular occasion the wicked Were-Wolf Dog gets the jump on everyone, tricking and destroying most of Santa's reindeer in an attempt to ruin Christmas for the children of the world. But one little reindeer survives to carry the White Bear on an agonizing search for substitute reindeer. The day is saved, of course, but not until the new reindeer are shamed into helping by an old grandfather seal who volunteers to hobble the whole distance to deliver presents to the children.

One other children's story from the *Home Monthly* period, so far uncollected, has been identified by Bernice Slote as Cather's. Published 26 November 1896, it dates from the same half-year as "The Burglar's Christmas," "The Strategy of the Were-Wolf Dog," and "The Princess Baladina." The story is titled "Wee Winkie's Wanderings," and tells about a little girl who, tired of her dollies and of being told what to do by her mother, decides to run away.[20] Her mother, in an effort to teach the little one a lesson, helps her pack a few things into a handkerchief and bids her farewell. After a long day of walking and sitting on the hilltop in front of her house, Wee Winkie returns home, tired and worn. Her mother washes and feeds her little daughter and puts her to bed, and neither of them, Cather concludes, "said a word about her running away."

As Slote points out, the setting for the story is very much like that of Cather's childhood home in Virginia, the same area described in *Sapphira and the Slave Girl,* and the incident may well be autobiographical. Wee Winkie is a shortened version of Wee Willie Winkie, a nursery rhyme character. Willa herself was nicknamed "Willie" by family and close friends, and, according to Slote, Cather's cousin Bess Seymour remembers that Willa was sometimes called "Winkie."

At least one more sketch, this one in the "Editor's Talk" column of the *National Stockman and Farmer* of 24 December 1896, is attributable to Cather.[21] More an anecdote than a short story, it is told by the editor as if it happened in his (her) family. And it probably did, for the chief characters are Jim and Elsie, and they correspond in age to Cather's brother Jim and her sister Elsie a few years earlier. The little sketch describes how six-year-old Jim tried to lower four-year-old Elsie down the chimney on a rope to see if the chimney would be wide enough for Santa.

III. THE STORIES FROM THE LEADER YEARS

Cather left the *Home Monthly* and went to Nebraska in June of 1897, but it was not long before she received and accepted an offer from the Pittsburgh *Leader.* She returned to Pittsburgh in September to an assignment on the newspaper's wire copy desk, and she also began writing drama criticism regularly for the *Leader.* In addition she sent material back to Lincoln, this time to the *Courier* instead of the *Journal,* under her old column title, "The Passing Show." And she continued to write stories for the *Home Monthly* and to do a book column for that journal under the pseudonym "Helen Delay," readily repeating *Leader* and *Home Monthly* materials in the *Courier.* Cather remained with the *Leader* until the spring of 1900, doing a fair amount of traveling as well as writing during that time. In the three years after she left the *Home Monthly,* Cather published only five known stories. Evidently her journalistic activities limited the time and energy she could devote to imaginative literature. Two of these stories appeared in the *Home Monthly,* two in the *Courier,* and one in *Cosmopolitan.*

A. The Cost of Art

Regardless of their artistic merits, or lack of them, "The Prodigies" (*Home Monthly*, July 1897) and "Nanette: An Aside" (*Courier*, July 1897) are important stories. They mark Cather's solid entrance into the world she had been exploring for some time as a journalist—the world of the artist. In them the young writer contemplates the excruciating cost of art for the artist, the nature of the conflicts the artist suffers, and the isolating consequences of the artist's dedication. These themes are important in later novels, particularly *The Song of the Lark* (1915) and *Lucy Gayheart* (1935). Both stories, and especially "The Prodigies," which is the better story, argue that the price of art is too high to pay for the value received.

In "The Prodigies," two children of exceptional talent are pushed by their mother's ambition beyond the endurance of their frail bodies. The little girl collapses during a performance, her voice strained beyond repair. Even then, apparently having learned nothing, the zealous mother passes the doubled burden to the narrow shoulders of her son. Art is no paradise, Cather says, especially for the young. Nelson Mackenzie, the physician who attends the stricken child, and who had witnessed her collapse, remarks bitterly to the children's mother about their European training: "Your foreign teachers have not been content with duping you out of your money, they have simply drained your child's life out of her veins" (p. 422). Not only was Cather adamantly opposed to the exploitation of young talent, but she also argues in numerous columns that genuine artistry generally comes only with maturity.[22]

Perhaps even more disturbing to Cather than premature overtures into art was the conviction that, to a large degree, a choice for art is a choice against human society. Thea Kronborg (*The Song of the Lark*) even missed her mother's funeral to grasp an opportunity that furthered her career. But as she grew older, she realized that she had given up a great deal in terms of human relationships to be an artist. Clement Sebastian (*Lucy Gayheart*) also contemplated at length the isolation he had necessarily suffered as the price of his art. So while art is in some sense a means for transcending the world, in another sense it makes life more difficult. In "The Prodigies," the children hunger to be like other children, but they are not allowed to be. They can only longingly pretend to be "just the common children of the 'new rich' next door" (p. 421). They look jealously at children snowballing in the street, and long to go, just once, to a dog show instead of an opera. Perhaps saddest of all, the prodigies have been exploited to gratify their mother's vanity. They are castaways on art's island while she moves about in society displaying them and their hard-won prizes before eyes that envy and minds that never count the cost.

Using a device that was destined to become a trademark of her work, contrast and juxtaposition, Cather provides another set of children whose mother is envious of the "success" of the prodigies. Harriet Mackenzie, less wise than her husband, feels cheated to have borne only "thoroughly commonplace" (p. 413) children while Kate Massey was blessed with prodigies. Kate is obviously destroying her children, and Harriet apparently longs for the chance to do the same to hers, who, luckily, were born without talent.

In "Nanette: An Aside," Cather introduces for the first time in her fiction the demanding, yet self-sacrificing woman of real talent who has denied herself nearly every impulse but the one toward art. This woman was to figure in several later stories, notably, "The Diamond Mine," "A Gold Slipper," "Scandal," and "Coming, Aphrodite!" as well as in *The Song of the Lark*. "A Singer's Romance," published just three years after "Nanette" appeared, follows basically the same plot line and repeats many of the details sketched out in the earlier piece. The main difference is that the German singer in "A Singer's Romance" is good, but not magnificent, while Tradutorri in "Nanette" is one of the best. For her, art must come first; there simply are no choices any more. Madame Tradutorri is shocked to learn that her personal serving woman, Nanette, wishes to marry. She cannot imagine a choice for love rather than art. But in the end Tradutorri gives Nanette her freedom, and her blessing, admitting that "there are women who wear crowns who would give them for an hour of" the love Nanette has found (p. 410).

More important than the narrative, however, is what Cather says in this story about art and the artist. The story becomes something of an essay. Tradutorri pulls from her dressing case an opera score for which she is to sing the title role and delivers this very important speech: "You see this, Nanette? When I began life, between me and this lay everything dear in life—every love, every human hope. I have had to bury what lay between. It is the same thing florists do when they cut away all the buds that one flower may blossom with the strength of all. God is a very merciless artist, and when he works out his purposes in the flesh his chisel does not falter" (p. 410). Perhaps Tradutorri's dismissing Nanette with a self-pitying comment is melodramatic, but the point must be made: the choice for art is a choice for loneliness and a denial of nearly all the usual domestic and social satisfactions. It is a great price to be paid by a human being under any circumstances, and Tradutorri weeps "lonely tears of utter wretchedness" (p. 410).[23]

"Nanette: An Aside" is important not only as a testimonial to the cost of art and the value of human association, but also for its explicit statements, absent from "A Singer's Romance," about the performing artist. Tradutorri's greatness is described in terms of her ability to repress and wall up emotion so that what the audience perceives is "stifled pain." Tradutorri's technique, thus, is to conserve "all this emotional energy; to bind the whirlwind down within one's straining heart, to feel the tears of many burning in one's eyes and yet not to weep." "This," says Cather, "is classical art, art exalted, art deified" (p. 408). Another kind of art, perhaps equally legitimate, has for its object "the generation of emotional power; to produce from one's own brain a whirlwind." Singers who ascribe to this kind of art sing with the senses while Tradutorri sings with the soul. These "other singers" mainly "vent their suffering"; they "pour out their self-inflicted anguish" (p. 408). Cather's own remarkable restraint in her mature art, her preference for understatement, her desire "not to use an incident for all there is in it—but to touch and pass on," probably derive from these early views. It is clear that the Duse-Tradutorri style was more congenial to Cather than the Bernhardt style.[24]

But regardless of the style, for Cather genuine art, even though it may increase the artist's suffering, also helps the artist and the sensitive members of his or her audience to understand their human suffering and momentarily rise above it, even if only briefly, in fleeting comprehension of the Divine.

B. A TOUCH OF DRAMA

In her next story, "The Way of the World,"[25] Cather leaves the world of artists and becomes again the oral storyteller, cleverly reconstructing in stage play fashion a microcosmic Eden in a children's backyard playtown. Cather handles point of view superbly, blending humor and pathos through the consciousness of a narrator (or stage manager) who appears both amused and saddened, but not the least surprised, at what he reports.

The narrator is the key to the story, the detached deity, if you will. He projects himself as all-wise and much experienced, and tells his tale in the form of a parable, a modern replay of the ancient drama in Eden. We can almost imagine him as a self-possessed and still-lively grandfather, telling this story to a group of his grandsons, supposedly to educate them to the ways of women in this world, but in reality teasing them without their knowing it. To his naive audience his bias is clear; it is the old bias derived from centuries of male interpretation of Genesis: the female creature, charming though she be, is fickle and heartless and will bring man to ruin. This attitude is articulated by one of the child actors who mutters, "Girls always spoil everything a boy's got if you give 'em a chance" (p. 400). But the wizened teller of the tale appears to have grown philosophical about what he cannot change.

The backyard playtown that the boys in his tale have constructed is called Speckleville after the town's founder and leading citizen; but as a bachelor stronghold which allows no females within its borders, it is Eden (peopled with several Adams) before the appearance of Eve.[26] As Eve might have done before her, Mary Eliza approaches the privileged domain and "peer[s] at" the boys "through the morning glory vines." Tomboy though she is, the narrator says with a wink, "the instincts of her sex were strong in her, and that six male beings should dwell together in ease and happiness seemed to her an unnatural and a monstrous thing" (p. 397). Then the narrator pretends to back off, declining "to rehearse all the arts and wiles by which Mary Eliza deposed Speckle and made herself sole imperatrix of Speckleville," but "rehearsing" at least 90 per cent of them. The narrator carefully connects Mary Eliza to Eve by indicating that her first appeal to the boys was through their "stomachs," adding, "When first a woman tempted a man she said unto him, 'Eat'" (p. 400).

Dangerous though Mary Eliza is, the story's acknowledged villain is the boy from Chicago whom the narrator calls "the tragic motif" and "the heavy villain" (p. 401) of the tale. The New Boy undoes Speckleville as the serpent undid the Garden, beguiling the woman and tempting her to betrayal. With her defection the town falls apart. Notwithstanding the importance of the serpent's role, the narrator is aware that woman has, through time, born a heavy burden of blame for the fall from Eden. Ever since Mother Eve reportedly destroyed Adam's happiness and lost him the Garden, woman has been regarded by man as his nemesis. And in the tradition of his fathers Cather's narrator pretends to perpetuate the myth. He represents the Edenic experience as a prototypical one that will be repeated in various forms and settings through time, noting particularly that the advent of woman and her civilizing influence in the West has spelled the demise of the rugged frontier. The whole human race, generation after generation, will relive the fall from paradise in one form or another.

Cather's narrator puts on a good show, shaking his head and clucking his tongue over Mary Eliza's deceit, but he secretly laughs at the boys in his audience who are too naive to see beyond the popular interpretation of the Fall. As he pretends to glean valuable lessons from the Edenic myth and the form it takes in Speckleville, the narrator drops enough negative observations to tarnish the splendor of an all-male society and raise questions about the authenticity of popular interpretation of the Edenic myth. For example, we can see the narrator smiling as he introduces his flawed young Adam, an anxiety-ridden Speckle: "Indeed, cares of state were weighing heavily upon Speckle, and he had some excuse for gravity, for Speckle was a prince in his own right and a ruler of men" (p. 395). "What matter if he had to peddle milk to the neighbor women at night? . . . Tomorrow he was the founder of a city and a king of men" (p. 397)! With the same gentle irony the narrator discloses how it happens that the town is in Speckle's backyard and that Speckle holds "all the important offices in the town." It seems, he says, that "Speckle's folks had been farming people, and regarded their backyard as the natural repository for such encumbrances as were in the way in the house; and Speckle was among them" (p. 396). We learn further that Speckle is a loan shark and that all the boys but one have weaknesses Speckle can exploit to get their approval of Mary Eliza. And we watch these once adamant males fall at her feet when she introduces smiles and sweets into Speckleville. We cannot forget, either, that the most sinister character in this drama is a male.

The narrator, then, uses his little production to reveal that he does not accept the standard interpretation of the Adam and Eve story. Both male and female in his drama willingly turn their Garden into a marketplace, and in so doing lose their youth and innocence as the opening verse of the poetic epigraph to the story testifies:

> O! the world was full of the summer time,
>   And the year was always June,
> When we two played together
> In the days that were done too soon. (P. 395)

And in spite of the narrator's good-natured horseplay, he knows that the loss of youth and innocence can leave a vacuum of loneliness as well as a head full of troubling knowledge.

Cather's next published piece, a trifling little dramatic sketch, has none of the cleverness and sensitivity exhibited in "The Way of the World." "The Westbound Train" (*Courier,* 30 September 1899), published while Cather was still with the *Leader,* is just slightly more consequential than the two juvenile dialogues that survive from her campus years in Lincoln.[27] The setting for "Westbound Train" is a railway station at Cheyenne, the plot a case of mistaken identity. Mrs. Sybil Johnston arrives to pick up passes only to discover that a Mrs. S. Johnson has already picked them up. This little sketch is either deliberate farce or an unsuccessful comic psychological venture which brings a woman into an unnerving confrontation with her presumptuous and snooty alter ego.

C. A PROMISE FOR THE FUTURE

Published just a few months after "The Westbound Train," "Eric Hermannson's Soul" (*Cosmopolitan,* April 1900) is a significant piece of work, blending tensions and conflicts from several sources into a complex weave of religious and sexual impulses. An important forerunner of Cather's prairie novels and later stories, this story, like Cather's earliest Nebraska stories, describes the Divide as a harsh world for Europe's lost children. The narrator grieves that the "arid soil and . . . scorching sun" have burned the more delicate responses out of "those Norwegian exiles," and that one could "watch the light die out" (p. 369) of their eyes and see a heavy shadow fall over them. This is the landscape of the opening section of O Pioneers!, savage and unyielding, but without even the promise of a munificent future in the care of a human heart that loves it. The plodding Oscar Bergson could almost have stepped out of the setting of "Eric Hermannson's Soul."

And if the land does not destroy a person's spirit, the unctuous Free Gospellers do, twisting religion into a punishing travesty of true worship. Cather of course presents some very positive images of religious devotion in books like *Death Comes for the Archbishop* (1927) and *Shadows on the Rock* (1931). But in *One of Ours* (1922) the spirit of the Free Gospellers finds muted expression in the religious attitudes of Brother Weldon and those who attend and administer the affairs of the Temple school where Claude Wheeler is unhappily enrolled. And like Eric Hermannson, Claude is one of the faltering "bad ones" who resists public conversion and a religion in which, as Claude observes, "the noblest could be damned . . . while almost any mean-spirited parasite could be saved by faith."[28] Pitiful as they are, the Free Gospellers are not without influence. Even Eric, wildest boy on the Divide, would eventually smash his beloved violin, "the final barrier between Eric and his mother's faith" (p. 361), and follow the holy and joyless life God seemed to require of him. The coming of Margaret Elliot from the East changes Eric's resolve, however. Forbidding himself the luxury of self-delusion, Eric willingly damns his soul, as he believes, for one night of music and dancing with her before she slips out of his life forever.

Implicit in Margaret Elliot's presence on the Divide is the East-West tug-of-war that was to characterize Cather's fiction and her life for years to come.[29] "Eric Hermannson's Soul" is important as the first of Cather's stories to portray this conflict, a conflict that would surface repeatedly in her novels. Beginning with *O Pioneers!* Cather creates a whole string of narratives that chronicle the struggles of sensitive, prairie-born characters who yearn for the advantages of the East's more civilized lifestyle, but who nevertheless have the more vital, if cruder, West in their blood.

Cather portrays this conflict graphically in this story by contrasting Margaret's absent fiancé against Eric, and by showing Margaret torn between them. The easterner enters the story by means of a letter, perfectly timed. It arrives on the heels of a frightening experience with wild horses in which Eric, through brute strength and courage and love, saves Margaret from certain injury or even death. Written by a man with "drooping shoulders, high white forehead and tight, cynical mouth" (p. 375), the letter, predictably, is an affected parcel of drivel. Ostensibly a love letter, it begins: "My Dearest Margaret: If I should attempt to say *how like a winter hath thine absence been,* I should incur the risk of being tedious. Really, it takes the sparkle out of everything. Having nothing better to do, and not caring to go anywhere in particular without you, I remained in the city until Jack Courtwell noted my general despondency. . ." (p.

373). Cather juxtaposes this insipid, self-conscious, sexless chatter against Eric's capacity for action and his vibrating, ingenuous avowal of love. Having determined that Margaret is unharmed from her encounter with the mustangs, Eric delivers an impassioned, rawly poetic speech that also shows damningly the difference between an elemental feeling for language and a precious taste for the artificial frippery that sometimes passes for clever writing:

> But if they [the mustangs] had hurt you, I would beat their brains out with my hands, I would kill them all. I was never afraid before. You are the only beautiful thing that has ever come close to me. You came like an angel out of the sky. You are like the music you sing, you are like the stars and the snow on the mountains where I played when I was a little boy. You are like all that I wanted once and never had, you are all that they have killed in me. I die for you tonight, tomorrow, for all eternity. I am not a coward; I was afraid because I love you more than Christ who died for me, more than I am afraid of hell, or hope for heaven. (P. 372)

When deeply moved, Eric finds speech beyond his ordinary capabilities. The immensity of his declaration of love is better appreciated by the reader than by Margaret Elliot, who would not understand Eric's religious commitment. But her "slow smile" at her fiancé's letter indicates that the difference between the two expressions of love, and between the two men, has not been lost on her.

The content of the letter as well as its style addresses the subject of art, another favorite Cather topic, and further reveals the duality in Margaret's nature. One paragraph describes two pictures which her fiancé has purchased. In the first, by Puvis de Chavannes, "A pale dream-maiden sits by a pale dream-cow and a stream of anemic water flows at her feet." The other picture, by Benjamin Constant, is characterized by "its florid splendor, the whole dominated by a glowing sensuosity" (p. 373). The pale picture is, of course, *his* favorite; he bought the voluptuous one because Margaret liked it. Beneath Margaret's civilized veneer is an elemental passion which heretofore had found expression only in such things as her taste in art. But it shows up now in the attraction she feels toward Eric whom she regards as a Sigfried of the plains. Carrying in her blood the primitive strain of "some lawless ancestor" (p. 375), she is thus clearly related to Bartley Alexander (*Alexander's Bridge*), Marie Shabata (*O Pio-*

neers!), Clara Vavrika ("The Bohemian Girl"), Thea Kronborg, and Godfrey St. Peter.

In still other ways the concern of "Eric Hermannson's Soul" for art, places it at the thematic center of Cather's work. Even for Eric, a semibarbarian on the scorching prairie, the yearning toward art becomes an expression of the desire for spiritual succor: "In the great world beauty comes to men in many guises, and art in a hundred forms, but for Eric there was only his violin. It stood, to him, for all the manifestations of art; it was his only bridge into the kingdom of the soul" (p. 361). And when Margaret plays the organ and sings for him, he is touched so deeply that he can verbalize for the first time his love for his little crippled brother now dead.

Cather's integrative handling of statements about art indicate an impressive achievement in technique in this work. Also impressive are her multiple use of incident and image and her careful control of rhetoric. The wild horse episode, for example, has significance beyond the contrast it engenders between Eric and Margaret's city man. It serves also to underline the turmoil that Margaret's coming has generated in Eric's Free Gospel-chastened soul and the turmoil that the prairie and Eric's primitive magnetism have generated in hers. Like the little horse newly broken to the saddle and highly susceptible to the ebullience of the mustangs, Eric finds that Margaret has awakened his deepest and truest yearnings—for music, for power, for love. All of his bottled-up passion comes roaring to the surface, and he dances with her though he burn in hell for it. She, too, is aroused. But as with the mustangs, Eric and Margaret's impassioned experience together is short-lived, leaving "as suddenly as it had come," sweeping in a "struggling, frantic wave of wild life . . . up out of the gulch and on across the open prairie" (p. 372).

If Cather's language sometimes seems overexuberant, there is nevertheless ample evidence that she is working by conscious design and with no little skill. There are three moments of climax in the story in addition to the horse incident, and at each of these moments, Cather adjusts the volume of her rhetoric to an appropriate level. The first climactic moment occurs when Eric elects to cast his lot with the Free Gospellers, renouncing his only pleasures, music and dancing. At the crucial moment of conversion he breaks his violin. The language reflects rising emotion, but is nevertheless precise and clean: "Eric Hermannson rose to his feet; his lips were set and the lightning was in his eyes. He took his violin by the neck and crushed it to splinters across his knee, and to Asa Skinner the sound was like the shackles of sin broken audibly asunder" (p. 362). The next moment of climax occurs when Eric agrees to dance with Margaret at her final party. She has no idea what she is asking him, and he fully believes that he is assenting to his own damnation. When she asks, he answers simply and quietly, though his eyes are flashing, "Yes, I will." But "he believed that he delivered his soul to hell as he said it" (p. 371). Here the emotion of the moment emerges through understatement. In the final climactic scene at the dance, Eric and Margaret have climbed the windmill tower. Nearly spent from excitement and inner turmoil, Margaret responds to instincts deep within her, and the once sarcastic narrator grows eloquent: "This woman, on a windmill tower at the world's end with a giant barbarian, heard that cry tonight, and she was afraid! Ah! the terror and the delight of that moment when first we fear ourselves. Until then we have not lived" (p. 377).

Every incident in the story has been building toward that moment on the tower, as if it were inevitable from the first time Margaret and Eric saw each other. Eric's is the ancient story of damnation and salvation, and he misinterprets its meaning. To him, his conversion to holiness is symbolized by the smashing of his violin, and his return to "evil" is signaled by his taking up that devil's instrument to play at the dance, and by his dancing with a woman. His damnation, he thinks, is confirmed by the kiss he and Margaret exchange on the windmill tower. While the reader understands that the two mortals are at this moment in tune with the universe, answering an urge that comes from "the bottom of things, warming the roots of life" (p. 377), Eric believes that he will pay for this night in hell, and he almost savagely exults in the prospect: "Ah, there would be no quailing then! If ever a soul went fearlessly, proudly down to the gates infernal, his should go. For a moment he fancied he was there already, treading down the tempest of flame, hugging the fiery hurricane to his breast" (p. 378).

Then suddenly the tempest ceases, as if a sexual climax has passed. The subdued rhetoric signals the change: "It seemed but a little while till dawn" (p. 378). Margaret boards the carriage that points her eastward, and Eric prepares for the day's work. Asa Skinner appears on schedule, but his convert is impervious to him. Eric's conviction that he has irrevocably lost heaven, that he has exchanged heaven for this one night, extricates him from Skinner's strangling grasp. If Margaret had not come, Eric might have shriveled into a joyless, guilt-ridden Free Gospeller. Regardless of his assumptions about the state of his soul, we perceive that by renouncing Asa Skinner's brand of religious piety, by answering the basic urges of creation, and by sacrificing himself for love and beauty's sake, Eric has found, not lost, his soul. He is calm, even cheerful, in the face of Asa Skinner's accusations.

Clearly, the story ends more positively than it had begun. In spite of their sorrow there remains in Eric and his fellow immigrants "something of the joyous childhood of the nations which exile had not killed" (p. 374). And for Eric, one breath of paradise is enough to offset countless millenia of suffering in both earth and hell. Margaret, on the other hand, may never achieve Eric's calm, but she leaves the prairie knowing more about herself than she did when she came. Her brush with elementalism has stirred the youth self in her toward almost uncontrollable desires. It is therefore Margaret again, even more than Eric, who adumbrates characters in Cather's later work, characters who are driven by desires they do not always understand. Margaret is one of those eternally restless souls who ache with the "desire to taste the unknown which allures and terrifies." She wants "to run one's whole soul's length out to the wind—just once" (p. 363), the same restless urge that visits Thea Kronborg on countless summer nights in Moonstone, Colorado.

"Eric Hermannson's Soul" is an important story in the Cather canon, something of a culmination of her earlier work and a promising introduction to her later work. If for no other reason than that she produced this story in her years with the *Leader,* those years were important in her development as an artist.

IV. *THE* LIBRARY *STORIES*

Cather resigned from her position with the *Leader* in the spring of 1900, and in the next few months published several stories in the *Library,* a Pittsburgh literary magazine of short life published by Charles Clark. George Seibel writes rather sarcastically about the magazine and his own connection with it, indicating that it was conceived when Clark found himself in possession of a $20,000 gift and decided that Pittsburgh needed a literary journal. Seibel says that he and Cather, who were good friends, began writing for Clark in exchange for "chunks of Chick's uncle's or grandma's coin."[30] Of the

five *Library* stories identified and collected, two, "The Affair at
Grover Station" and "The Sentimentality of William Tavener," deserve lasting attention.

A. Two Murder Stories

"The Dance at Chevalier's" (*Library*, 28 April 1900) and "The Affair at Grover Station" (*Library*, 16 June 1900) both develop murder plots; the latter even depicts the return of the victim's ghost.
"The Dance at Chevalier's" is a slight piece, probably entertaining
enough if told aloud, but rather thin and almost juvenile. "The Affair at Grover Station," on the other hand, is a skillfully wrought
mystery story, not as good as Cather's more mature work, but having considerable merit.

Through the symbolic use of dancing Cather creates a link between "Eric Hermannson's Soul," "The Dance at Chevalier's," and
"The Affair at Grover Station." Each of the stories features a dance,
and each dance is conducted at a different level of social sophistica-
tion. The first is a Norwegian dance, the second a French, and the
third an American inaugural ball. The Norwegian dance is a rather
primitive affair, soul-stirring, if coarse. The Chevalier dance, however, is much brighter, for the French immigrants are not so dehu-
manized by their battles with the soil as are their Norwegian counterparts. Nevertheless, Cather's narrator cannot help noting that
these folks, though livelier, are anything but pure French; their
blood is an impure mixture of French, Canadian, and Indian ("red
squaw") sources. In fact, the narrator regrets, they retain their
Frenchness only in "their names, and their old French songs, and
their grace in the dance" (p. 551). Finally, in "The Affair at Grover
Station," when the Anglo-Saxons throw a dance, frontier amenity
reaches its peak. The event described, the inaugural ball for the governor of Wyoming, requires formal attire and flowers for the wom-
en.[31]

"The Dance at Chevalier's" never rises above the popular piece it
is advertised to be in its opening lines: "It was a dance that was a
dance, that dance at Chevalier's, and it will be long remembered in
our country" (p. 547). Nevertheless, it foreshadows the much happier Catholic fair sponsored by the French immigrants in *O Pioneers!*
This story develops a standard love triangle plot with Denis, the
handsome primitive Irishman, vying against the evil "Signor" for
the affections of the beautiful Severine Chevalier. The Signor gives
Denis a poison drink, blackmails the French beauty into granting

him a kiss before Denis's incredulous eyes, and then rides off into the night. With the poison coursing through his body, Denis dances a final dance with Severine, a grotesque rendering of the Dance of Death. He dies believing her unfaithful. As strictly a folk tale, the story might have succeeded. The Signor's slow poison is straight out of folk literature, home brewed according to a recipe from "an old, withered Negro from the gold coast of Guinea." But Cather does not sustain the story's oral folk atmosphere; the storyteller tends to drift in and out, now controlling the narrative, now relinquishing control.

In some sense, "The Affair at Grover Station," a story which prefigures Cather's repeated use of railroad workers and incidents in her novels, also features a dance of death. While the victim's friends are dancing, he is killed and hidden in a box car.[32] The plot is similar to that of "The Dance at Chevalier's" with a devilish rejected suitor killing his rival in love. Larry O'Toole, a railroad man from up the line, was to have made Cheyenne on a late train and escorted the lovely Miss Masterson to the governor's ball. When he fails to appear, his good friend "Terrapin" Rodgers, narrator of the murder tale, worriedly calls for Miss Masterson, assuring her that O'Toole must be coming on a later train. O'Toole, of course, never comes. The villainous Freymark arrives very late at the dance, "effusively gay" (p. 344), but interrupted in his attentions to Miss Masterson by the appearance of O'Toole's wounded dog who throws himself howling at Freymark's feet. The next morning at Grover Station, stymied in his search for clues, Rodgers falls into an exhausted sleep in the railroad office where O'Toole worked. He wakes in paralyzed terror to see the dead man's ghost, in formal attire, scratching the vital clue to his body's whereabouts on the chalkboard. When the body is found, it is not difficult to tie the murder to the nefarious Freymark.

Not only is the plot intriguing, but the whole production, and it is a production, is handled with impressive grace. The opening sentence is nearly perfect as the narrator of the frame story sets the stage: "I heard this story sitting on the rear platform of an accommodation freight that crawled along through the brown, sun-dried wilderness between Grover Station and Cheyenne" (p. 339). No laborious dredging up of suspense here, no self-conscious storytelling; only the solid, but plastic, style of a teller sure of his tale and a writer sure of her craft. Exercising an infallible sense of pace, Cather and her narrator take time to set the mood, to draw Rodgers out, and to allow him ample room to tell the story however he wishes.[33] With calculated restraint, the narrator introduces Rodgers and relates his

tale, withholding none of the horrors but underplaying them to just
the right degree. With Poe-esque deliberateness the plot advances
step by logical step toward the final climactic detail—the revelation
that the corpse of the murdered man, when finally found, has blue
chalk dust on the fingers of its right hand.

B. A Solid Achievement

A story of this period which bears little resemblance to those just
described is a short but excellent piece called "The Sentimentality of
William Tavener" (*Library,* 12 May 1900). It charts briefly and quietly the awakening of a long dormant tenderness between a married
couple grown distant through many years of husk-building habits.
Accustomed to an almost adversary relationship in which his wife
has regularly aligned herself against his implacability as an advo-
cate for her sons, William Tavener denies the boys money and permission to attend the circus the next day. But the occasion has
seeded fertile ground, and that night the two adults find themselves
exchanging memories of a long ago circus. Softened by their newfound consonance, he pulls out ten dollars so that the boys can build
a few of their own circus memories. The boys indeed get their wish,
but they realize that something has changed. In their mother's unexpected admonition not to waste their father's hard-earned money
is the revelation that "they had lost a powerful ally" (p. 357).

Cather's growing sense of how much to say and how much to leave
unsaid, her increasing skill at delineating a character with one
stroke, her almost uncanny ability to define a relationship with a
single apt observation, and her marvelous feeling for low-keyed humor are evident. For example, in the scene where William Tavener
sits calmly refusing to acknowledge the agitation of his wife and the
moodiness—even muffled sobs—of his sons on the eve of the circus,
Cather captures the man with one sentence: "But William Tavener
never heeded ominous forecasts in the domestic horizon, and he never looked for a storm until it broke" (p. 354). Similarly, one sentence
tells us a great deal about his wife Hester: "The only reason her husband did not consult her about his business was that she did not
wait to be consulted" (p. 353). Beneath the hard rock of their individual inexorability, however, we divine an immense well of mutual regard: "William set his boys a wholesome example to respect their
mother. People who knew him very well suspected that he even admired her" (p. 353). The almost miraculous resurrection of that old
set of long-forgotten feelings is lovely, but Cather reminds us that

some things lost cannot be wholly restored. There are wasted years of emptiness that cannot be recovered and filled. Hester's somewhat pensive joy at meeting her husband again on old grounds is marred by "a painful sense of having missed something, or lost something" (p. 357) over all those lonely years when they had merely lived together like "landlord and tenant" (p. 356).

Set in farming country and describing people who might well have been Virginia-born relatives of the Burdens in *My Ántonia,* "The Sentimentality of William Tavener" is familiar material for Cather, and she uses it readily and gladly. A fine companion piece to "Eric Hermannson's Soul," it reveals another aspect of life on the Divide. While "Eric Hermannson's Soul" abounds in fiery, elemental passion, this story concentrates quietly on habitual human relationships. Calm and yet deep, "The Sentimentality of William Tavener" suggests a new solidity, a gentle tone that would be felt again in the stories of Ántonia and Rosicky and Bishop Latour.

The other two stories of the *Library* group, "A Singer's Romance" and "The Conversion of Sum Loo," were described earlier in connection with stories treating similar materials.

Thus in these groups of early stories, produced by the young journalist in Nebraska and Pittsburgh, lie the seeds for a rich art that was already showing its genius. In these earliest stories Cather is, for the most part, the observer who maintains a distant, rather impersonal perspective. Willa Cather, the developing artist, is in these stories, but Willa Cather, the woman, generally is not. Here she observes the phenomena, the human race struggling through its sentence of exile, and reports it. As yet, she herself is not in the struggle, but she is beginning to understand its terms. And she is beginning to see the loss of Eden as something of a total metaphor for describing human experience. The barren landscape and the lonely human being are the dominant images in the more serious of the stories. And while their basic movement chronicles loss, they chart a countermovement of recovery, of search for the Eden that has been lost—or of search for the human relationships and values that can reconcile humankind to its loss. In the next group of stories there is a noticeable change in perspective as Cather continues to develop her basic theme. In some of the *Troll Garden* stories, she shortens the distance between herself and some of her characters. She begins to care in a more personal way about them and about her subject matter.

NOTES

1. "Peter" was apparently edited lightly by Cather's English teacher, Herbert Bates, and sent off for publication without her knowledge. The *Hesperian* was a student magazine at the University of Nebraska, and the *Sombrero* was the University's yearbook. The *Mahogany Tree* and *Overland Monthly* were commercial journals.

2. Woodress, *Willa Cather: Her Life and Art,* p. 60. Slote in "Willa Cather as a Regional Writer," p. 10, observes that "Willa Cather's stories have at least a double view of the new world, and sometimes even greater complexity.

3. Bradford ("Willa Cather's Uncollected Short Stories," pp. 540–41) makes such a comparison, noting particularly the differences between Ántonia's "gentle father" and the "drunken, dirty old man named Peter Sadelack."

4. Faulkner, *Willa Cather's Collected Short Fiction,* p. 542. Unless otherwise noted, all page references to stories through 1912 are from this volume as previously documented (page references are in parentheses in the text). I am also indebted to Mildred Bennett's introduction to this volume and to the editor, Virginia Faulkner, for other facts and dates pertinent to these stories.

5. Francis Sadilek, Annie's (Ántonia's) father, apparently committed suicide in just this way. Cather heard the story many times after she arrived in Nebraska.

6. Bohlke ("Beginnings: Willa Cather and 'The Clemency of the Court,'" pp. 138–43) discusses the similarities between the details in Cather's story and those surrounding the death of a convict as reported and editorially exercised in the *Journal* early in 1893 when Cather was in her sophomore year at the University of Nebraska. The event caused quite a scandal and an intense investigation of punitive practices at the Nebraska State Penitentiary at Lincoln.

7. In Faulkner, *Willa Cather's Collected Short Fiction,* p. 481, "Conversion of Sum Loo" is described as a reworking of "Son of the Celestial."

8. Ibid.

9. Slote, *Kingdom of Art,* p. 104. On a strict chronology this story comes between "Son of the Celestial" and "Clemency of the Court." It appears unsigned in the *Hesperian* of 15 April 1893, and is reprinted in appendix 2 of *Kingdom of Art,* pp. 437–41, as well as in the revised edition of Faulkner's *Willa Cather's Collected Short Fiction.* In an editing note, p. 437, Slote suggests that the fact that Cather was literary editor of the *Hesperian* at this time may explain why the story does not bear her signature. In her introduction to *The Kingdom of Art,* pp. 104–206, Slote discusses the obvious connections between the contextual details of this story and Cather's Virginia background, as well as connections with Cather's later fiction.

10. Slote, *Kingdom of Art,* p. 437.

11. Ibid., p. 438.

12. *Tommy* suggests a scant likeness to the young Willa Cather. She is a bit mannish, and she is more at home among the old men of the town than among the young.

13. For the Brownville article as it appeared in the *Journal,* 12 August 1894, see Curtin, *The World and the Parish,* pp. 102–12. Some details from Cather's visit there also appear in a 1900 article in the *Library,* titled "The Hottest Day I Ever Spent." Cather signed this piece with a pseudonym, "George Overing." See Curtin, *World and the Parish,* pp. 778–82. Mariel Gere, a friend of Cather's who visited Brownville with her to gather material for the article, wrote to Mildred Bennett in a letter dated 6 February 1956, of her embarrassment at the rather brash young Cather's "journalistic" methods. Cather on that occasion apparently sought out examples of deterioration rather than points of pride. Mariel Gere worried over the disappointment the article must have been to the governor and the local people who thought they were going to get some lovely publicity out of Cather's visit. One incident in particular distressed Mariel. Cather reportedly piled all the kneeling benches in one end of a chapel she visited, and asked Mariel to photograph the room that way. (Letter in Nebraska State Historical Society archives in Lincoln.)

14. Elizabeth L. Seymour is one of several pseudonyms that Cather used in the early years of her career. Like some others, it is derived from a family name, in this instance the name of a cousin, Bess Seymour, who stayed in the Cather home in Red Cloud. For a discussion of Cather's journalistic pseudonyms, see Hinz, "Willa Cather in Pittsburgh," pp. 190–207. Faulkner, in *Willa Cather's Collected Short Fiction,* describes the pseudonyms briefly (p. 546) and indicates that Hinz was sometimes in error (p. 593).

15. Buchanan is a forerunner of the peripheral character-narrator who appears several times in Cather's later work. Jim Burden is the most obvious example of the type.

16. Cather's oft-quoted statement in "The Novel Démeuble" describes what she in some measure achieved in her own work as she matured as an artist: "Whatever is felt upon the page without being specifically named there—that, one might say, is created. It is the inexplicable presence of the thing not named, of the overtone divined by the ear but not heard by it, the verbal mood, the emotional aura of the fact or the thing or the deed, that gives high quality to the novel or the drama, as well as to poetry itself." The essay is printed in two collections of Cather essays, *Willa Cather On Writing* and *Not Under Forty.*

17. Woodress, *Willa Cather: Her Life and Art,* p. 82. Mildred Bennett, who identified "The Strategy of the Were-Wolf Dog," tells of mentioning her discovery to Cather's younger sister, Elsie, and of Elsie's excitement over it. Elsie later wrote to Mrs. Bennett that she remembered hearing the story when she was a child; it was another of the much-loved White Bear tales

that Roscoe and Willa used to tell to the other Cather children. Elsie was too young to have heard the story from Willa, but Roscoe repeated to the younger Cather children the stories he and Willa had told to the others years before. See Bennett, "A Note on . . . The White Bear Stories," p. 4.

18. According to Faulkner (*Willa Cather's Collected Short Fiction*, p. 546), the pseudonym "Charles Douglass" is a combination of the first names of Cather's father Charles and her brother Douglas. At Cather's request, apparently, Douglas adopted her spelling preference and began adding a second "s" to his name. This double "s" spelling appears again in the story, "The Treasure of Far Island."

19. *Century* and *Harper's* both ran serial stories about princesses in 1895 which drew Cather comment in the *Journal*. Perhaps she decided to join the fray with her own princess story. For excerpts from Cather's *Journal* remarks, see Curtin, *World and the Parish,* pp. 152–53.

20. The story first appeared in the *National Stockman and Farmer,* a weekly which listed the same address as the *Home Monthly,* and for which Cather apparently also wrote while she was with the *Home Monthly.* The page titled "Our Young Folks" seems to have been her particular responsibility, for the material on that page in 1896–97 bears her stamp. This is explained by Slote in a short introduction to the reprinted story and in her essay, "Willa Cather: The Secret Web," delivered at the Merrimack Symposium and published in Murphy, *Five Essays on Willa Cather,* pp. 5–8. The story was first reprinted in *Vogue* (June 1973), p. 113, with a note by Slote.

21. This sketch is reprinted with "Wee Winkie's Wanderings" and is also introduced by Slote.

22. In an 1895 column in the *Courier,* however, Cather writes of being enthralled by the performance of the Dovey sisters, ages ten and twelve, who are apparently the sources for the slightly older children in "The Prodigies" (see Slote, *Kingdom of Art,* pp. 146–49). A week later in a column on Josef Hofmann, a young pianist who returned to America to thrill concertgoers a second time, Cather makes a more typical comment. She offers her congratulations that Hofmann is no longer a prodigy. She says, "As long as he was a prodigy he could never be an artist, indeed not a musician even. There have been certain great men, Mozart and Paganini chief among them, who have been able to live down the fact that they were once prodigies, but they had to be great indeed to do it." For Cather there was even something grotesque about a child's performance. She spoke of it as a "sacrilege to childhood" and a "blasphemy to art" (*Courier,* 26 October 1895; Curtin, *World and the Parish,* pp. 185–86; and Slote, *Kingdom of Art,* pp. 148–49).

The whole subject of the youthful artist is an interesting one, for while Cather was a young woman, and even as late as 1925 when she published "Uncle Valentine," she seemed to feel that with few exceptions, like those of Alexandre Dumas, who began doing great work at age twenty, and the

Menuhin children whom she met in 1930, significant artistic achievement comes only with age and experience. The Dovey sisters are precious and extraordinary, but who can tell whether or not they will eventually be true artists? Time after time Cather quotes Helena von Doenhoff: "Art does not come at sixteen." Speaking of singers, Cather says that an artist does not arrive at a full realization of self until after age thirty (*Journal*, 27 January 1895; Curtin, *World and the Parish*, p. 175). In these early columns Cather worries over youngsters who become performers too early, who "go too soon into an artificial atmosphere, an atmosphere where there is no time for silence and reflection and in which study is unknown" (*Courier*, 26 October 1895; Curtin, *World and the Parish*, p. 186). She has especially strong opinions about youthful novelists. In a *Journal* column in October 1894, she says, "The practice of youthful novel writing has done as much as any other one thing to weaken and vitiate literature. The notion seems to have gone abroad that a man can write before he has lived . . ." (Curtin, *World and the Parish*, p. 131). Still later, in May of 1895, she stresses again that one must live before one can write. She insists that "glorious and beautiful" as youth is when it is sincere, it cannot produce great novels.

   23. Cather certainly saw both sides of this issue, and displayed at least some ambivalence toward an exclusive choice for art. Sometimes she seemed to suggest that the gifted artist had an obligation to give all for art, and other times she applauded the artist who turned aside from art in favor of love and domesticity. In a *Journal* column (27 January 1895) she speaks regretfully of Helena von Doenhoff's choice for marriage and bids her a somewhat sarcastic "long farewell." Admitting that "the lonely and homesick time of life" is apt to come on a great singer in her early thirties, Cather says that the only "thing that can save her" is her loving "art better than success." Cather insists that "in art it is only the player who stakes all who wins, and that complete self-abnegation is the one step between brilliancy and greatness, between promise and fulfillment. If Doenhoff were a few years younger she might afford to take a few years off to dabble in matrimony, but she is now at the crisis where a slackening of the tension means the end" (Curtin, *World and the Parish*, pp. 175–76). In later columns, however, Cather pays a tribute to Mary Anderson who retired from the stage and married happily. Cather speaks admiringly of this woman who exemplified "the charms of wise and noble living, which is the highest art of all. . . ." She describes the kinds of things a great artist can call up in an audience and then says, "There is only one thing greater—to give them up. Many have been bold enough to win glory, but few have been strong enough to renounce it. Having won the best the world has to give, then to quietly put away all the glamour and brightness and intoxication of it because there is still a higher life unfilled, to have been a queen and then to be merely a woman, that is indeed greatness. It was Anderson's greatest creation" (*Journal*, 21 July 1895; Curtin, *World and the Parish*, pp. 201–2). Nearly a

year later Cather qualifies this statement by praising Mary Anderson Navarro as a person, but lamenting the loss art suffered through her defection. Navarro, she says, had the good sense to estimate the rewards of a life dedicated wholly to art at their true value and turn her back on them and live her life. "It was this clear vision, this correct estimation of the values of things that ennobled her as a woman and sadly limited her as an artist. . . . If all artists could end so it would be happy indeed for them, but sad, sad for art" (*Journal*, 3 May 1896; Slote, *Kingdom of Art*, p. 158; and Curtin, *World and the Parish*, p. 202).

Cather was to return to this theme again and again in her columns and in her fiction. Especially eloquent in her praise of actress Eleanora Duse, Cather points to Duse's awareness of "the loveliness and lovelessness and desolation of art. Of the isolation . . . of all creative genius. Of the loneliness which besets all mortals who are shut up alone with God. Of the gloom which is the shadow of God's hand consecrating his elect." Speaking of genius, Cather says, "Solitude, like some evil destiny, darkens its cradle, and sits watching even upon its grave. It is the veil and the cloister which keep the priesthood of art untainted from the world" (*Journal*, 16 June 1895; Curtin, *World and the Parish*, p. 208).

24. Cather describes this same dichotomy of style in a column that compares Eleanora Duse and Sarah Bernhardt. The two schools of art, she says, are the schools of senses and soul. Duse's acting is "done in marble just as Bernhardt's is done in color. . . . Bernhardt's acting is a matter of physical excitement, Duse's of spiritual exaltation. . . . Art is Bernhardt's dissipation, a sort of Bacchic orgy. It is Duse's consecration, her religion, her martyrdom" (*Journal*, 16 June 1895; Curtin, *World and the Parish*, p. 207).

The phrase cited here is from a letter Cather wrote to the editor of *Commonweal* in answer to a request for information about *Death Comes for the Archbishop*. Her reply, titled "On *Death Comes for the Archbishop*," appears in *Willa Cather on Writing*, pp. 3–13. See p. 9 for the quotation cited above.

25. Cather may have borrowed her title from William Congreve's Restoration comedy by the same name. She at least superficially treats Congreve's concern over the problem of human relationships, particularly between the sexes, and concludes that it is difficult for honest affection to flourish in an atmosphere of artificiality and shallow fashion.

26. Willa Cather created a playtown called "Sandy Point" in her backyard. She was thirteen at the time, and became mayor as well as editor of the town newspaper. The shops were set up in packing boxes, and transactions were conducted with pins and Confederate money brought from Virginia as packing material. In many details the town matched Speckleville, except that in Willa's town all the proprietors were female, probably by choice rather than decree. Bennett (*World of Willa Cather*, pp. 172–73) describes the Sandy Point operation.

27. Cather's interest in drama and dramatic forms was lifelong. In *The World of Willa Cather*, pp. 169–212, Bennett describes that interest. As a youngster Cather loved to write and produce and act in plays. The first of the campus pieces, titled "A Sentimental Thanksgiving Dinner: In Five Courses," appeared in the *Hesperian*, 24 November 1892. The second is a biting satire on Greek-letter fraternities titled "Daily Dialogues; Or, Cloak Room Conversation as Overheard by the Tired Listener" (*Hesperian*, 15 February 1893). Apparently, the catalyst for this awkward bit of satire was a not-so-friendly rivalry between the literary societies and the "Greeks." See Shively, *Writings from Willa Cather's Campus Years*, p. 17.

28. Cather, *One of Ours*, p. 50.

29. Cather was always pulled toward the West, even though she knew that she was to make her life in the East. In an interview cited by Bennett, *World of Willa Cather*, p. 140, Cather calls the tug toward Nebraska the "happiness and curse of my life."

30. Seibel, "Miss Willa Cather from Nebraska," pp. 205–6. Seibel recalls that Cather still "wrote under a variety of *noms de plume,* as she had done for the *Home Monthly.*" He remembers specifically that one was "Nickelmann [*sic*], borrowed from a folklore figure in Gerhart Hauptmann's *Sunken Bell,* which we had read once." The full name was Henry Nicklemann, which, according to Faulkner in *Willa Cather's Collected Short Fiction* (p. 546), "appeared on some seventeen articles," including "When I Knew Stephen Crane," which was "credited to Nicklemann in the *Library*," but "signed Willa Sibert Cather when it appeared in the Lincoln *Courier*." "The Dance at Chevalier's" was signed Henry Nicklemann.

31. It is sometimes painful to read in Cather what today would be regarded as openly racist comments. We must remember that such treatment was common among early writers of "realism." Cather unblushingly, really unconsciously, repeats demeaning racial stereotypes in these early stories. As she matured, slurring racial references disappear, or when they do appear they are usually intended as a judgment against whoever utters them. In many novels, she speaks fondly and respectfully of immigrants from Europe as well as of Mexicans and Indians, although some comments and characterizations might be regarded as anti-Semitic. Certainly, American movies traded on these old racial stereotypes long after Cather no longer felt inclined to use them.

32. "The Affair at Grover Station" was probably inspired by a summer visit Cather paid to her brother Douglass, then a railroad station agent in Cheyenne. See Woodress, *Willa Cather: Her Life and Art*, pp. 96–97. Bennett, *World of Willa Cather*, p. 36, says the story "was written with his assistance"; presumably he provided the railroading details.

33. Anticipating the narrative device she was later to employ in *My Ántonia,* Cather creates a narrator who repeats someone else's story. And,

as in *My Ántonia*, the story begins with a train ride. In *My Ántonia*, however-
er, we encounter the third party only in the "Introduction" where he (or she)
meets Jim Burden, a childhood friend, on a train. The two reminisce about
Ántonia, and months later Jim drops off a manuscript for his old friend to
read. The manuscript is the novel. In "Affair at Grover Station," the narrator reports the story as it was told to him.

TWO

Refining the Gift: 1901–1905

I. A TIME OF TRANSITION

Cather left the *Leader* sometime during the spring of 1900 and went to visit her cousins in Washington, D.C. There she did some editing work before returning to Pittsburgh. In March 1901, she accepted a position teaching English and Latin at Pittsburgh's Central High School then later moved to Allegheny High School. By the time Willa Cather began teaching in Pittsburgh she had written more than many writers produce in a lifetime. It is estimated that by then, in addition to numerous short stories, poems, and an unpublished volume of drama criticism, Cather had written "more than five hundred columns, articles, reviews, and feature stories."[1] It was during Cather's teaching years that she composed and published *The Troll Garden* stories, a remarkable collection for a writer little known in literary circles. The four stories of this period that precede the *Troll Garden* group date from the spring of 1901 to the fall of 1902. They lack the crisp energy and control of "Eric Hermannson's Soul" and "The Sentimentality of William Tavener." It was also at this time that Cather became acquainted with Isabelle McClung with whom she was to enjoy a lifelong friendship. That same spring she moved out of her boardinghouse and into the McClung home where she was accorded the privacy and atmosphere she needed for her writing.[2] And Cather continued writing, in spite of a demanding teaching schedule.

A. AN ABUNDANCE OF SENTIMENTALITY

The four stories alluded to above have a particular flavor, something of a genteel sentimentality, a self-consciousness that had not fretted the best of Cather's earlier stories. One is tempted to credit some of this genteel intrusion to the move from the bumpy cadences of boarding house living to the more gracious rhythms of the McClung household. Two of the stories, "Jack-a-Boy" (*Saturday Eve-*

37

ning Post, 30 March 1901) and "The Treasure of Far Island" (*New England Magazine,* October 1902), are highly romantic. The other two, "El Dorado: A Kansas Recessional" (*New England Magazine,* June 1901) and "The Professor's Commencement" (*New England Magazine,* June 1902), are less sentimental, but tend to be overwritten. Nevertheless, these four stories have a memorable quality; they stick in the mind. Perhaps Cather was just reaching the age where she could begin to be nostalgic about childhood, for both "Jack-a-Boy" and "The Treasure of Far Island" are quite different from her earlier treatments of childhood themes.[3] "Jack-a-Boy" is written like a juvenile tale, fraught with characters like "The Woman Nobody Called On," but its little hero is almost oppressively Greek. This is not to suggest, however, that the story is without charm. On the contrary, Cather's facility with language rhythms and sounds mesmerizes the reader as the Golden Age luxuriates across the story's pages like a banquet comprised solely of desserts.

The child Jack-a-Boy moves with his parents into an apartment house verging on decay and wins the hearts of its most crabbed and lonely occupants. But he grows sick with a fever and dies. Cather's narrator (a lonely female occupant of the building) sentimentally describes the boy's passing in terms of his rejoining "some joyous spirit with whom he had played long ago in Arcady." Noting that "the flowers and the casket and the dismal hymns" are "cruelly inappropriate for such a glad and beautiful little life," she bravely tries "to forget all that, and to remember only that Jack-a-Boy heard the pipes of Pan as the old wood gods trooped by in the gray morning, and that he could not stay" (pp. 319–20). Another neighbor, an old professor who is immersed in the scholastic dry dust of the Classical Age, is as prodigal as the narrator with his sentimental indulgences, avowing that "sometimes the old divinities reveal themselves in children," radiating "that holiness of beauty which the hardest and barest of us must love when we see it" (pp. 320–21).

The story has another problem too, a problem with taste. As it draws to a close the old classicist suggests that the young lad was an instance of Walter Pater's assertion that "the revelation of beauty" is perhaps, after all, "to be our redemption." Taking her cue from the professor, the narrator frames a less than subtle comparison between the boy and the Savior. In light of the story's theme, this comparison is not offensive, but in a context of wood nymphs and Greek divinities frolicking in the fields of Arcady, such an allusion jangles the sensibilities. The story's chief value lies in its poetic fluency and its thematic affirmation of human caring as an antidote for loneliness.

"The Treasure of Far Island," no less exuberant and sentimental, is not so quaintly storybookish as "Jack-a-Boy," and hence less justified in its excesses. It is the story of Douglass Burnham, a successful eastern playwright who returns to his childhood home on the Divide to recapture his youth and his love. With his somewhat reluctant pirate playmate of yore, the now lovely Margie Governor, Douglass rows on the appointed day to their childhood island to dig up the treasure they had buried many years ago. For a time, Margie is the pessimistic counterbalance to Douglass's optimism, but Douglass gradually breaks down Margie's reserve and together they recapture the world of their childhood where "the meadows . . . were the greenest in all the world because they were the meadows of the long ago; and the flowers that grew there were the freshest and sweetest of growing things because once, long ago in the golden age, two children had gathered other flowers like them, and the beauties of vanished summers were everywhere" (p. 276). Their world is shot through with celestial fire and furbished with romantic profusion:

> The locust chirped in the thicket; the setting sun threw a track of flame across the water; the willows burned with fire and were not consumed; a glory was upon the sand and the river and upon the Silvery Beaches; and these two looked about over God's world and saw that it was good. In the western sky the palaces of crystal and gold were quenched in night, like the cities of old empires; and out of the east rose the same moon that has glorified all the romances of the world—that lighted Paris over the blue Aegean and the feet of young Montague to the Capulets' orchard. (P. 282)

The self-imposed curbs and low-keyed restraint that distinguish Cather's later work are absent here, but we can readily recognize in these lines an early manifestation of the lyrical impulse that invigorates Cather's novels.

This story is also interesting because it foreshadows setting and theme in Cather's later work, especially *My Ántonia* and *Lucy Gayheart*. The river and the island described here and in the novels are part of her own childhood memories of adventures on the Republican River. And like many of Cather's works, "The Treasure of Far Island" testifies that youth is the best time, the time of power, the time of aliveness, the time most worth living, the time too soon gone forever. This theme carries through many of the novels and into later stories like "The Joy of Nelly Deane," "Uncle Valentine," "Double Birthday," "Two Friends," "The Old Beauty," and "The Best Years." So convinced is Cather of the value of youth over age that several of her young characters die in almost merciful escape from the disillusionment that accompanies age. Claude Wheeler, Tom Outland, Nelly Deane, and Lesley Ferguesson ("The Best Years") are all granted that fate.

Thinking of "the other gallant lads who sailed with us then," Margie sighs, "It is very sad to grow up." Douglass counters, "Sad for them, yes. But we have never grown up. . ." (p. 277). As the two continue to discuss their child selves, Margie cries out that the pirate's treasure they so carefully saved "was really our childhood that we buried here, never guessing what a precious thing we were putting under the ground" (p. 280). Douglass agrees that the burial rites marked the end of their golden childhood days, but he insists that they can find youth again. Margie, however, charges him with losing it for them in the first place by growing up and taking on "the ways of the world" (p. 281). This appears to be an authorial allusion to the earlier story of that title in which Cather traces the calamity wrought in the child world by a sellout to a materialistic ethic. "The Treasure of Far Island" reverses the tragedy of "The Way of the World," recouping the loss and returning its characters to freedom and light and childlike sharing.

B. BEGINNINGS AND ENDINGS

The titles of the other two stories in this group, "El Dorado: A Kansas Recessional" and "The Professor's Commencement," suggest an interesting contrast which, in fact, is reversed in the stories themselves. "El Dorado: A Kansas Recessional" ironically ends with an upturn toward a new life while "The Professor's Commencement" moves steadily downward, confirming again that youth once lost is gone forever. The abundant optimism of "The Treasure of Far Island" is absent from these stories, but Cather is as munificent in describing Desolation as she was in describing Arcady. Cather opens "El Dorado: A Kansas Recessional" with a grim picture of the Solomon Valley through which "a turbid, muddy little stream . . . crawls along between naked bluffs, choked and split by sand bars" (p. 293), until it plays itself out. The abundance of desolate detail is in absolute contrast to the description of setting in "The Treasure of Far Island" and harks back to the dreary landscape of Cather's early prairie stories. Here again, she peoples the landscape with the most solitary of characters.

Completely alone in the world, Josiah Bywaters sits in his store, the sole inhabitant of El Dorado, a town advertised as "the Queen City of the Plains," to which he had come from Virginia, like Cather's people, to make a new life. Instead of finding wealth, he found himself the victim of a land fraud. When the other losers pulled out, he stubbornly remained, and watched angry creditors dismantle the town board by board, stone by stone. In the end, however, when the man who had bilked him returns on a sentimental errand, Bywaters discovers him killed by a rattler. He pockets the ten thousand dollars he finds on the body, burns the store, and heads east without looking back.

The story picks up one of Cather's dominant motifs, isolation. It occurs not only in story after story, but in most of the novels as well. Bywaters' store is the town's "solitary frame building," and it is "the solitude rather than any other hardship" (p. 294) that makes him suffer. He is "a sort of 'Last Man' . . . stranded on a Kansas bluff" (p. 295). Left there alone, he had become "almost a part of that vast solitude, . . . homesick for his kind" (p. 295). Even the land "seemed as lonely as himself and as unhappy. No one cared for it." God himself seemed to have grown tired of it and deeded "it over to the Other Party" (p. 303).

The final story of this group, "The Professor's Commencement," treats both the isolation and the youth themes. Although the professor has the companionship of his widowed sister and various colleagues and friends, he is essentially a solitary man. Facing retirement, he glumly attends the high school commencement services that formally mark the end of his daily communion with teachers and students. Emerson Graves, another of the multitude of Cather characters who mourn the passing of youth, has harbored the conviction that if he could somehow retain his youth, he could forever fend off loneliness. Interacting daily with literature's lyric poets and with high school students had, he felt, "prolonged his youth well into the fifties," and anyone observing the professor's mouth would note that it "was as sensitive and mobile as that of a young man" (p. 284). Graves fancies himself as one whose "real work had been to try to secure for youth the rights of youth; the right to be generous, to dream, to enjoy; to feel a little the seduction of the old Romance, and to yield a little" (p. 287). The professor regrets that even while his students are still in school the industrialism that will eventually devour them is so close that it fills the classroom with its ravenous sounds, eager to feed upon these youngsters. This is the same industrial threat that Cather describes later in "The Namesake" and "Uncle Valentine."

The professor faces retirement with a heavy heart, feeling "like a ruin of some extinct civilization," for "he had been living by external stimulation from the warm young blood about him." Now, with "the current of young life . . . cut away from him" he feels "horribly exposed," drunk dry by "those hundreds of thirsty young lives" (p. 289). In his sense of loss that seems inevitably to accompany the passing of years, Emerson Graves foreshadows Godfrey St. Peter. And just as the discouraged St. Peter thinks on his youth self, so Graves before him asks himself what he has done with his own bright youth and remembers with mixed pleasure and pain his one remarkable student. St. Peter, too, has such a student, Tom Outland, and Cather gives the whole center section of *The Professor's House* (1925) to "Tom Outland's Story" as St. Peter reads through Tom's notebook one solitary summer. Tom might have been devoured by the material world, as Graves knows his students will be, but Cather rushes him off to war where, like Claude Wheeler, he is killed before the brightness of his youth can be tarnished.

With the facile rhetoric of one who has not yet been there, Cather eloquently describes the bitterness of aging felt by the professor and his colleagues: "With youth always about them, they had believed themselves of it. Like the monk in the legend they had wandered a little way into the wood to hear the bird's song—the magical song of youth so engrossing and so treacherous, and they had come back to their cloister to find themselves old men—spent warriors who could only chatter on the wall, like grasshoppers, and sigh at the beauty of Helen as she passed" (p. 290). Professor Graves tries to recapture his youth self and even correct its mistakes by repeating the poem he had delivered at his own commencement, a recitation he never finished because his memory failed him at a critical moment. Everyone in the audience appreciates the significance of his attempting the poem again some forty years later. Predictably, he stumbles on the same line, time's merciless reminder that the past is irredeemable.

II. *THE BLOSSOMING:* THE TROLL GARDEN

A. THE LURE OF THE GARDEN

Two of the best pieces of fiction Cather ever wrote appeared in 1905, in *McClure's* separately and as part of her first collected volume of prose, *The Troll Garden*. Surely, "The Sculptor's Funeral" and "Paul's Case" deserve the respect they have earned as hallmarks in American fiction. "A Wagner Matinee," which appeared in 1904 in *Everybody's Magazine* before it was collected in *The Troll Garden*, also shows the sure touch of a first-rate writer of fiction.[4] The whole collection, probably written in the two-year span from the fall of 1902 to the fall of 1904,[5] demonstrates that for Cather a long and productive apprenticeship was over. In fact, nothing Cather wrote in the subsequent six or seven years is better than the best of this collection, or even as good. Gone is the somewhat stylized literary pose of the "Jack-a-Boy" group and the rather superficial treatment of serious themes.

Perhaps the wisest approach to *The Troll Garden* collection is through a consideration of its title and the two epigraphs with which Cather introduces it. One epigraph, appearing on the title page, is from Charles Kingsley's *The Roman and the Teuton: A Series of Lectures Delivered Before the University of Cambridge*. More specifically, the lines Cather borrows come from a parable titled "The Forest Children" which Kingsley repeats in one of his lectures.[6] This is the epigraph as Cather uses it: "A fairy palace, with a fairy garden; . . . inside the trolls dwell, . . . working at their magic forges, making and making always things rare and strange." The other epigraph, appearing opposite the title page, is a stanza from Christina Rossetti's "The Goblin Market":

> We must not look at Goblin men,
> We must not buy their fruits;
> Who knows upon what soil they fed
> Their hungry thirsty roots?[7]

Cather elides a few words from the Kingsley quotation which, when included, cast a very different light upon the epigraph and indeed upon the whole volume of stories. The parable as Kingsley tells it opens, "Fancy to yourself a great Troll-garden, such as our forefathers dreamed of often fifteen hundred years ago;—a fairy palace,

with a fairy garden; and all around the primeval wood. Inside the
Trolls dwell, cunning and wicked, watching their fairy treasures,
working at their magic forges, making and making always things
rare and strange; and outside, the forest is full of children; such children as the world had never seen before, but children still. . . ."[8]
In appropriating that passage, Cather preserves references to the
magic and the creativity of the trolls, but omits references to their
evil natures. And, she does not mention the children outside in the
forest.

E. K. Brown takes the passage with its elisions at face value. In
his view, the pair of epigraphs define the two thematic strands of the
book: first, the artist and second, the forces which are unsympathet-
ic and even destructive to art. Brown identifies the artists as the "industrious" trolls, while the "evil-working" goblins are the enemies of
art; and each story in the collection, he believes, illustrates the conflict between these two forces. Brown distinguishes between what he
calls the "baleful" strand and the "sunny" strand, the baleful strand
portraying the defeat of the artist, and the sunny strand portraying
the artist at work "in relation with persons of great wealth." Brown
believes that the first six stories deal alternately with the two inter-
woven themes, and that "Paul's Case" stands as a coda to the two
sets. Stories one, three, and five—"Flavia and Her Artists," "The
Garden Lodge," and "The Marriage of Phaedra"—show "artists or
persons with artistic temperament" working "amid the wealthy" to
produce "things rare and strange"; this is the troll, or sunny, strand.
Stories two, four, and six—"The Sculptor's Funeral," "A Death in the
Desert," and "A Wagner Matinee"—which comprise the goblin or
baleful strand, are "tales filled with an undercurrent of malaise and
a sense of nightmare," the consequences of venturing "into the goblin market" where the goblins destroy with their poisonous fruits.[9]

Bernice Slote, however, pointing to Cather's ardent interest in
myth and history, argues convincingly that Kingsley's parable says
essentially the same thing as Rossetti's poem. Trolls and goblins
alike display their dangerous enticements temptingly before the
eyes of childish innocence. Slote also insists that Cather's intent is
not merely to invoke the conflict between artist and society that her
critics are so fond of describing. Slote points out that in Cather "the
greedy and insensitive are everywhere, and even in art there are
both Trolls and Forest Children (the overrefined versus the genuine,
the real desire versus the false)."[10] Cather uses the two epigraphic

items, it appears, less to define the dichotomy (which certainly is present) of the book and the individual stories in it than to give double emphasis to the threat of materialistic seduction. As Slote says, "*The Troll Garden* is about corruption, the distortion of values; in every human sense there may be goblin fruit to desire, and Trolls who guard their riches."[11]

Before *The Troll Garden,* Cather had defended her values boldly in columns and reviews, but had only occasionally moved beyond simple sentiment or intrigue or entertainment in her fiction. But with her first collection of stories[12] we detect a new sense of obligation to use art as a weapon against its enemies, against the trolls and goblins of this world. Edward A. Bloom and Lillian D. Bloom see *The Troll Garden* as a battleground where the artist struggles incessantly with a society that is hostile to both art and artist. In keeping with the general thesis of their book, the Blooms regard the collection of stories as "primarily an extended colloquy between the artist as hero and a personified middle-class society as the villain."[13] While their position has merit, particularly as it describes a story like "The Sculptor's Funeral," the force of it is diminished by the truth of Brown's important observation about the stories: "Artists do not often appear practicing their art, or theorizing about it, or never do they attempt either theory or practice at length; they appear in their relations with others, usually either with non-artistic persons or with persons who are merely appreciative." The problem is "that artists are crucially unlike other beings," and this "unlikeness often brings havoc into the lives of those who surround the artist."[14] The Blooms also speak of the social separateness of the artist, but chiefly in terms of the artist's self-immolation, a sacrifice which could never be understood by "'normal' ungenerous individuals." Because the artist has given all, he must be granted special dispensations by society for behavior that would not be tolerated in the ungifted. Hence, "the mutual suspicion" between artist and society in general is probably to be expected.[15]

It must be remembered, however, that the *Troll Garden* stories are not stories of struggling artists. They are, rather, stories that deal with human values and relationships played against genuine art as an index of value. In them Cather is concerned with a much broader value system than that of art for its own sake. She is talking about both art *and* humanity, refusing to separate the two, insisting that whatever works against art works also against humanity. The connection she discovered and described in *The Troll Garden,* the connection between aesthetic (or artistic) sensibility and meaningful human life and interaction, became the foundation upon which she built for a lifetime. The troll garden was to become for Cather forever the territory of the enemy, the country of materialism and false art, and hence the country where the artist and the nonmaterialist would forever be aliens. It is this country that Cather explores in the *Troll Garden* stories, warning against its false fruits, enchantingly delicious, but destructive to art and humanity alike.

B. THE AMBIGUITY OF ART

The first story in *The Troll Garden* is "Flavia and Her Artists," appropriately named for the flamboyant woman who adores artists and is happy only when her house and life are filled with them. Assuredly, Flavia's house is the seductive troll garden which lures artists, pseudoartists, and other people of arty or intellectual reputation to partake of its worldly pleasures and in turn to bestow the privilege and the prestige of their company upon their eager hostess. Imogen Willard, the handsome and scholarly daughter of Flavia's friend, arrives as a houseguest, one of Flavia's "chosen" personalities, each one selected because of some supposed talent or celebrity value. Another guest is the square-shooting actress, Jemima "Jimmy" Broadwood. Flavia is married to the sensitive Arthur Hamilton who owns, by virtue of inheritance, a highly successful farm machine manufactory. Some of the guests are trolls themselves, having come in their cunning to exploit Flavia; others, like M. Roux, appear to be genuine, if less than gracious, artists.

Arthur has a blind spot where Flavia is concerned and would even sacrifice his relationship with her to save her from pain. Roux is not similarly handicapped. Though somewhat perplexed at first, Roux comes to some uncomplimentary conclusions about Flavia which he publishes in a newspaper interview in order to punish her and women like her for using him as a showpiece. He had wondered why she gathered artists about her, for he had perceived "at a glance" what the narrator already knew, "namely, that all Flavia's artists have done or ever will do means exactly as much to her as a symphony means to an oyster; that there is no bridge by which the significance of any work of art could be conveyed to her" (pp. 164–65). Flavia is both troll and forest child, both temptress and wide-eyed innocent.

Ambitious, demanding, oblivious to her own blindness, she lives parasitically off the borrowed light of those whom she persuades to accept her sumptuous hospitality.

The narrator, who grants that Flavia is a "remarkable woman," nevertheless characterizes her in rather harsh terms at times. Flavia's inclinations toward people tend to smack of "violence" and "vehemence and insistence." Her "enamel" face "a perfect scream of animation" (Jemima Broadwood's term), Flavia lives in constant anxiety for fear that "the fabric of her life" might "fly to the winds in irretrievable entanglement" (pp. 156–57). Flavia, who thinks she is in complete harmony with the artists of the world, strikes Imogen as one who projects a note which is "manifestly false." And apparently, Flavia's weakness is not simply a matter of ignorance. These people whom she regards as "her natural affinities" she also regards as "lawful prey" (p. 149), a term which carries ugly suggestions. Unable to construe opinions of her own, Flavia adopts the positions of others and argues them with fervor. The "most worn word in her vocabulary" is "best" (p. 150); the creed she repeats daily is that one must seek "the best" and give "the best."

In her house Flavia's great ambition has been realized, to provide an "asylum for talent," a "sanitorium of the arts," terms which unmistakably suggest a harbor for the diseased or unhealthy. Still, for Flavia the house is "the mirror of her exultation; it was a temple to the gods of Victory, a sort of triumphal arch" (p. 152). The sneer is obvious in the voice of the narrator in this description of Flavia and her dream for her artists: "A woman who made less a point of sympathizing with their delicate organisms, might have sought to plunge these phosphorescent pieces into the tepid bath of domestic life; but Flavia's discernment was deeper. This must be a refuge where the shrinking soul, the sensitive brain, should be unconstrained. . ." (p. 152).

This story is not simply a dramatization of the conflict between the artist and society. Flavia, who believes herself to be the very soul of art appreciation, but who is in fact shallow and foolish, is in many ways a more likeable character than the "artists" who know what she is, but pretend to admire her in order to enjoy the material advantages Arthur's money provides. Thus, though they scale the wall and enter her troll garden, they perhaps are the greater beguilers. Even M. Roux, who is certainly more worthy of the title of artist than the hack novelist Frank Wellington, cruelly betrays Flavia after eating at her table. Jemima's obvious scorn for all the celebrities who devour Flavia's goblin fruit carries significant weight in the reader's mind, for she has an uncanny ability to tell things straight. The "artists," in fact, have beguiled Flavia into believing that they have magical powers and extraordinary sensibilities which she would do well to nurture and even worship. Then too, Hamilton's regard for his wife speaks in her favor as well as his.

It seems clear that Cather's main concern is not with art per se, but with the attitudes and behavior of human beings, some of whom happen to be artists. Art can and often does suggest a standard of truth for human thought and action, but in this story it is Arthur Hamilton, manufacturer, not the artists, who becomes the measuring stick. It is Hamilton, who resists the false attractions of materialism and exploitive art alike, against whom Cather judges both artists and plebeians. It is he who acts instinctively and selflessly out of love and human caring. And it is he who is therefore destined to be misunderstood and to dwell as a stranger in his own home. In this story Cather demonstrates the principle she had come to believe and avow with increasing fervor: the exploitive instinct is destructive to both art and humanity, and it isolates human beings from their most salutary sources of sympathy.

"The Sculptor's Funeral," the next story in the collection, presents a shining still-life portrait of the nonexploitive artist, the true artist who may appear to have been selfish because of his single-mindedness, but who in fact has offered a kind of total sacrifice of self on the altar of art and humanity. It was surely not by accident that Cather chose to juxtapose Flavia and her perfidious artists against the sculptor, damning them by the integrity of his example. And in some ways, the hostile environment of the small Kansas town to which Harvey Merrick's body returns for burial is no more pernicious than the hothouse corruption of Flavia's "asylum" for "delicate organisms" and "shrinking souls."

"The Sculptor's Funeral" is a landmark in Willa Cather's career. Not only is it her first truly great story, but it is the first story in which she herself is totally involved. Cather is writing from the heart about things that are so terribly true for her that the whole force of her personality and her belief resonates through the lines. Perhaps for the first time the vitality of her mind and art speaks more convincingly than the content of her words or the grace of her style. Cather seemed to recognize the story's quality, for she selected it to appear in a later collection of short stories as well as in her collected works; and she allowed it to appear in anthologies, a rare concession for her.

"The Sculptor's Funeral" is Cather's most important fictional statement to date on what were for her the enduring values of human life. The coffin of the sculptor is in some sense a monument to those values, like the tombs of ancient monarchs. In life, however, the sculptor was regarded as an embarrassment to his father. The townspeople pitied Harvey Merrick's father for trying to run a farm with a son who aspired to an education and advanced training in art rather than property and money. Even as a youngster Harvey could not be trusted to tend cows responsibly because he might be distracted by a sunset. The sculptor's body is shipped home where the "successful" men of Sand City come to sit through the night with it, cackling over Harvey's prodigalities and failures, completely unaware of the meaning of the palm on his coffin.[16] The sculptor, dead before reaching middle age, is a world-renowned artist who had somehow miraculously sprung up in their midst.

Jim Laird, who went off to college with Harvey and returned to be the shyster lawyer his townsmen wanted him to be, in a fit of anger and self-hatred bursts in on the watchers and delivers what is probably the most powerful speech Cather ever wrote. In that speech she clearly draws the battle lines for what was to be a lifelong effort to fortify the things of the spirit against material incursions. Jim Laird, who is really the central character of the story, knows that he succumbed to the trolls' enticements while Harvey resisted, and he throws his self-disgust back at his fellow townsmen in a verbal cyclone: "There was only one boy ever raised in this borderland between ruffianism and civilization, who didn't come to grief, and you hated Harvey Merrick more for winning out than you hated all the other boys who got under the wheels. Lord, Lord, how you did hate him! Phelps, here, is fond of saying that he could buy and sell us all out any time he's a mind to; but he knew Harvey wouldn't have given a tinker's damn for his bank and all his cattle-farms put together; and a lack of appreciation, that way, goes hard with Phelps" (pp. 183–84). He attacks what he calls the "sick, sidetracked, burnt-dog, land-poor sharks" such as "the here-present financiers of Sand City" mercilessly and praises Harvey Merrick, who "wouldn't have given one sunset over your marshes for all you've got put together" (p. 185).

In some sense Jim Laird is both the protagonist and the antagonist of the story. The central conflict is not between the sculptor and
the townspeople, for Harvey Merrick has already won the old battle
and is safely out of the fray. The central conflict is between Jim's
better nature and the self that prospers by serving scoundrels. The
return of Harvey's body has stirred to the surface a side of Jim's nature that he has repressed for many years, a side that values all that
Harvey stands for. It is as if Harvey's body had to come home to deliver its silent message to Jim Laird. More specifically, the return of
his friend's body for burial is the symbolic return of Jim's own conscience which is then promptly buried with the sculptor. So the
"sculptor's funeral" is indeed the most important event in the story.
It precipitates the awakening of conscience that some years ago
might have saved Jim Laird; but it also brings him face-to-face with
what he has become, and the shame of it is too painful to bear. Too
drunk to attend the funeral, Jim awards the victory over his soul to
the antagonist within him whom he despises.

Jim, as the central character, is subtly played against the other
characters in the story. The rather nondescript Steavens who accompanies his master's body home could never speak so passionately for
personal integrity as Jim Laird, nor could he fall so miserably into
the service of the enemy. Jim's townsmen, unlike Jim, are too dense
to see the evil in their natures. But Harvey's mother is particularly
important because she is like an exposed nerve someone has stepped
on, Jim's nerve. Cather's description of her is superb, terrible and
superb, complete in just a few lines. The woman's face is brutally
handsome, "but it was scarred and furrowed by violence, and so col-
oured and coarsened by fiercer passions that grief seemed never to
have laid a gentle finger there." Steavens perceives that "she filled
the room; the men were obliterated, seemed tossed about like twigs
in an angry water." Even he "felt himself being drawn into the
whirlpool" (p. 176). Jim has some of that same raw power, but with
him it is usually tempered by expediency. Besides Jim, only the feeble old father and the family's mistreated housegirl seem to have
sensed the sculptor's quality.

During the wake Cather allows each of the watchers to reveal
himself through his smug comments. What better way to show an
artist's fineness than to bring him mute into the company of all that
is sordid and crass? And what better way to show what Jim Laird
has sold out to? In reporting that Jim does not attend his friend's fu-

neral services, the conclusion reconfirms that the story's central concern is Jim Laird's self-division and the successful repression of his better nature: "The thing in him that Harvey Merrick had loved must have gone underground with Harvey Merrick's coffin; for it never spoke again, and Jim got the cold he died of driving across the Colorado mountains to defend one of Phelps's sons who had got into trouble out there by cutting government timber" (p. 185).

The next story in the collection, "The Garden Lodge," works in still a different way with the troll garden theme. The distinctions between trolls and forest children are deliberately blurred in "Flavia and Her Artists," with troll-like characters appearing everywhere. But the distinctions are lucid in "The Sculptor's Funeral" where the self-satisfied trolls flourish with little outside interference. "The Garden Lodge," however, exposes no *evil* trolls; its only trolls, in fact, live in the garden of art. Cather admits, through allusion and direct statement too, that art itself can be a form of sorcery, a garden of incorporeal delights that may tempt the innocent to sorrow and even destruction, or hold out promises that forever elude. "The Garden Lodge," a ready confession that art is both agony and ecstasy, is an important story for Cather. She makes it plain that art scarcely guarantees the devotee glamour or material ease or a lifetime of emotional high tides, though at various moments it can bring all of those. Art can spell poverty and pain and social censure as well as wonder. To have risen to the top and received worldwide acclaim as the sculptor had done is one thing; to have sacrificed everything to one's artistic desire and reaped only hardship, "petty jealousies," and a "cowardly fear of the little grocer on the corner" (p. 189), as Caroline Noble's father had done, is quite another.

Determined first of all to survive, Caroline has consciously rejected the sentimental and molded herself into what her friends perceive as a "cool-headed" and "disgustingly practical" woman who is "always mistress of herself in any situation" (p. 187). What her friends do not know, of course, is what she had endured as a youngster:

> She had grown up in Brooklyn, in a shabby little house under the vacillating administration of her father, a music teacher who usually neglected his duties to write orchestral compositions for which the world seemed to have no especial need. His spirit was warped by bitter vindictiveness and puerile self-commiseration,

and he spent his days in scorn of the labour that brought him bread and in pitiful devotion to the labour that brought him only disappointment, writing interminable scores which demanded of the orchestra everything under heaven except melody. (P. 188)

This, she learned, was what art meant: a mother "who idolized her husband as the music lord of the future," a brother who "had inherited all his father's vindictive sensitiveness without his capacity for slavish application" (p. 188), and a house that "had served its time at the shrine of idealism," brought "low enough" by "vague, distressing, unsatisfied yearnings" (p. 189). She remembers that in that house where a "mystic worship of things distant, intangible and unattainable" prevailed, the family nevertheless always had "to come down to the cold facts of the case; to boiled mutton and to the necessity of turning the dining-room carpet" (p. 189).

After the deaths of her brother and mother, Caroline had assumed control of the household, and by giving lessons and eventually playing recital accompaniments, she managed to pay the bills and take life in hand. She met and married a widower, a successful businessman, and for the first time she "paused to take a breath"; finally, with him, she felt "entirely safe" (p. 190). But the world of art eventually intrudes upon her hard-won peace. Secure and decidedly unsentimental, she scarcely expects to be thrown off balance by the visit of opera star Raymond d'Esquerré who elects to rest, study, and practice for a month at the Nobles' home, singing many hours in the garden lodge with Caroline accompanying him. Until her husband suggests after d'Esquerré's departure that they tear down the garden lodge and build a summer house there, she had not known what deep lodes of her essential being had been tapped by the singer's presence and his art. Her initial reaction favors preserving the lodge because d'Esquerré had sung there. That night, unable to sleep, Caroline goes to the lodge, vulnerable to a flood of throttled feelings and memories. While a storm holds itself in poised abeyance, she plays from the last music that the artist had practiced there. Finally, she breaks down sobbing; and the storm, as if on cue, crashes around her. After so many years of studied control, Caroline begins "fighting again the battles of other days," helplessly entertaining long-buried ghosts from her past. By the next morning, however, she has successfully collected and ordered her feelings again. When her husband asks her if she has come to a decision about the lodge, she calmly votes to raze it. She has not fallen in love with the man for whom she played accompaniments as Lucy Gayheart does, but she is momentarily caught in his spell. Older than Lucy, and far less impulsive, she is less vulnerable, but she is also less vital and appealing.

The focal point of the story is Caroline's experience in the garden lodge on the night of the storm. There she is visited by a vestige of her young self, and also by the realization that the things she had come to believe in as realities were perhaps only shadows after all. And "the shadows of things, always so scorned and flouted," were in fact "the realities." Even more painfully, she realizes that "her father, poor Heinrich [her brother], even her mother, who had been able to sustain her poor romance and keep her little illusions amid the tasks of a scullion, were nearer happiness than she." This realization is reinforced by an allusion, the second in the story, to Klingsor's garden: "Her [Caroline's] sure foundation was but made ground, after all, and the people in Klingsor's garden were more fortunate, however barren the sands from which they conjured their paradise" (pp. 195–96).[17]

So, the contest is not between the sordid money-grubbing world and the heaven of pure art, but rather it is between the practical and the imaginative impulses which can quicken inside anyone. But given a choice, who would not finally prefer the excesses of the imagination? The story develops an interesting paradox on this point. D'Esquerré, who creates an enchanted world for his largely female audiences, seeks relief "near a quiet nature, a cool head, a strong hand" (p. 190), while Caroline, who has committed herself to matter-of-factness, has her moment of truth in the realms of feeling and imagination. D'Esquerré is only too aware that with his art he escorts women aching for his magic into the garden of the trolls, or in this case, of the sorcerer Klingsor. The sorrow, of course, is that the garden of the imagination is enchanting chiefly to those outside it. Only occasionally is d'Esquerré stirred to "believe again." For the most part he lives with a "tacit admission of disappointment under all this glamour of success—the helplessness of the enchanter to at all enchant himself" (p. 194). True artists do not fool themselves, do not partake of their own goblin fruit, except in rare moments when their audiences give it back to them with "fervent and despairing appeal" (p. 194).

C. THE WAGES OF ART

The next story in *The Troll Garden,* "A Death in the Desert," is generally regarded as an important story even though it is not so strong stylistically nor so credible as "The Garden Lodge." In "A Death in the Desert" Cather warns again that the garden of art can be a sorcerer's garden which, though it seems to promise perennial youth and the rarest of sweet fruits, may, in fact, deliver a bitter harvest of isolation and death.

By accident of his passing through Cheyenne, Everett Hilgarde becomes a watcher with Katharine Gaylord and her brother Charlie during the last weeks of her life. Although Everett had loved her for many years, she had loved only Everett's look-alike brother, Adriance Hilgarde, her teacher and fellow performer who is now safely abroad. Her continuing futile passion for the talented and self-serving Adriance only adds to Everett's distress as he watches her die. Katharine's anguish is overstated almost to the point of melodrama, and we become aware that this story is less the account of a woman's pitiful dying than it is the tragedy of a man's being subsumed in the identity of a famous brother whom he has the misfortune to resemble. Katharine Gaylord's approaching death provides a set of circumstances under which Everett's bitter lifelong eclipse can be revealed.[18] Everett, not Katharine, is the story's main character, just as the main character in the Robert Browning poem of the same title is not the dying man, but the one who ministers to the dying man.[19] Katharine's "death in the desert" has momentary significance, chiefly as it affects and elucidates Everett's life. Everett's death is continual.

"A Death in the Desert" begins and ends with Everett's being mistaken for his older, yet more youthful, brother, of whom he is a somewhat crudely molded copy. All his life, people have noticed or loved Everett chiefly because of his resemblance to Adriance; all his life they have preferred Adriance to him. Everett's chief value has been his ability to call up the apparition of his brother for the artist's worshipful admirers. The opening scene of the story introduces Everett's everlasting predicament. The setting is a westbound train in Colorado where a traveling man mistakes Everett for Adriance and plies him with questions about his famous brother, "the only subject that people ever seemed to care to talk to Everett about" (p. 200). Never free from his own face nor his brother's fame, Everett no sooner steps from the train in Cheyenne than a "woman in a phaeton uttered a low cry and dropped the reins." Embarrassed, Everett "lifted his hat and passed on. He was accustomed to sudden recognitions in the most impossible places, especially by women" (p. 201).

This particular woman, of course, is Katharine Gaylord. Answering her pleading summons, Everett is greeted with an all too familiar exclamation: "How wonderfully like Adriance you are" (p. 206)! Always on the periphery of Adriance's life and career, Everett resentfully recalls that as a young man he was habitually enlisted for backstage emergencies, but no one paid him any attention, "unless it was to notice the resemblance" he bore to Adriance (p. 207). He recalls bitterly that even his mother, in her loneliness for Adriance, "used sometimes to call me to her and turn my face up in the light . . . and kiss me, and then I always knew she was thinking of Adriance" (pp. 207–8).

As Everett's days with Katharine in Wyoming stretch into weeks, he realizes that even here, with the woman he loves present and Adriance an ocean away, he remains, as always, a stand-in, or, as the narrator says, "a stop-gap." In everything, he has found "himself employed in his brother's business, one of the tributary lives which helped to swell the shining current of Adriance Hilgarde's." He sorrowfully realizes that his vigil with Katharine is only another "commission from his brother," and that "his power to minister to her comfort . . . lay solely in his link with his brother's life" (p. 210).

Cather reminds us again of the consequences of consuming the enticing fruits of art. Art takes its toll on the character of the artist who may, like Adriance, be so absorbed in himself that he is unconscious of another's love or suffering. It also takes its toll on a person like Katharine who gives all for it, but is quickly forgotten when she can no longer meet its demands. Finally, it takes its toll on a person like Everett who is swallowed up by it because of simple proximity and accident of birth and countenance. Katharine is a victim once, but Everett is a victim again and again, for there are many Katharines in the overspill of a life like Adriance's. Everett's eternal agony is to be nothing to anyone except a look-alike for the wonderful Adriance. Even the woman he loves, in her last living moments, touches his hair, looks into his face, and whispers, "Ah, dear Adriance, dear, dear" (p. 217). As Everett at last boards the train to leave Wyoming, the story comes full circle, for a huge German woman rushes up to him ecstatically, thinking he is Adriance. He must say again, "I see that you have mistaken me for Adriance Hilgarde. I am his brother" (p. 217).

Cather carefully creates a cyclical effect in this story, suggesting that what we have seen is just one episode in a series that endlessly repeats itself in Everett's life. Although it does not make Katharine's pain any easier to bear, her story will be repeated in the lives of others, each one suffering only his (or, more usually, her) individual fate. Everett's story, however, will be repeated again and again in his own life. Since he is something of a second self for Adriance, he becomes a conscience for his brother, accepting responsibility for the rejected, easing the pain Adriance has managed to sidestep. It is unjust, surely, but perhaps such injustice is inevitable if the truly gifted artist is to rise. The Blooms insist that, being "several cuts above ordinary people, the artist must be willing to be preoccupied with himself,"[20] and Cather would be the last to argue against the hard and sometimes damaging choices the artist must make. Understanding the necessity for the artist's selfishness, Katharine absolves Adriance from blame, insisting, "It wasn't in the slightest degree his fault. . . . I fought my way to him, and I drank my doom greedily enough" (p. 215). But Everett has swept up too many broken pieces of human lives to accept that analysis wholeheartedly. At the end, he boards the train, fully expecting his next "commission" from Adriance to present itself before long, fully expecting to be erased himself, again and still again.

Cather seems to be saying that the immolation of Everett is a high price to pay for the privilege of Adriance. Even in *The Song of the Lark* the artistic gains Thea Kronborg makes by willfully denying some of her tender impulses are offset to some degree by the losses that she suffers as a human being, and that others suffer through her neglect. And though she has to separate from her family in order to become an artist, she has also to rediscover those old ties in order to find peace and self-renewal. Cather had learned, as Brown puts it, that "there was disillusionment in the garden and danger in the marketplace."[21]

"The Marriage of Phaedra," the fifth story in *The Troll Garden,* is probably the least memorable in the collection.[22] The point of view is essentially that of an American in London, but the story is not really his, and he is no Jamesian American abroad. In fact, the story has no convincing central figure; perhaps that is why it seems somewhat anemic and out of focus. "The Marriage of Phaedra" does, however, treat rather straightforwardly the conflict between society and art. If it contains a forest child, that child is the late Hugh Treffinger, a painter known for his extravagant personality and his equally extravagant artistic methods. He had ventured into the troll garden of high society to pursue and win the attractive, if brittle, Lady Ellen. Unable to resist the tempestuous charm of his courtship, she married him, only to watch him lapse into his old habits and social preferences. Experimental and courageous in his art, he attracted a school of devotees, but Lady Ellen had absolutely no feeling for his work. His best painting, *The Marriage of Phaedra,* was never finished, and on his deathbed, Treffinger made it understood that the painting was never to be sold. James, Treffinger's personal valet and loyal servant, steals the painting when he learns that Lady Ellen, on the brink of a second marriage, plans to sell it to an unscrupulous art dealer from Australia. James carries the painting to the American artist, MacMaster, who convinces James that the painting would be recovered regardless of their efforts to hide it. MacMaster makes a feeble effort to save it by appealing to the Lady Ellen, but she rebuffs him, and the painting is sold. The sale of the precious painting by one who has no interest in it other than its monetary value foreshadows Roddy Blake's selling to a foreign art dealer the Indian relics he and Tom Outland had found (*The Professor's House*). In both cases, the art pieces are taken away from the one who values them most.

The most interesting and puzzling aspect of the story is its title, the same title attributed to the painting which James believes precipitated the strokes that killed Treffinger. The Theseus-Phaedra-Hippolytus allusion is a puzzle because it has no clear application to the story. Cather's work testifies to her conviction that art and marriage make a difficult mix, and perhaps this notion is hinted at in Treffinger's painting where Phaedra turns from her husband for a stealthy glance at Hippolytus, the object of her helpless passion. If one's desire is bent in a particular direction, one is helpless to change it. For the artist, art can be the only consuming passion, marriage and mate notwithstanding.

D. TWO OF THE LOST

Two of Cather's finest stories, "A Wagner Matinee" and "Paul's Case," complete the *Troll Garden* collection. Both deal with sensitive characters whose environments shackle their artistic spirits. Although it portrays the East-West conflict that is prominent in Cather's work, especially in books like *The Song of the Lark* and

Lucy Gayheart where the artist is particularly sensitive to the strictures of western family life and mentality, "A Wagner Matinee" is not so much about the contrasting worlds of Boston and Nebraska as it is about Aunt Georgiana and what those worlds have in turn made of her. As a young woman she had taught music in the Boston Conservatory, but she turned her back on that world when she fell inexplicably in love with a shiftless young New Englander and went west with him to stake out a homestead in the rugged prairie lands of Nebraska. After thirty years of unrelieved toil, she returns to Boston to settle the matter of a small legacy from a deceased relative. She is met there by a nephew who as a youngster had lived with her family and worked for her husband on the Nebraska farm. He has planned a surprise for her, a Wagner concert, the first real music she has heard in half a lifetime. She is moved immeasurably as the artist in her nature, so long asleep, trembles to consciousness. When the concert is over she cannot bear to leave, because "just outside the door of the concert hall" is the world she must take up again, "the tall, unpainted house, with weather-curled boards; naked as a tower, the crooked-backed ash seedlings where the dish-cloths hung to dry; the gaunt, moulting turkeys picking up refuse about the kitchen door" (p. 242).

This story may be, as some have suggested, chiefly an indictment of "the toll exacted by the land,"[23] but more than that it is a revelation of human love and appreciation. A nephew discovers a new depth of feeling for an aunt who, in spite of the narrow circumstances of her own life, taught him an appreciation for the fine and the beautiful, gave to him gifts she could not give to herself, opened doors for him that were forever closed to her. Out of this young man's memory a wonderful, almost heroic, portrait takes shape; this portrait is the woman, and this woman is the story. Georgiana arrives in Boston, black with soot and sick with travel, a "misshapen figure" in a "black stuff dress." Her nephew Clark, so terribly aware of her oddness, nevertheless regards her with unmistakable "awe and respect" (p. 236). Every detail, even down to her bent shoulders, "sunken chest," "ill-fitting false teeth," and "skin as yellow as a Mongolian's" (p. 236), is mellowed by his loving regard for her. Seen through another pair of eyes she would have been a country caricature, but seen through his eyes, she becomes a symbol of the pioneer spirit.[24]

Through Clark's memory Cather reconstructs incidents that define Georgiana's character. His earliest recollections must have

come to him secondhand, perhaps as an old family story. He remembers hearing that as "an angular, spectacled woman of thirty," she
conceived an "extravagant passion" for "a handsome country boy of
twenty-one" and eloped with him, "eluding the reproaches of her
family" by going to the Nebraska frontier where, through incredible
hardships, she and Howard Carpenter managed to establish themselves. Georgiana becomes for Clark something like what Ántonia
was to become for Jim Burden, heroic and wonderful, if not mythic.
In spite of coarse outward circumstances, she retained a fineness of
spirit with which she unconsciously and continually blessed his life.
He reflects gratefully, "I owed to this woman most of the good that
ever came my way in my boyhood, and had a reverential affection for
her" (p. 236). He remembers the countless times that she stood at
her ironing board at midnight, after the day's chores were over and
the six young children were in bed, drilling him on Latin verbs, or
listening to him read Shakespeare. He recalls further, "She taught
me my scales and exercises, too—on the little parlour organ, which
her husband had bought her after fifteen years, during which she
had not so much as seen any instrument, but an accordion that be-
longed to one of the Norwegian farmhands" (p. 237). It was she who
gave Clark "her old text-book on mythology," the first book he ever
owned. It was she who listened to him practice, counting out the
time with him. Once as he struggled with an old piece of her music
he had found, she came up behind him, put her hands over his eyes,
and drew his head to her shoulder. With trembling voice she
warned, "Don't love it so well, Clark, or it may be taken from you.
Oh! dear boy, pray that whatever your sacrifice may be, it be not
that" (p. 237).

   Now, years later, he wonders if the concert will mean anything to
her, wishing "for her own sake . . . her taste for such things quite
dead, and the long struggle mercifully ended at last" (p. 237). Her
chief concern as they travel the city she had once known so well is
for "a certain weakling calf" at home, and "a freshly-opened kit of
mackerel in the cellar" which could spoil in her absence. But when
the music begins, she meets it in a rush of combined anguish and joy.
By turns she clutches at Clark's coat sleeve, or moves her "bent and
knotted" fingers across an imaginary keyboard on her old dress, or
weeps silently. Clark knows then that the feeling "never really
died," that "the soul that can suffer so excruciatingly and so intermi-
nably; it withers to the outward eye only; like that strange moss

which can lie on a dusty shelf half a century and yet, if placed in water, grows green again" (p. 240).

However much this story discloses the irreclaimable loss suffered by a woman who exchanged her artistic loves and drives for the cruelties of frontier life, however painful the experience in the concert hall is for all of us who sit with Clark beside Aunt Georgiana, we are not back "on the Divide" with Canute Canuteson. Even in our grief we are in an atmosphere of human caring and appreciation; we are in the presence of genuine feelings unashamedly expressed. Cather evokes these feelings through the momentary collision between the world of music and culture which Georgiana had rejected so long ago and the stark, barren world she chose out of love. Her two worlds pause in equipoise as the concert ends and the musicians exit, "leaving the stage to the chairs and music stands, empty as a winter cornfield" (p. 241). And, as Clark observes, just outside that door in Boston is Nebraska waiting to claim its stepchild.

After thirty years, Aunt Georgiana has tasted again of the goblin fruit, the luscious nectar that never satisfies, but only increases the appetite. Again the lure is the world of art, quite different from the evil materialism of the fabled troll garden, but a lure nevertheless. Appropriately, Cather leaves the story at the door of the concert hall, with the return to Nebraska as inevitable as the winter prairie wind. The cold, harsh world of the Divide may yet again scar over the wound newly opened, and Georgiana may slip gratefully into the somnambulant routine of her life in Nebraska; but for the moment she is caught hopelessly between the two worlds that have shaped her life. Clark's mournful observation at the beginning of the Pilgrim's chorus (*Tannhauser* overture) seems to define the mood of the story in terms of opposition, change, and loss: "With the battle between the two motives, with the frenzy of the Venusberg theme and its ripping of strings, there came to me an overwhelming sense of the waste and wear we are so powerless to combat; and I saw again the tall, naked house on the prairie, black and trim as a wooden fortress. . ." (p. 239).

"Paul's Case," the final story in *The Troll Garden,* is drawn from Cather's experiences as a high school English teacher and lower-middle-class neighborhood dweller in Pittsburgh. It was the only story for some time that Cather allowed to be anthologized. Published seven years before Cather's first novel would appear, it remains one of her most widely read and acclaimed works.

Eccentric, maybe even half-crazy, Paul abhors the dull respectability of his neighborhood on Cordelia Street and his high school. He finds his only pleasure as an usher at Carnegie Hall and as a hanger-on with the stock theater company where he can bask in the artificial glow emanating from stage lights which never play on him, from hotel lobbies he is forbidden to enter, from music and paintings he does not understand, and from the lives of performers he completely misinterprets. By comparison, school and home are drab, unbearable; he cannot be bothered with them. After a minor inquisition in which his teachers "fell upon him without mercy" (p. 244), Paul still shows no inclination to study or to be agreeable. It is decided finally that he must quit school and go to work, and that he must forego Carnegie Hall and the stock company.

Thus imprisoned in Cordelia Street with all legitimate avenues of escape effectually closed, Paul commits a desperate act. Entrusted to deliver his company's weekend bank deposit, Paul makes his decision and takes flight. Structurally, the story is as bold as Paul. Part 1 ends with the adult collusion that separates Paul from the only things he loves; part 2 begins in abrupt juxtaposition with Paul on a train bound for New York. Once in New York he lives for several marvelous days the life he had always believed he was suited to live, the life of a wealthy boy in a luxurious room at the Waldorf, wearing fine clothes, eating elegant food, and surrounding himself with flowers.[25] But those self-indulgent days make it impossible for him to return to Cordelia Street. When Paul learns from the Pittsburgh newspapers that his father has repaid the stolen money and is en route to New York to retrieve him, he takes a ferry to Newark and a cab out of town. Then he dismisses the cab and struggles through deep snow along the bank beside the Pennsylvania tracks. When the train comes he leaps into its path. In the instant before he dies, however, he suffers a heartbreaking realization: he had been too impatient in grabbing his one moment of splendor; he should have gone to exotic lands across the seas.

A fitting climax to the *Troll Garden* collection, "Paul's Case" is the most overt treatment of the troll garden/goblin market theme in the book. Paul is obviously the hungry forest child who is utterly helpless before the luscious appeal of the garden, represented for him in the trappings of wealth and in his adolescent perception of the artist's world. For Paul there is no reasoned choice, no weighing of alternatives and consequences, no will to resist; for him there is only ugliness and the garden, and he must have the garden. But Paul is also Cather's ultimate alien. He belongs nowhere, and can never belong. Expanding the theme she had introduced in her early stories on the Divide, Cather portrays in Paul a being who is alienated by more than environment and lack of human contact and understanding. Peter, Canute, Serge, and Lou could all have been saved by altered environmental circumstances and human caring, but not Paul. He thinks an environmental change is all he needs, but he is wrong. And he will admit no need for the love of mere mortals.

Paul knows that he is unsuited for Cordelia Street; what he does not know is that he is unsuited for the worlds of art and wealth as well. Paul is an alien because he has a warped perception of everything; he is unable to see anything in his world as it really is. His mind reconstructs the world in his image of it, and then he tries to inhabit the world he conceives. Since in truth one segment of Paul's world is better than he imagines it to be, and the other is worse than he imagines, he is always out of step no matter where he is. Cordelia Street is repulsive to him, utterly ugly with its "grimy zinc tub[s]" and "cracked mirror[s]" (p. 251) and its insufferable monotony. Cather indicates, however, that Paul's view is not necessarily correct. Cordelia Street is a respectable neighborhood where semisuccessful white collar workers and their wives rear great broods of children and attend ice cream socials at church. The fact that Paul's father can readily make good Paul's theft suggests that he is far from destitute.

Paul wants to believe that Cordelia Street and his high school represent the very antithesis of the world for which he was made, the world of wealth and glamour. What he fails to perceive is that the ideals of Cordelia Street are identical with his own. He only thinks his values are out of place there; in actuality they are not. Cordelia Street, like Paul, worships glamour and money and the things money can buy. Its gods are the wealthy business magnates for whom the men on Cordelia Street work. Up and down the street people like Paul's father sit on their front steps and exchange "legends of the iron kings," tales of their bosses who cruise the Mediterranean but still keep office hours on their yachts, "knocking off work enough to keep two stenographers busy." The street fairly buzzes with "stories of palaces in Venice, yachts on the Mediterranean, and high play at Monte Carlo," stories absorbed greedily by the underlings of the "various chiefs and overlords" (pp. 249, 250) whom Paul would like to emulate. Cordelia Street constructs a golden vision of the world Paul longs to enter.

The only thing within Paul's reach that approximates that fairy world is the world of art—music, drama, painting. It seems to offer what he seeks.[26] But he is just as wrong in his perception of that world as he is in his perception of Cordelia Street. He mistakes its stagey glitter for its essence. Like Flavia, he knows nothing of true art. Since mere finery is what he craves, "symphonies, as such," do not mean "anything in particular to Paul"; but he loves them for their show just as he loves paintings and the theater. For him art is the soloist's "elaborate gown and a tiara, and above all . . . that indefinable air of achievement, that world-shine" (p. 246). He longs to enter what he perceives to be a tropical world of shiny, glistening surfaces and basking ease" (p. 247). But not being an artist himself he has no real place in that spangled world.

Cather makes it clear that not only is Paul not an artist, but his perception of the artist's life and the artist's glittering world is miles from the truth. The artists in this story have no delusions—and no wealth. Scarcely the "veritable queen of Romance" that Paul believes her to be, the German soloist is, in fact, "by no means in her first youth, and the mother of many children" (p. 246). Paul's notions about the stock company players is equally distorted, and they, "especially the women," are "vastly amused" when they learn of the romantic stories Paul has told about them. "They were hardworking women, most of them supporting indigent husbands or brothers, and they laughed rather bitterly at having stirred the boy to such fervid and florid inventions." It is a further irony that Paul's idols "agreed with the faculty and with his father that Paul's was a bad case" (p. 253). His alienation from the world of art is complete.

Paul's last desperate effort to find place, to be where "his surroundings explained him" (p. 257), is also destined to failure, again because he mistakes artificial sheen for reality—and because he can make no distinction between the radiance of art and the shimmer of the Waldorf. The latter is just another version of the opera house to him. Art equals shine; shine equals wealth. To him it is all one desire. In New York, with a thousand dollars at his disposal, he believes he is home at last, for "on every side of him towered the glaring affirmation of the omnipotence of wealth." Here, he thinks, is the center of life; ". . .the plot of all dramas, the text of all romances, the nerve-stuff of all sensations was whirling about him like the snow flakes." He glides easily about the Waldorf, at last with "his own people," feeling "as though he were exploring the chambers of an enchanted palace, built and peopled for him alone" (p. 256).

But Paul has merely purchased the sensation of home, played his only ace for a few days of belonging. With stolen money he buys an artificial environment in which to enclose himself—linens, suits, gorgeous people, a fine room, and the hotel itself. Even Central Park is not real, but is "a wonderful stage winterpiece" (p. 256). The Waldorf encasing Paul is the final symbol of his alienation because its artificial splendor isolates him from encroaching reality. Cather represents the Waldorf and its displaced occupant in repeated references to the alien hothouse flowers that bloom "under glass cases" on the streets of New York, all the "more lovely and alluring that they blossomed thus unnaturally in the snow" (p. 256). Like Paul, the flowers can survive for a time if they are protected by artificial light and heat. But even then, their days are limited, and if they are ever removed from their heated cases, they wither and die.

In the story's final scenes, Cather continues to equate Paul symbolically with flowers out of place in a harsh environment. Walking along the tracks, having made the decision never to return to Cordelia Street, Paul notices that "the carnations in his coat were drooping with the cold, . . . their red glory over. It occurred to him that all the flowers he had seen in the glass cases that first night must have gone the same way, long before this. It was only one splendid breath they had, in spite of their brave mockery at the winter outside the glass; and it was a losing game in the end, it seemed, this revolt against the homilies by which the world is run" (p. 260). As if prompted by this symbolic description of his own brief moment of splendor and its inevitable end, Paul buries a blossom in the snow, acknowledging his death in a cold world that holds no lasting home for him.

Paul misconceives the garden of art as a glittering world of wealth and ease, and he fails to perceive that the chief difference between Cordelia Street and the Waldorf is the difference between wanting and having—a difference not of kind but of degree. Understanding these worlds so little, he has no home in either of them. Only in his death, when he "drop[s] back into the immense design of things" (p. 261), does the alien child appear to find place.

Thus, the pursuit of art and the pursuit of wealth exact their tolls. One by one the stories in *The Troll Garden* show the consequences of such pursuits, whether misguided or true, whether understood by the seekers or not. And then, in the climactic story, "Paul's Case," the two are seen as one goal, a final impossible and intolerable irony in which Paul equates God and mammon.

NOTES

1. Faulkner, *Willa Cather's Collected Short Fiction,* p. 264. Unless otherwise noted, all page references to stories through 1912 are from this volume (page references are in parentheses in the text).

2. Isabelle was the daughter of a distinguished Pittsburgh judge, Samuel A. McClung.

3. Bennett, *World of Willa Cather,* p. 38, indicates that Cather's youngest brother was called "Jack-a-boy" as a youngster, and that in the story Cather "described her admiration" for him. "She told friends that she would give anything just to look into his eyes for ten minutes." The sentimentality of the story may be partly attributable to Cather's feelings for Jack. Her continuing fondness for him is apparent in a letter to Frances Cather (Aunt Franc), dated 17 November 1914 (presumably), Nebraska State Historical Society archives. Jack had been staying with her in New York, attending school, and she speaks proudly and affectionately of her little brother who is becoming so manly.

4. "The Sculptor's Funeral," "A Death in the Desert," "A Wagner Matinee," and "Paul's Case" also appear in *Youth and the Bright Medusa.*

5. These composition dates are suggested in Faulkner, *Willa Cather's Collected Short Fiction,* p. 148.

6. Charles Kingsley, *The Roman and the Teuton: A Series of Lectures Delivered before the University of Cambridge* (London and New York: MacMillan & Co., 1891), pp. 1–5. Bernice Slote discovered this source. In an appendix to *Kingdom of Art,* pp. 442–44, she reprints the entire "Forest Children" story.

7. In a tribute to the deceased Rossetti in a *Journal* column, 13 January 1895, Cather describes "Goblin Market" as Christina Rossetti's "one perfect poem," and she quotes from it and discusses it at some length.

8. Slote, *Kingdom of Art,* pp. 442–43.

9. Brown, *Willa Cather: A Critical Biography,* pp. 113–15.

10. Slote, *Kingdom of Art,* p. 95. See also Bradford ("Willa Cather's Uncollected Short Stories," p. 545) who says, "A reading of the uncollected

stories dealing with artists reveals that Miss Cather's attitude toward the artist was more complex than might be supposed from reading only the accepted stories."

11. Slote, *Kingdom of Art,* pp. 95–96.

12. She also published her only volume of poetry during this period, *April Twilights* in 1903.

13. Bloom and Bloom, *Willa Cather's Gift of Sympathy,* p. 117.

14. Brown, *Willa Cather: A Critical Biography,* p. 118.

15. Bloom and Bloom, *Willa Cather's Gift of Sympathy,* p. 149.

16. Slote ("Willa Cather as a Regional Writer," p. 11) suggests that even though the inhabitants of Sand City are crude and materially corrupt, " 'The Sculptor's Funeral' cannot be taken altogether as a judgment of the small town in the west; it is based on more general observations." She notes that the situation in the story is actually based on an incident that occurred in Pittsburgh, the return of the body of artist Charles Stanley Reinhart for burial. Bennett ("Willa Cather in Pittsburgh") was the first to make the connection between the short story and an early newspaper column in which Cather describes the Reinhart homecoming.

17. See Wagner's *Parsifal.* When Parsifal breaks the sorcerer's spell, Klingsor's garden, like that of the trolls, collapses in ruins.

18. The Blooms (*Willa Cather's Gift of Sympathy,* pp. 148–49) interpret the story to be Katharine's. They speak of the "sacrificial motif" in the story, of the artist who destroys herself in creating beauty for a world that is largely disinterested. They even describe Katharine's disease-wracked body as "the personification of the artist's self-immolation." Woodress, *Willa Cather: Her Life and Art,* also believes that if the story contains tragedy, Katharine's life is that tragedy, while Everett's life is only pathos. Several Cather letters make it clear that she had serious doubts, both early and late, about the quality of "A Death in the Desert." Still, she elected to include it in *Youth and the Bright Medusa.*

19. Bradford ("Willa Cather's Uncollected Short Stories," p. 544) makes the interesting comment about both poem and story "that attending an artist is as destructive of one's personal life as attending a saint."

20. Bloom and Bloom, *Willa Cather's Gift of Sympathy,* p. 146.

21. Brown, *Willa Cather: A Critical Biography,* p. 123.

22. The idea for this story comes from a visit Cather made to the studio of artist Sir Edward Burne-Jones on her first trip to England in 1902. That visit is described in an account she sent back to the *Journal.* It has since been collected in Kates, *Willa Cather in Europe.* As Kates says, "... it is with no great surprise that we find the entrance lodge, the 'bare tank' of the studio itself, and, above all, this active-minded talkative guardian—even with his own name [James]—eventually reappearing in further work" (p. 66). There was also an unfinished picture in the Burne-Jones studio, not on

the Phaedra subject, which caught Cather's attention and became the central concern of her story.

23. See Bloom and Bloom, *Willa Cather's Gift of Sympathy,* p. 8, for example.

24. See Bennett, *World of Willa Cather,* note, p. 254, and Woodress, *Willa Cather: Her Life and Art,* pp. 116–17, for references to the ire Cather's portrait of Georgiana raised in Nebraska when "A Wagner Matinee" first appeared in 1904. Cather, distressed over the reaction of local people to her picture of life on the Divide, softened the portrait of the old woman for the *Troll Garden* collection and cut the offending paragraph describing Georgiana altogether for the *Youth and the Bright Medusa* collection (1920).

25. At least two sources suggest that Cather used two different models for her portraits of Paul in Pittsburgh and Paul in New York. In a 15 March 1943 letter to John Phillipson (Willa Cather archives in Red Cloud), Cather says that the Pittsburgh Paul was a boy she had taught in her Latin class, and the New York Paul was herself. The boy was high-strung and erratic like Paul, and tried to make people believe that he was a favorite of a theater stock company. So far as she knew, he never ran away or jumped under a train. She indicates that the New York Paul reflects her own feelings about New York and the Waldorf-Astoria when as a young woman in Pittsburgh she made occasional visits there. Cather also says that sometimes a character develops from a writer's grafting another person onto herself. Seibel, in his recollections ("Miss Willa Cather from Nebraska," p. 205), reports that he read "Paul's Case" and insisted to Willa Cather "that the Paul of the first pages would not act like the Paul of the closing pages." He says, "Paul was not drawn from one boy in her high school classes, but from two boys—hence the dualism I sensed and she later admitted."

26. Slote (*Kingdom of Art,* pp. 96–97) speaks of Paul's "genuine if excessive feeling for art" and later describes him as "a Forest Child who desires things rare and strange, but to excess and with no one to help him."

THREE

Finding A Fictional Stance: The McClure's Years, 1906–1912

When the school year ended in the spring of 1906, Willa Cather resigned from her teaching job at Pittsburgh's Allegheny High School and moved to New York to take a position with *McClure's Magazine*. She had been wooed away from Pittsburgh by S.S. Mc-Clure, "that dynamic publishing genius," who had made a special trip to meet the author of *The Troll Garden* and offer her a job on his lively muckraking and literary journal.[1] By 1908 she was managing editor and traveling widely on assignments and material-gathering excursions for *McClure's*. During the years she was associated with that magazine, from 1906–1912,[2] she published nine stories, three of which stand out as singularly original—"The Enchanted Bluff" (*Harper's*, April 1909), "Behind the Singer Tower" (*Collier's*, May 1912), and "The Bohemian Girl" (*McClure's*, August 1912). At least one more, "The Namesake" (*McClure's*, March 1907), is worthy of special mention. The other five, not without their good points and their appeal, do not measure up to the best stories in *The Troll Garden*.

Although by this time Cather had written a number of stories, notably those in *The Troll Garden*, that showed her independence as a writer and her ability to draw upon materials close to her own experience, during the time she was with *McClure's* she wrote several stories that have a distinctly Jamesian flavor. They, and even some later stories, pick up themes James liked to treat—art as a subject for art, the conflicting demands of public and private life, marriage as a difficult institution at best and doubly difficult for the artist, "being" versus "doing," and the foolishness of an artificially engendered and maintained social construct. Situations and moments in these and earlier stories recall James: there are ghosts in some of

68

them, and James, too, wrote of the supernatural; the old man in "The Count of Crow's Nest" makes a moral decision to place honor above other considerations, the kind of decision a Jamesian protagonist would make; "The Marriage of Phaedra" centers around the possible sale of a famous painting as does James's last novel, *The Outcry*. Nevertheless, there are differences between the two writers' handling even of similar themes and materials. Although Cather admits that the artist is sometimes careless, for her the artist generally has more integrity than the consumer of art. In *Roderick Hudson* and other works, however, James portrays the consumer of art as being more careful than the artist. James also tends to write novels and stories of situation rather than of character. When Cather does that, she is more likely to resemble James than when she does not. Part of finding her own stance as a writer seems to have been the recognition that her forte is the creation of characters and landscapes rather than the exploration of situations or manners. And even though the strongest stories in *The Troll Garden* concentrate on character rather than on situation, Cather did not capitalize on this strength as fully as she might have while she worked for *McClure's*. And even after those years, at least until "Uncle Valentine," it was in the novels and not the short stories that she focused on character and landscape and produced her most original work.

I. THE MOTIVES FOR ART

"The Profile" (*McClure's,* June 1907) and "The Willing Muse" (*Century,* August 1907) were published within months after "The Namesake," the first story from the *McClure's* years, appeared. Both show the influence of Henry James: they describe the unfortunate marriages of artists, and they probe sensitively into human nature, exploring the mystery of human relationship.

A. THE MOTIVE OF PITY

"The Profile" is about a reputed artist, a specialist in women's portraiture commissioned to paint a young woman whose face is horribly disfigured on one side by a scar. Their growing fondness leads to marriage and the birth of a frail, unattractive daughter whom they name Eleanor. The painter, Aaron Dunlap, had hoped that Virginia, his wife, would confide in him, share with him the burden of her deformity; but in her vanity she will never admit to it, and a painful estrangement results. Staying with the Dunlaps is a cousin of Virginia's, a student whose name is also Eleanor. On one occasion the miserable Dunlap seeks Eleanor's sympathy with a spontaneous handclasp. Stunned and embarrassed, she soon announces an early departure for America. Virginia senses the reason and haughtily leaves the country herself, but not before arranging an ingenious piece of revenge. The night Virginia departs, Eleanor's bed lamp explodes, burning her badly on the face and arms. Once Dunlap's divorce is final, he marries Eleanor, taking for a second time a wife whose face is disfigured by a scar.

It might appear at first reading that all our sympathy should go to the suffering Dunlap and all our blame to the heartless and proud Virginia, but careful analysis reveals that Dunlap himself is responsible for much of the change he regrets in her nature. Living with a man like him would be next to impossible for a proud woman. Dunlap, "preferably a painter of women," has always seen himself as a gallant protector of what he deems to be the weaker sex. His portraits invariably reveal "a certain quiet element of sympathy, almost of pity, in the treatment" (p. 125), a desire to protect the beautiful face he painted "from the cruelty of the years" (p. 126). Dunlap had grown up wincing at the suffering of women, in "a country where women are hardly used." His own "mother had died of pneumonia contracted from taking her place at the washtub too soon after the birth of a child," and he had watched his drunken grandfather beat his grandmother with cobbling leather. Experiences like these from his childhood "had left him almost morbidly sensitive" (p. 126), and his years in Paris had "quickened in him a sense of the more slight and feminine fairness in things" (p. 127).

Although by nature Dunlap is all tenderness where women are concerned, especially women who have known deep pain, his inordinate interest in misery borders on the grisly. When Virginia begins to sit for him, with the lovely side of her face toward him, he finds an excuse to slip around her and tinker with the window shades in order to examine her scar undetected. Dunlap takes pleasure in pondering Virginia's supposed courage, his heart aching all the while "at the injustice" of her burden. After the first sitting he is "overcast by a haunting sense of tragedy," and his thoughts turn to "his mother and grandmother [and] his little sister . . . as if they were creatures yet unreleased from suffering" (p. 128). Pity leads to love, and Dunlap marries Virginia.

Like Hawthorne's artist Aylmer in "The Birthmark," Dunlap has a neurotic fixation on his wife's one mark of imperfection. Early in the relationship, Virginia seems ignorant of the real source of his attraction, unaware that "he was drawn to her by what had once repelled him [the scar]. Her courageous candor appealed to his chivalry, and he came to love her, not despite the scar, but, in a manner, for its very sake. He had some indefinite feeling that love might heal her; that in time her hurt might disappear, like the deformities imposed by enchantment to test the hardihood of lovers" (p. 129). It is not enough that she is lively and responsive and seems to love him. Seeing himself as some kind of storybook hero, Dunlap mistakenly believes that Virginia must want just such a lover as he is determined to be. He thinks, "Was she not living for the moment when she could throw down the mask and point to it and weep, to be comforted for all time? . . . The moment must come when she would give him her confidence; perhaps it would be only a whisper, a gesture, a guiding of his hand in the dark; but however it might come, it was the pledge he awaited." So sure is he of the healing power of his Messianic love that "during the last few weeks before his marriage, the scar, through the mere strength of his anticipation, had ceased to exist for him. He had already entered to the perfect creature which he felt must dwell behind it" (p. 129). But, of course, had she been perfect, he would not have been drawn to her.

Hurt and disillusioned by Virginia's refusal to indulge his sympathetic attentions, he never seems to realize that from the first he had constructed a set of expectations which, by her very nature, she could not meet. Even motherhood does not dismantle the fortress that was shielding her inner being from him, for her sickly, unbecoming child is only another blemish that Virginia refuses to acknowledge. Obsessed by the scar now, seeing only the scar when he looks at her, he at last dares to mention it, to criticize her for wearing clothing that makes an ostentation of it. But with her convulsive shudder, he is immediately "sick with pity," feeling as a man might "who has tortured an animal" (p. 134). That dreariest of emotions, pity, is perhaps the deepest feeling of which Dunlap is capable. He is more grotesque than she; he must poke the sick animal with a stick to see it writhe.

Surely, Virginia had begun to sense early in their marriage that his love was based mainly on pity, and that the thing she hated passionately was the thing he found most alluring in her. The only door through which he wanted to enter the relationship was the one door she could not open to anyone, least of all to one who came exuding pity in the name of love. She has to leave him to preserve her integrity, to assert her right to be a person rather than a deformity. Dunlap learns nothing from the experience. He never changes. Out of what must have been the same impulse that led to his first marriage, he enters his second, with the scarred Eleanor.

B. THE MOTIVE OF SUCCESS

The Jamesian overtones are evident in "The Profile," but they are still more evident in "The Willing Muse." Artists are the subjects for several of James's early stories, and the sympathy of the artist for his subject is emphasized in a story like "The Real Thing." Perhaps even more pertinent here is what S. Gorley Putt calls James's fascination with "emotional cannibalism." He says that in a novel like *The Sacred Fount* and a maudlin story called "Longstaff's Marriage," "self-abnegation is exposed as the most chilling demonstration of possessiveness." Putt adds, "James had a sharp nose for that kind of superior suffering which is inseparable from moral blackmail."[3] Aaron Dunlap is certainly guilty of the sort of emotional violation seen in James.

"The Willing Muse" bears a very close relationship to at least two of James's novels and a few short stories. Not only does Cather appear to have borrowed the idea for her title from James, but Nick Dorimer and Miriam Rooth in *The Tragic Muse* are prototypes for Kenneth Gray and Bertha Torrence. Though Dorimer is a painter and Miriam is an actress while both Gray and Bertha are writers, Gray's art is private and self-absorbing like Dorimer's, and Bertha's is social like Miriam's. As with Dorimer, there is some question as to whether Gray is an artist at all. The performance of both is anything but impressive. Bertha's enervating effect on Gray is also prefigured in *The Sacred Fount* in the relationship between Mrs. Brissendon and her husband. Like Mrs. Brissendon, Bertha seems increasingly youthful and energetic while her husband seems increasingly sapped of his youth and energy. Both women appear to drain the very life out of their mates, to live by drawing lifeblood from them. In Cather as in James, marriage can be killing. Short stories by James like "The Lesson of the Master," which shows the conflict between marriage and literary effort, and "Greville Fane," which describes a woman who writes vulgar best-sellers, also have corresponding elements in Cather's story.

In "The Willing Muse" Bertha Torrence cheerfully buries Kenneth Gray under the reproachful pages of her own efficiently prodigious output. The sensitive Gray, who has always been protected and coddled by people like the narrator, Philip, and another friend named Harrison, is recognized as having a rare and valuable artistic gift. After Gray and Bertha are married, her productivity and reputation soar while his creative activity dwindles until he functions mainly as her assistant, handling correspondence and reading proofs and manuscripts. Some years later he simply disappears, and the narrator and Harrison, having some notion of where he is, resume their protective roles by keeping his secret.

Cather's purpose in the story is at least partly to play the mentality of the conventional popular artist against an ethereal, flighty, but truly remarkable nature like Kenneth Gray's. Cather asserts that the kind of talent that hammers out best-sellers in assembly line fashion bears little resemblance to the talent which creates art, or has the capability to create art. A marriage between Bertha and Gray, who represent the two kinds of talent, is as impossible as a marriage between artificial art and genuine art.

Perhaps feeling some guilt about having almost gratefully abandoned Gray to Bertha's influence and lifestyle, Philip decides that he is duty-bound to instruct her in the proper treatment of so delicate an organism as Gray. The ensuing conversation is a classic exercise in noncomprehension. If Philip, as protector of Gray, is tactless and manipulative, Bertha is blind and insensitive. She sees little but the fact of Gray's talent, and can understand nothing of the creative paralysis which strangles him. For her, "The problem is simply to make him mine his vein." Philip then suggests that success might be destructive to Gray, and confesses in deliberately niggling language that he had never dared urge Gray too much because of the artist's obvious "chosenness." She, of course, will not hear of it. A man with talent will produce: "What he needs is simply to keep at it" (pp. 115–16).

During the first years of their marriage, Bertha continues to spin off two books per year, written, Philip has to admit, very well, "indeed, rather better and better." It is hard to criticize Bertha, unless it might be for her "intrepid, whole-hearted, unimpeachable conventionality. One could not exactly call her unscrupulous; one could only observe that no predicament embarrassed her; that she went ahead and pulled it off" (p. 117). When Gray finally disappears, Bertha is incredulous, even astonished. Harrison, however, believes he knows exactly why Gray left: serving the cause of pseudoart was draining the soul out of him, and there was no way for him to remain with Bertha and not serve that cause. Bertha, like Flavia, is a parasite that feeds upon and depletes an artist.

Cather makes her point about pseudoart, but she does not merely demolish the world's Bertha Torrences. In fact, Philip and Harrison's admiration for Bertha, if somewhat grudging, is real. Bertha does write well, and the final lines of the story pay her a genuine tribute: "'For after all,' sighed Harrison, . . . 'Bertha is a wonderful woman—a woman of her time and people; and she has managed, in spite of her fatal facility, to be enough sight better than most of us'" (p. 123). It is well to remember, too, as Bernice Slote observes in *The Kingdom of Art,* that as a young columnist Cather admired the energetic performer, on stage and in books and in life. The more delicate, even if more perfect, artists sometimes lack spirit and feeling.[4]

In addition to presenting the conflict between genuine and spurious art Cather also makes an implicit comment about the relationship between Bertha and Gray. Almost totally ignorant of self and each other, they enter into marriage, each expecting the union to spur them on to wonderful things. Gray never seems to have suspected what life with Bertha would be like; Bertha never seems to notice that serving her interests is destroying Gray. Bertha's mind is inoperative in realms of uncertainty and ambiguity, and Gray's cannot function on a plane of practical certainties. Bertha has no conception of what true art is, and Gray is completely baffled by Bertha's businesslike productivity. There is virtually no understanding between them and apparently no thought that such understanding might be sought.

II. THREE PERSPECTIVES ON THE PAST

Since Cather was soon to begin work on what was to be *Alexander's Bridge,* whose central motif is the protagonist's attempt to recapture his lost youth and the past, it is perhaps no surprise that several of Cather's stories from the *McClure's* years would deal with the past. In "The Namesake," "Eleanor's House," and "The Enchanted Bluff," Cather examines three different perspectives on the past, three different uses of it. The first story, "The Namesake," argues for the inestimable value of one's personal past, of blood relationships through which one finds oneself and perhaps even the key to one's creative energies. On the other hand, "Eleanor's House" shows the uselessness and even the danger of an inordinate devotion to a particular past which makes the present a betrayal and the future an impossibility. "The Enchanted Bluff" anticipates some of the best of Cather's subsequent fiction by exploring the healthy fascination of a group of youngsters for the legends and peoples of long ago. Thus, in these three stories Cather asserts the value of human ties, to one's own progenitors and to the human race as a whole, throughout time. She also warns against petty assumptions about anyone's claiming exclusive rights to segments of the past.

Cather's debt to James is very apparent in "Eleanor's House" and nonexistent in "The Enchanted Bluff." The frame story of "The Namesake" is set in Europe and centers around an artist; to that extent it may be said to bear resemblance to the work of James.

A. THE RECOVERED PAST

"The Namesake" is about a sculptor who tells a group of aspiring young artists in Paris of a journey he made to his ancestral home in America many years ago. His story recounts his birth as an artist through an apocalyptic spiritual union with a youngster he had never known, but whose blood he suddenly felt coursing in his own veins. Like "The Enchanted Bluff," "The Namesake" presents a layered past, with the narrator looking back on an event that opened to him a still more distant past, thus creating a present, a middle past, and a distant past. Called to America as a young man to care for an aging aunt left alone by the death of her father, Lyon Hartwell left his studies in Europe and took up temporary residence at the old Hartwell homestead in western Pennsylvania. Having lived in Europe with his artist father all his life, Hartwell felt himself an alien in the old house: "Within the house I was never at home. Month followed month, and yet I could feel no sense of kinship with anything there. Under the roof where my father and grandfather were born, I remained utterly detached" (p. 143).

The only link Hartwell felt with his past was through a portrait of the boy-uncle for whom he was named, a boy who, at a very tender age, lost his life while carrying the colors for his regiment in the Civil War. This boy is surely a brief sketch of the character who

would become Claude Wheeler in *One of Ours*. He, like Claude, is totally idealistic, totally committed to the cause for which he fights.
For him, war in the name of human freedom is a glorious thing. Like
Claude, he is fearless in battle and remains at his post even after he
is fatally wounded. And like Claude, he is spared postwar disillusionment by losing his life in heroic action while still in his youth.
Again, as she had done in numerous letters and works of fiction,
Cather pays tribute to the faith, beauty, and courage of youth. And,
as much as her letters reveal her hatred of war and its destruction,
in both *One of Ours* and "The Namesake," she demonstrates her affection for the young men who serve on the battlefront.

Looking for a flag to display on Memorial Day, Hartwell found a
trunk in the attic bearing the name given to the boy and later to
him, Lyon Hartwell. Inside were the boy's clothes, his books, his
army letters, and various other articles. But it was in a well-worn
copy of the *Aeneid* that Hartwell discovered the living boy. In finding his young ancestor, he also discovered himself, found his spiritual roots. The catalyst for his revelation was a sketch of the federal
flag drawn by the boy-uncle in that book, a sketch with these words
written above it in "a slanting, boyish hand":

> Oh, say can you see by the dawn's early light
> What so proudly we hailed at the twilight's last gleaming?

As Hartwell looked at the drawing, he felt in a "rush of . . . realization" that he knew the boy "as he was then" (p. 145). Deeply moved,
he raced out to the garden, to the locust tree which the boy had
planted; he could almost feel the boy's presence there. In emotion-
filled rhetoric Hartwell divulges the meaning of his discovery:

> The experience of that night, coming so overwhelmingly to a
> man so dead, almost rent me in pieces. It was the same feeling
> that artists know when we, rarely, achieve truth in our work; the
> feeling of union with some great force, of purpose and security, of
> being glad that we have lived. For the first time I felt the pull of
> race and blood and kindred, and felt beating within me things
> that had not begun with me. It was as if the earth under my feet
> had grasped and rooted me, and were pouring its essence into me.
> I sat there until the dawn of morning, and all night long my life

seemed to be pouring out of me and running into the ground. (P. 146)

In this passage, spoken with the same passion that characterizes similar expressions in *O Pioneers!, The Song of the Lark, My Ántonia,* and *One of Ours,* Cather says that the miracle of art is made possible through the miracle of human understanding and relationship. This new sense of relationship, of human understanding, of connection with past, is the key to unlocking the self. It released the artist in Hartwell and gave him a subject. The Civil War henceforth provided him with both historical and emotional material for numerous sculptures, the last and best of which portrays his boy-uncle "running, clutching the folds of the flag, the staff of which had been shot away" (p. 139).

Hartwell's finding his life as an artist through union with his past anticipates Thea Kronborg's discovery about her relationship with an even older past, with the ancient potsherds of the southwest desert. In the moment that she first comprehends their yearning for art, she gains an understanding of her own compulsion, and her artist self is sprung free. For Thea, the past is no longer an abstraction; it is people, human beings like herself. The revelations experienced by Thea and Hartwell are, in a very real sense, a homecoming. And it is no exaggeration to say that art very often chronicles humanity's efforts to find home, place, roots, and connections. The home motif is particularly strong in "The Namesake." Hartwell's unusual candor with his young adulators, his unexpected willingness to share a personal experience with them, is prompted by the fact that one of them has been called home, just as he himself was called home so many years ago.

The story also contains a counterthrust that prophesies the loss of home in the wake of industrial expansion, a perennial concern for Willa Cather. The Hartwell homestead, originally built on a river's high banks in gentle green country, is now completely surrounded by industrial desecration. The timber-stripped hills are peppered with oil derricks, gas wells, and coal shafts. The rivers and skies are polluted. The great manufactories are almost at the doorstep. In the midst of "tumultuous life," a "glare of relentless energy" (p. 141), the old homestead, now only house, garden, and orchard, stands like an island of tranquility. But even on this island the remaining trees "had the look of doomed things." They "bent a little toward town and seemed to wait with head inclined before that oncoming, shrieking force" (p. 142). Home will undoubtedly be lost again, but the boy who lost his life in battle will not have to suffer that agony. And the most important legacy the sculptor inherited, an emotional "home," remains intact.

B. THE MANUFACTURED PAST

"Eleanor's House" (*McClure's,* October 1907), in giving another perspective on the past, warns against the mindless sacrifice of everything, especially a living human being, to a notion of the past that has little validity in the present. The past, valuable as it is, can be a lie, Cather warns, and trying to live such a lie can destroy one's humanity. "Eleanor's House" is not one of Cather's best stories, but it is one of her most fascinating and most sophisticated to date, demonstrating a subtle psychological complexity that shows, perhaps more than any other of her stories, the influence of Henry James.

Not only does Cather portray Americans living abroad, but her point-of-view character, Harriet Westfield, might have walked out of a number of James's works. The most obvious links are with *The Spoils of Poynton* and *The Golden Bowl.* Mrs. Gereth, who lives in the dower house while her son and his rather vulgar fiancée, Mona Brigstock, have their residence at beautiful Poynton, surely suggests the character of Harriet Westfield who cannot bear the thought that Harold Forscythe's supposedly clumsy second wife, Ethel, might inhabit Harriet's (actually Forscythe and dead Eleanor's) beloved Fortuney. Fleda Vetch, Mrs. Gereth's choice for her son, prefigures Eleanor in that she is admired by Mrs. Gereth just as Eleanor was admired by Harriet. And Cather's story is focused through Harriet's eyes just as James's is perceived through Mrs. Gereth's. In the end, however, Harriet is able to recover Fortuney, while Mrs. Gereth burns Poynton to prevent Mona from getting its treasures. There is also in Harriet something of Fanny Assingham from *The Golden Bowl.* Like Fanny, Harriet wearies her husband with discussions about what is happening in the relationships of others.

At first glance "Eleanor's House" recalls "The Willing Muse" which immediately precedes it in the Cather canon. Both stories feature a marriage which is expected to save a gifted male from the weaknesses of his own character. But surprisingly, the marriage between Eleanor and Harold Forscythe in the later story was apparently a perfect one, until Eleanor suddenly became ill and died. Now the desolate husband has taken a second wife, Ethel, whom he coldly keeps at a distance because she attempts to heal his pain rather than just console him over his loss. Made bold by her own desperation, in the end she follows him to the house where he had lived with Eleanor and forces him to choose between her and the dead woman. Ultimately, he chooses the living Ethel, and they make plans to return to America and begin a new life.

Chief mourner over the death of Eleanor and the sorrows of Forscythe is Harriet Westfield; and, since she is the story's center of consciousness, point of view unexpectedly becomes the story's most important fact. It is through point of view that Cather discloses that her central concern is not the relationship between Forscythe and Ethel, but rather the relationship between Harriet and the dead Eleanor. As Harriet's attitudes and opinions are reported, her perplexing biases and her almost insane devotion to the memory of Eleanor surface. It becomes apparent that the story is designed as a delicately fashioned revelation of one woman's possessiveness and jealousy and her obsessive devotion to the past. Forscythe and Ethel, we realize, are only minor figures, important mainly as they threaten or otherwise affect Harriet's inflated image of Eleanor.

Cather accomplishes several important things in establishing Harriet as her point-of-view character. For example, she creates reader trust in Harriet and Harriet's assessments of people and situations. This allows the eventual revelation of her true nature and function in the story to strike with unusual force. Toward the close of the story, as Harriet's endless petty observations and suspicions about Ethel accumulate, we begin to see Harriet for the jealous, reactionary person she is. In the end, because of what we know about Harriet, we realize that there is nothing left for her to do but buy a piece of the past—Fortuney, the only segment of life she really believes in—and slip out of the present which she is powerless to affect or understand.

Then too, Cather's use of Harriet as the point-of-view character conceals Ethel's true nature and potential until the end of the story. Harriet despises Forscythe for marrying someone less than Eleanor, and she despises Ethel with a terrible, almost unspeakable antipathy for not being Eleanor. Ethel is clearly the outsider whom Harriet cannot admit into the charmed circle, although she feigns a certain sympathy for Ethel and attributes some of her own negative feelings to Forscythe. She describes Ethel as a "poor, limp, tactless,

terrified girl" who even walks in an "exasperating way," and assumes that Forscythe "hates the way she likes what she likes, and
he hates the way she dislikes what she doesn't like" (p. 97). At the
end, the reader is no less surprised than Harriet to discover that under Ethel's influence Forscythe has found himself, has abandoned
Eleanor's ghost, and will go on to be still "finer and finer" (p. 111).
We come to the rather abrupt realization that Ethel is not the grace-
less rag we had thought her to be. In fact, she emerges as a worthy
successor to Eleanor, and Harriet is buried in the nostalgia that had
blurred her vision from the first.

By using Harriet as her point-of-view figure, Cather is also able
to create the inescapable presence of Eleanor. Harriet's goddess is
indeed immortal, and Harriet is her prophetess, preaching in her
name, worshiping her, demanding like worship from fellow believ-
ers, and interpreting her will on numerous occasions. Forscythe is a
convert to the faith, one whose apparent defection is a grave disappointment to Harriet; Harriet can keep the faith even in Eleanor's
absence, but Forscythe cannot. His first blunder, Harriet perceives,
is his choice of a second wife who is a mere mortal: "He can't do anything well without her [Eleanor]. You see, he couldn't even do this
[marry intelligently]" (p. 97). The story is filled with Eleanor. Nearly every page contains a reference of some sort, either direct or indi-
rect, to her or to Fortuney. But since Eleanor was only mortal, after
all, this morbid devotion, this enthusiastic misery, this calling of the
congregation to repentance and worship, seems finally inappropriate and even bizarre. The reader, like Forscythe and Ethel, is glad to
escape, guiltily happy to leave Harriet in the quicksand of a past
that finally no one but she could believe in.

What bothers Harriet most about Forscythe's marriage to Ethel is
that Ethel might have aspirations not only toward Eleanor's place
in Forscythe's affections, but also toward Eleanor's house at Fortuney. A foray onto that holy ground, where "a union of the gods" (p.
98) had transpired, would be intolerable to Harriet. She complains
to her husband, "And, mark my words, she is bent on Fortuney. . . .
The girl has fixed her eye, made up her mind . . . and she's circling
about it; she can't endure to be kept out." As his wife grows "more
and more vehement," Robert Westfield remarks sympathetically on
Ethel's difficult situation and her terrifying uncertainty. Through
Westfield's sane responses we come to realize that we cannot rely on
Harriet's perceptions about any matter involving either Eleanor or
Eleanor's house. Harriet sniffs, "The figure she'd cut in a place of

such distinction" (p. 96)! She accuses Ethel of feigning meekness in order to win her way into Fortuney and to supplant the peerless Eleanor. "I've known her kind before!" she cries, eyes flashing. "Can't you see what she wants? . . . She wants to be to him what Eleanor was; she sees no reason why she shouldn't be!" Westfield replies, "Well, why, in Heaven's name, shouldn't she be? He married her. What less can she expect" (p. 98)? Later, when Harriet agrees to go with Ethel to Fortuney in pursuit of the Eleanor-haunted Forscythe, Westfield catches her in an involuntary slip which reveals her real reason for going: " 'Ah, so it's to keep her out, and not to help her in, that you're going,' Westfield deduced" (p. 107).

Finding Forscythe lying heartsick in Eleanor's room at Fortuney is too much for the distraught Ethel. She collapses, and Forscythe at last awakens to the fact of Ethel. He discovers her grief—and her pregnancy—and somehow comes to his senses. He decides to pull out with Ethel, leaving Eleanor and Eleanor's house to Harriet. It will not be quite the same without him, for he had become a part of Harriet's Eleanor myth, but it is nevertheless with a sense of gratitude that Harriet bids the pair goodbye and decides "to buy Fortuney and give up to it" (p. 110). She will never understand Forscythe's "giving up everything" to go with Ethel, for in Harriet's mind, she herself and Forscythe belong together. They alone are "left over from another age—a lovely time that's gone" (p. 110). Still more puzzling to Harriet is the fact that Forscythe now appears to have "come up to his possibilities for the first time, through this silly, infatuated girl, while Eleanor, who gave him kingdoms—" she pauses and does not finish what would have been an impossible admission. Instead, she sighs thankfully that Fortuney, "all that's left of them [Eleanor and Forscythe]," will be hers. And, in particular, she is glad once again to have the uncontested property rights to "my Eleanor" (p. 111)! Gratefully, she sinks back into the past where she can worship her gods in the cloistered safety of Fortuney.

Cather clearly regards Harriet's appropriation of the past in order to escape painful reality as folly. And she prefers symbols of timelessness—the rock, the mesa, the land itself—over monuments to the past.

C. THE SYMBOLIC PAST

It is just such a timeless symbol that Cather creates in "The Enchanted Bluff" and again later in "Tom Outland's Story." The first of her great fictional rocks, the blue mesa of the ancient cliff dwellers inspires reverence for its majesty and appreciation for the silent message it bears from the past.[5] Although Cather had produced some exceptionally fine work prior to "The Enchanted Bluff," with it she opens a new door, finds access to a new set of feelings. This is not the first time, of course, that she uses Nebraska as a setting, but it is the first time that she uses it both tenderly and honestly. Some of the very early Nebraska stories, like "On the Divide" and "Lou, the Prophet," and even stories like "The Sculptor's Funeral" and "A Wagner Matinee," paint perhaps an unfairly harsh picture of life on the prairie, while "The Treasure of Far Island" distorts it in the other direction. Somewhere between these two extremes Cather found the stance that was to inform her fiction for the rest of her life. "The Enchanted Bluff," which finds middle ground, is pivotal in Cather's work. In this story Cather at last looks on Nebraska with ungrudging, yet realistic, affection and begins to use its offerings in a personal way. She describes the Republican River, which she knew intimately in every mood. She writes from a firsthand acquaintance of the seedlings that sprang up in a single season on its mud banks and the children who haunted its bluffs and sand terraces on summer nights. The Divide could be unpredictable and harsh, testing even the hardiest to the very limit; but at the same time it could be lovely, almost temperate in the glow of human dreaming and caring, utterly breathtaking in the cry of a night bird.

As Cather became more aware of her own past and its particular value for her as a writer, she seems to have become increasingly aware of the general potential value of the past for all of us if we have an appropriate attitude toward it. The incidents in this story which are echoed later in her novels almost invariably focus on the past. As the boys of "The Enchanted Bluff" lie on their river island looking up at the stars, their chatter leads into the same subjects that occupy Jim Burden and the hired girls when the day closes on their picnic by the river in *My Ántonia*. Talk among the Sandtown boys ranges from Napoleon to the Aztecs and the early Spanish explorers. In *My Ántonia*, Jim Burden ponders these same legends, telling the hired girls whatever he can remember "about Coronado and his search for the Seven Golden Cities."[6]

The coming of night and the speculations about long ago lead the boys of Sandtown on a mental journey to the faraway western desert where their imaginations settle on the Enchanted Bluff. It becomes their place of desire, the object of their youthful dreams. Tip's uncle, a drifter, had seen the bluff and told Tip stories about the peace-loving Indians who had built a cliff city on it long ago. Steeped in mystery and beckoning to the adventuresome, it is this same mesa that draws Tom Outland like a pin to a magnet in *The Professor's House.* The mesa becomes something of a religious sanctuary for Tom, mainly because of its power to connect past and present. The Sandtown boys do not see the bluff's unifying power in overt terms, but they seem to experience some intuitive sense of it. For Tom, the realization of his oneness with the ancient cliff dwellers, a relationship which crosses the barriers of time, comes in a flash of sacramental wonder. The same thing happens for Thea Kronborg. And when Jean Latour visits the mesa of Ácoma in *Death Comes for the Archbishop,* he is overwhelmed by its timeless antiquity.

So vivid are the narrator's opening descriptive paragraphs in "The Enchanted Bluff" that we are scarcely prepared to learn that what he is describing happened twenty years ago. The past has two dimensions in this story, that of the personal boyhood past of the narrator and that of the historical past that belongs to every human being. Cather's usual method is to put her central tale inside a frame story so that from the beginning the relationship between past and present is apparent. This story, however, opens with the central tale, creating the illusion that the past is the present, vivifying the past and asserting its ever-presentness. There is also something distinctly elegaic about this story, a tone that is enhanced by the juxtaposition of present with personal past, and by the added perspective of two or three layers of ancient past. The childhood past of the Sandtown boys is centered in one great dream, to explore the Enchanted Bluff. But the present confirms the loss of that dream. The vision dies as does one of the principal dreamers, and the others lapse into dreamless adulthood in an unromantic prairie town. Cather counters the loss, however, through the rebirth of the dream in Tip Smith's son, Bert, who "has been let into the story, and thinks of nothing but the Enchanted Bluff" (p. 77). The continuity is always there, reaching backward and forward through time.

III. HOME TERRITORY AND TWO EXPERIMENTS

A. NEBRASKA AGAIN

Two other stories of the group written while Cather was associated with *McClure's,* "The Joy of Nelly Deane" (*Century,* October 1911) and "The Bohemian Girl" (*McClure's,* August 1912), are set in Nebraska and accompany the launching of Cather's career as a novelist. At this time, *Alexander's Masquerade* was appearing in installments in *McClure's,* and Cather was at work on a short novel, *Alexandra.* The first piece was to become *Alexander's Bridge;* the second, in combination with another story, "The White Mulberry Tree," was to become *O Pioneers!* "Nelly Deane" provides a tender, heartwarming, somewhat sentimental early portrait of Lucy Gayheart. Nelly is more carefree than Lucy, full of "unquenchable joy" (p. 56), loved by all in spite of themselves, and not to be denied under any circumstances. If not quite real, Nelly is still irresistible—to the narrator, to the reader, and to the sullen Scott Spinney who doggedly courts this little "grasshopper" when a "pushing ant" (p. 62) would surely have been more to his style.

Nelly and her friend Margaret, after a joyous girlhood together, singing in musical programs, skating on the river, exchanging secrets late at night, take separate paths. Margaret learns after several years, through the faithful Mrs. Dow, that Nelly has remained in Riverbend, and is still pursued by Scott. Apparently Nelly lost the suave Guy Franklin, a traveling salesman who had promised to marry her. Nelly's course seems set now, a dismal one toward marriage with Scott that will end in her early death in childbirth.

Cather sets the story in a town resembling Red Cloud and employs characters and themes that appear regularly in her work. Two of her most frequently used character types are represented in Nelly and Margaret; they are, respectively, the extraordinary female character who is seen through the eyes of an admiring narrator, and the admiring narrator who is almost painfully conscious of her own deficiencies in verve and daring and charm. Established from the beginning as a foil for the impetuous Nelly, Margaret views her story's central figure with frank appreciation, a large dose of apprehension, and no little awe. Even the three older women in town who especially dote on Nelly approve of her friendship with Margaret because Margaret is "quiet" and "a good influence" (p. 57) on the mischievous, headstrong Nelly. Margaret, however, as Mrs. Dow observes, is "inclined to take a sad view of life" (p. 62). At any rate, Mrs. Dow and Margaret both feel protective toward Nelly, as if they recognize instinctively that she has a rare and fragile gift.

There are other characters, too, whom we meet elsewhere in Cather's fiction. The impractical Jud Deane prefigures Hillary Templeton in "Old Mrs. Harris" and James Ferguesson in "The Best Years." Guy Franklin resembles Larry Donovan, the railroad man who disappoints Ántonia; and Scott Spinney, as will be noted in the discussion of "The Bohemian Girl," is a type who appears in later novels and stories. Even though Nelly is most like Lucy Gayheart, she also resembles Thea Kronborg and Claude Wheeler in their compelling desire for life and youth.

Among the recurrent Cather themes appearing in this story is a recognition of the polarity between East and West, here played between the city and the small prairie town. When Nelly repeats Guy Franklin's glowing tales of Chicago to Margaret, the two girls can hear that city "throbbing like great engines, and calling to [them]." The lure of "that faraway world" comes in "a pulsation across all the miles of snow. The winter silence trembled with it, and the air was full of something new that seemed to break over [them] in soft waves" (p. 61). Ironically, it is Nelly who has the loftiest dreams, but Margaret who ultimately leaves Riverbend.

Accompanying Margaret's awareness of the attractions of city life, however, is a strong sense of foreboding. In this story, as in others, Cather recognizes that the passage of time brings painful change and loss. Lying in bed next to Nelly, feeling the tug of Chicago's promises, Margaret also senses "imminent change and danger," and feels "somehow afraid for Nelly" (p. 61). Like a number of other Cather characters, Jim Burden in particular, Margaret does not want to face the fact of change. She does not want to see a different Nelly when she returns, nor does she want to hear Nelly speak of what has happened: ". . . I was afraid—afraid of what she might tell me and of what I might say" (p. 63). Before Margaret comes back a second time, Nelly is dead. Nelly thus becomes another of those Cather characters who are spared further disillusionment and loss through a sad but merciful death. They are a special breed, in some ways too full of hope and life, and yet also too delicate, to survive in a world that seems bent on reduction of spirit and conformity to community expectations.

Cather's most important theme in the story, however, is not a sorrowful one. It is, rather, a glad one suggested by the title, "The Joy of Nelly Deane." It is the theme of rebirth and restoration. Cather represents this theme through images of baptism, which signify death, and images of birth, which signify new life after death and the restoration of things lost. The actual baptism of Nelly into Scott Spinney's church prior to their marriage is foreshadowed in Nelly's twice breaking through the ice while skating in perilous abandon on the river. On hearing of the second incident, her three old admirers "declared that she was trying to be a Baptist despite herself" (p. 56). Later, after her performance in a musical program at the Baptist Church, Scott waits glumly for her "at the baptistry door" (p. 57). Baptism is repeatedly associated with Nelly's forthcoming "burial" in marriage with Scott.

As it turns out, Nelly is baptized officially during Margaret's winter vacation from college. In Margaret's mind the event is clearly a symbolic death. She notes that "the baptistry was a cemented pit" (p. 62) and that "the minister said the words about being buried with Christ in baptism." As Nelly is immersed in "the dark water," Margaret thinks, "It will be like that when she dies" (p. 63). Nelly comes out of the water, not to new life, but to living death with a joyless man. But when Margaret returns many years later, after Nelly's death, she discovers happily that baptism can go beyond burial, for the spirit of Nelly has been reborn in Nelly's two children. They have given the old Mrs. Spinney new life, "made her quite young again"; and as Margaret thinks of the children, the young, vibrant Nelly is reborn in her mind.

Appropriately, it is Christmas, the time of miraculous birth. Margaret meets her namesake, Nelly's little Margaret, on the sledding hill and notes the child's elastic energy. Then she enters the church where Christmas preparations are under way. There, beneath "the lesson-picture of the Wise Men," she sees the three old friends, "the three white heads . . . bent above the baby" (p. 67). Thus Nelly's baby boy is the center of a nativity scene, and Margaret feels as she holds him the rebirth of the joy of Nelly Deane: "He was so warm and tingling with life, and he had the flush of new beginnings, of the new morning and the new rose. He seemed to have come so lately from his mother's heart! It was as if I held her youth and all her young joy" (p. 68).

More realistic, if less joyful, than Nelly is Clara Vavrika Ericson, "the Bohemian girl." Clara is another of Cather's spirited women who end up marrying men singularly ill-equipped to appreciate their rare qualities, men who in fact resent them for such qualities. Alexandra Ebbling ("On the Gulls' Road") and Marie Shabata (*O Pioneers!*) share Nelly's and Clara's fate. Scott Spinney is morose and stolid, Olaf Ericson is heavy and silent, Lars Ebbling is thick and easy to anger, Frank Shabata is ill-tempered and difficult. The link between Clara and Marie is especially strong. Both are Bohemian, both have a close relationship with natural things, both are energized by an internal flame that cries for life at all costs, both risk the quenching of that fire by marrying men who cannot appreciate or tolerate it, and both give their love to a more compatible spirit. Marie cannot help loving Emil, and finally surrenders to that love the night Frank finds them and shoots them. Clara is more fortunate. She and Nils succeed in escaping together.

Clara is thirty, and some of her early gusto has been reduced to bitterness by life among the Ericsons where the only virtues are perpetual work and opportunistic propriety, and the chief pleasures are money in the bank and a new barn. Clara's greatest fear is that she will lose spirit. She cannot bear to hear that she has changed or has lost her spunk, or to face a future when her father would die and leave her completely at the mercy of her husband's people.

"The Bohemian Girl" opens with the return to Nebraska of Nils Ericson, the one Ericson brother who managed to break away and try his fortune in the outside world. Nils was the "different" one; the others, with the possible exception of young Eric, all bear the unmistakable brand of their mother, a driving, capable, no-nonsense woman who at seventy still has little use for dalliance or for Bohemians. Nils finds his childhood sweetheart, Clara, unhappily married to his older brother Olaf, a scowling man who is wealthy, crafty, and politically ambitious. When Nils asks Clara why she married Olaf, she replies: "I suppose I really did it to oblige the neighbors. . . . I've discovered that most girls marry out of consideration for the neighborhood" (p. 22). As the story moves through a variety of situations that bring Nils and Clara together, including a barnwarming and an afternoon of music at old Joe Vavrika's, Nils determines on a course of action. He waits for Clara in the road the night he is to leave and whisks her away with him. One almost wishes Cather had ended the story there, but she adds a section in which young Eric, always partial to the spirited Nils, runs away to join him and Clara, but loses his nerve and returns home.[7]

"The Bohemian Girl" is probably a fairly good index to Cather's feelings about Nebraska at this stage in her life. As "The Enchanted Bluff" illustrates, she had begun to get a new perspective on her own experience there and was discovering new ways to look at the materials she had already drawn from quite freely. She dramatizes that new perspective through the character of Nils Ericson. Now that Nils has been away, he finds he can look at the home of his youth with a generous degree of allowance. He can chuckle at his mother's stubbornness and amusedly watch her barrel about the countryside in one of the few automobiles in the county. Much as he may have chafed against it in his youth, he now finds himself wryly admiring her relentless spirit. And at the barn dance, his admiration for the "grandmothers" who prepare the food and vicariously enjoy the action is frank and warm.

For Clara Vavrika, however, Nebraska holds no such charms. She has never left it, and has no hope of leaving it. She feels the prairie and the Ericsons in a stranglehold about her neck, a grand conspiracy to choke off her life. But even Clara, brought unexpectedly to the irrevocable choice of going or staying, can scarcely bear to leave the land. There is a moment when she knows that to part with the land may be a greater agony than to stay and be depleted. The land, after all, holds one's past, even one's sorrow, and to leave it is to leave the very essence of one's being. Cather describes the anguish of Clara's indecision in highly charged language:

> The great silent country seemed to lay a spell upon her. The ground seemed to hold her as if by roots. Her knees were soft under her. She felt as if she could not bear separation from her old sorrows, from her old discontent. They were dear to her, they had kept her alive, they were a part of her. There would be nothing left of her if she were wrenched away from them. Never could she pass beyond that skyline against which her restlessness had beat so many times. She felt as if her soul had built itself a nest there on that horizon at which she looked every morning and every evening, and it was dear to her, inexpressively dear. (P. 37)

In some sense, Clara is the young Willa Cather, aching to leave and aching to stay as well, hopelessly caught between the great pull that is Nebraska and everything else out there, beyond Nebraska. Nils is the older Cather, ready to come back as an appreciative visitor, but still recognizing the great truth, the overpowering necessity, of his going.

In fact, the polarity between Nebraska and "the world" is illustrated in the contrasting settings of "Behind the Singer Tower," also of this period, and "The Bohemian Girl." One setting is characterized by harsh vertical lines, the other by long horizontal lines. One is the essence of activity and bustle; the other is the essence of everlasting sameness and quietude. Nils and Clara feel the pull of both worlds, as Willa Cather did, for each world answers one side of their inner natures. Clara's choice is particularly difficult; Nils made his long ago. Understanding Nils and Clara so well, as parts of her own self, Cather seems to have known instinctively how they would respond to one another. He would make love to her by describing their youth selves, by telling her to snatch life at any cost, by promising her nothing but the freedom to be herself. She, on the other hand, would make love to him by pounding the countryside on her horse Norman, by finally tearing herself away from the earth and running with him, by choosing life rather than a slow death.

Nils and Clara become for Cather almost a personification of the life force. Working against them are the forces of materialism—the Ericson landholders, with mother Ericson in command, who never loved the land but only wanted it, who fear that Nils has come home to claim a share of his father's legacy, who cheat young children out of their inheritance in order to save or make a dollar. Nils and Clara vibrate together, in their mutual scorn of the material and their mutual "capacity for delight" (p. 35). Cather applauds their recklessness, for without it, Clara would have been destroyed. She also recognizes in the parallel love affair between Emil Bergson and Marie Shabata that recklessness can sometimes kill, but that death is not the worst thing that can happen to one.

B. An Experiment in Romantic Fiction

Unlike Cather's other stories of this period that deal with the past, "On the Gulls' Road" (*McClure's,* December 1908) concerns itself *only* with the past rather than with the effects of the past on the present or its relationship to the present. It may have been influenced by a couple of James stories, "The Patagonia," which features a shipboard romance with the woman dying a suicide, and "The Solution," which features an American diplomat. A difficult sort of story for Cather, it is essentially an account of a maudlin memory trip into an isolated segment of the past which holds the narrator in its grip but gives him no handle on the present. The story focuses on one incident, a romantic love affair doomed from the first, perhaps possible only because it was doomed. And upon that one incident a lonely bachelor feeds his melancholy some twenty years later. The event described provides no sense of continuity, no sense of truth, even, for time and temperament have colored it until its only value

is sentimental. Sarah Orne Jewett, who at first saw much to admire
in the story, later blamed its weaknesses on the problems inherent
in a woman writer's trying to create a male narrator.[8] But Cather
was to use male narrators many times, with remarkable effective-
ness. There is something in this particular narrator that suggests a
mocking imitation of a romantic hero, and this story may be an unconscious parody on the popular sentimental novels and plays so
prevalent in her time.[9]

The highly contrived plot lends credence to that possibility. Its
heartrending events occurred twenty years ago on an ocean liner
bound from warm, sunny Mediterranean waters to the cold, stormy
seas of the North Atlantic. Subtitled "The Ambassador's Story," the
tale is narrated by a man who fell in love and never recovered from
the experience, and never intends to recover. He, then a clerk in the
diplomatic service, and she, the unhappy wife of the ship's engineer,
were perhaps destined to meet. She, who is reminiscent of
Katharine Gaylord in "A Death in the Desert," is dying of a heart
ailment; he is alive in the full flush of health and youth. Slowly and
discreetly, with scarcely an unprogrammed emotional outburst,
they fall in love, confessing it only as the voyage draws to an end. In
New York harbor she emerges from her quarters to give him a part-
ing gift, a box which he is not to open until he receives word; then
she departs almost immediately for Finmark, her father's home. On
a wet, dreary day many months later, he learns from her father's letter that she is dead. He opens the box she had given him and finds a
lock of her magnificent hair. The story ends in the present, twenty
years later, with the ambassador still in a revery at dusk, removing
"a thick coil" (p. 94) of her hair from its box and watching it curl almost sensuously around his arm.

Regardless of Cather's intent, this is certainly the stuff of which
popular romances are made. Lars Ebbling, the bearded husband-
villain of the piece, is charming and indulgent in shipboard flirta-
tions, but cruel and ugly when his will is crossed. The clerk and Mrs.
Ebbling play romantic hero and heroine in an ill-fated love. Their
most dramatic scene occurs when she refuses to run away with him.
Hurt, he cries, "You meant to cut me adrift like this, with my heart
on fire and all my life unspent in me?" Her despondent reply is, "I
am willing to suffer—whatever I must suffer—to have had you. . . .
Ah, don't begrudge it to me! If I have been wrong, forgive me." At
that moment, he recalls, "She bowed her head and pressed my fin-

gers entreatingly. A warm tear splashed on my hand." Alexandra
Ebbling concludes the conversation with a shivering plea: "Do you
grudge it to me? You are so young and strong, and you have everything before you. I shall have only a little while to want you in—and
I could want you forever and not weary." In their last moments together, he kisses her and she takes his hand. Recalling the moment,
he reflects, "We sat silent, and the moments came and went, bringing us closer and closer, and the wind and water rushed by us,
obliterating our tomorrows and all our yesterdays" (pp. 90–92).
Even nature contributes to the general misery, growing more forbidding with each passing day of the fated journey, turning on its pa-
thetic showers for the arrival of the black-edged letter and for the
revery that produces the tale.

Probably the most difficult passage to explain if one tries to read
"On the Gulls' Road" as a straight treatment of its theme is the concluding paragraph which describes the ambassador alone with a
lock of Alexandra's hair and his memories:

> The dusk had thickened into night long before I got up from my
> chair and took the little box from its place in my desk drawer. I
> opened it and lifted out a thick coil, cut from where her hair grew
> thickest and brightest. It was tied firmly at one end, and when it
> fell over my arm it curled and clung about my sleeve like a living
> thing set free. How it gleamed, how it still gleams in the firelight!
> It was warm and softly scented under my lips, and stirred under
> my breath like seaweed in the tide. This, and a withered magno-
> lia flower, and two pink sea shells; nothing more. And it was all
> twenty years ago! (P. 94)

The ambassador-narrator fits all too well the stereotype of the lover
in popular fiction—all youth and exuberance and optimism in the
early days of his love, all tears and sitting about in the twilight after
it is over. And his beloved, in spite of her boast that she is a realist,
has enjoyed playing the role of romantic heroine, even contriving
one more heart-rending scene after she is gone.

The story is perplexing for the reader, mainly because Cather's
stance is difficult to determine. Is she writing romance, or parodying
it? She herself was both a romantic and a realist. In her early columns and reviews she defends romance over realism, preferring
writers like Stevenson and Poe a hundred times over realists like

Howells (she thought him dull) or Zola (she thought him offensive). But she also has harsh words for what she regarded as nonlegitimate romance, irresponsible trading on a standardized, manufactured set of feelings; and she had a high regard for many realists, including Sarah Orne Jewett.[10] What, then, did Cather intend in "On the Gulls' Road"? A touching (if unsuccessful) story about lost love? A spoof on popular sentimentality in literature? An exploration of the excessively romantic temperament which conjugates life only in the past tense? Her intentions are simply not clear.

C. An Experiment in Social Criticism

Providing a stark contrast with "On the Gulls' Road" is a remarkably fine story published a few years later, "Behind the Singer Tower" (*Collier's*, May 1912).[11] In this story the protagonist also reaches into the past, but he does so in an attempt to find clarification of the present and insight into the future. He does not isolate the past and bathe it in pity as the ambassador does. Somewhat oddly out of place in this group of stories from the *McClure's* period, but reflecting a social consciousness fully compatible with the editorial spirit of *McClure's*, "Behind the Singer Tower" was published the same year as *Alexander's Bridge*. Some readers have felt that the two are related because each features an engineer and the failure of a great architectural structure. But while questions of cutting corners in construction costs and using substandard materials arise in both, for the most part the two pieces have very little in common. The central conflict in *Alexander's Bridge* is within Bartley Alexander, between the youth self that beckons him and the self that is approaching middle age, a married and highly successful engineer. In "Behind the Singer Tower," however, the central conflict is over a principle, a value system, and it is represented in the natures and characters of two men, engineers Fred Hallet and Stanley Merryweather.

What Cather is examining in this story is "the New York idea," the dream of a city of skyscrapers, and the necessity and cost of pursuing it. Like Thoreau, Cather in this story reminds us that the cost of a thing can be measured by the amount of human life expended in acquiring it; and by this standard the cost of the New York dream is staggering. The dream even takes on religious overtones as men struggle to raise great towers in the air. Old Hughie MacFarlane, a pioneer steel construction engineer, "dreamed the dream. When he was a lad working for the Pennsylvania Bridge Company, he saw Manhattan just as it towers there tonight" (p. 47).

He has some of the same nobility that Cather ascribes to the early western railroad men—pioneers in their own right. In *A Lost Lady,* Captain Forrester and his generation of pioneering capitalists are courageous and fine; as in this story, it is the later generations who lose sight of the original dream and compromise its principles. But regardless of the magnificence of its original conception, a great many human lives are paid to purchase a steel and concrete dream.

The story opens with Fred Hallet and a few others aboard a launch in the Manhattan harbor. The great Mont Blanc skyscraper hotel has burned that day, killing at least three hundred people—ambassadors, opera singers, presidents of business trusts, governors, and other people of importance. Water, even in a busy harbor, seems to offer the only antidote for all that burning, and the men on board Hallet's launch are grateful for the relief it brings. Hallet, who had worked for Stanley Merryweather in preparing the Mont Blanc foundation, glumly relates the story of a rather tiny tragedy from the past which foreshadowed the large one in the present. Because Merryweather was too tightfisted and too careless to replace a worn cable, six of the twenty Italians working for Hallet in the hot pit of the Mont Blanc foundation were crushed by a clamshell full of sand when the cable snapped above their heads. Hallet had a special attachment to one frightened little Italian who worked for him, Caesar—nicknamed Caesarino because of his size. After the deaths of Caesarino and his five comrades, Hallet broke with Merryweather, who saw no particular loss in the accident except for the insignificant cash settlements paid to the families of the dead men.

With that long-ago incident the story's essential dichotomy emerges, humanity versus the machine. Admitting that a man like Merryweather, who "made amazing mistakes, harrowing blunders," also "made the wheels go round," Hallet pronounces one of the standard Merryweather maxims: "Men are cheaper than machinery" (p. 51). The narrator observes that Hallet "was a soft man for the iron age," sure to be "beaten . . . in the race" (p. 50) by someone like Merryweather. In the wake of the Mont Blanc disaster, Hallet reflects bitterly that the Mont Blanc burning is regarded as a disaster because people of supposed consequence have been destroyed; but the hundreds of nameless little people, principally foreign immigrants, who are pulverized daily by the machinery of progress are virtually ignored. No one had worried much about fires in skyscrapers because "heretofore fires in fireproof buildings of many stories had occurred only in factory lofts, and the people who perished in

them, fur workers and garment workers, were obscure for more rea-
sons than one; most of them bore names unpronounceable to the
American tongue; many of them had no kinsmen, no history, no record anywhere" (p. 45).[12]

Hallet, giving vent to cynicism, jabs almost ruthlessly at the one
"foreigner" among the group on the launch, a Jewish doctor named
Zablowski. In a premeditated stab at Zablowski, Hallet comments
about the foreign heathenistic look of the Singer Tower and the cov-
ert "racial characteristics" in Merryweather, adding, "something
that you would recognize, Zablowski" (p. 47). As Hallet continues to
peck away, Zablowski responds by putting "his hand penitently to
his forehead" (p. 48). The story ends with Hallet taking another obvious swipe at Zablowski, and a newspaperman named Johnson
complaining, "Zablowski, . . . why don't you *ever* hit back" (p. 54)?
Hallet's cruelty is an expression of his own pain. He is angry at
Zablowski's vulnerability, angry that Zablowski can be the butt of
such jokes as his, angry that the immigrant comes to this country
and naively offers himself as a sacrifice to the inhuman, if
compelling, New York idea. Certainly, no one perceives better than
Hallet that racism is one clear manifestation, is perhaps even the
hallmark, of a system that devalues human beings.

After the Mont Blanc disaster the city is "enveloped in a tragic self-consciousness. Those incredible towers of stone and steel
seemed, in the mist, to be grouped confusedly together, as if they
were confronting each other with a question" (p. 44). And that question has to be asked. Is a city of this sort justified? Is the cost in human lives never to be counted? And where does the blame lie when
calamity strikes? "One might fancy that the city was protesting,
was asserting its helplessness, its irresponsibility for its physical
conformation," for the fact that, "squeezed in a vise," it could only
have "shot upward" (p. 44). Merryweather, who is clearly arrogant,
careless, and unfeeling, can be blamed, of course; but how about
Hallet, whose livelihood also depends upon the construction of skyscrapers, whose life has been consecrated to the New York idea?
Hallet always speaks of *our* kind of building, and worries that such
buildings will now lose credibility in the eyes of the world. The Mont
Blanc is "the complete expression of the New York idea" (p. 44), the
value system that builds towering cities at outrageous costs. Even
after the fire "it was still standing there," on Hallet's foundation,
"massive and brutally unconcerned" (p. 44).

As Hallet observes, almost willfully we throw our lives into fueling the flame of an idea such as old MacFarlane (Merryweather's uncle) imagined some generations ago. And sometimes that flame becomes a fire that destroys, as with the Mont Blanc. Cather's central image in "Behind the Singer Tower," other than the tower itself, is fire, or light—representing variously the flame of desire, the almost gaudy glare of accomplishment, and the consuming blaze of destruction. Hallet looks at the New York idea, at the fact that "our whole scheme of life and progress and profit was perpendicular" (p. 46), and realizes that it may have been "overdone." As he observes "the great incandescent signs along the Jersey shore, blazing across the night the names of beer and perfumes and corsets," it occurs to him that "a single name, a single question, could be blazed too far." Johnson says that all "lit up" as it is with its "incandescents," the Singer Tower looks like a Jewish high priest. Demurring, Zablowski says that the Singer Tower is more like a Persian, "a Magi or a fire-worshiper of some sort" who is "watching over the city and the harbor like a presiding Genius." This flaming tower, echoed by the burning Mont Blanc, urges mortals to worship the heathen fire. And somehow, the Statue of Liberty, for all "her high-mindedness," spawned that "great heathen idol." Now, holding her "feeble taper" (p. 46) of idealism, she can scarcely compete with that other all-consuming flame.

Recognizing our helpless compulsion toward the flame, Hallet keeps asking why, why. "Here we are," he says, "six men, with our pitiful few years to live and our one little chance for happiness, throwing everything we have into that conflagration on Manhattan Island, helping, with every nerve in us, with everything our brain cells can generate, with our very creature heat, to swell its glare, its noise, its luxury, and its power. Why do we do it?" And why do the immigrants come? Why did Caesarino leave his tranquil island existence; ". . . why did he come so far to cast his little spark in the bonfire? And the thousands like him, from islands even smaller and more remote, why do they come, like iron dust to the magnet, like moths to the flame" (p. 53)? Then, Hallet's impassioned oration takes a turn; he begins to insist that there is, after all, something magnificent about a dream, about almost any largely conceived idea. And if old MacFarlane's dream led to dehumanization and death under the stewardship of men like Merryweather, then we must capture a new and better vision which may be just over the horizon. Even Caesarino, at an intuitive level, must have sensed its imminence. Hallet continues, "There must be something wonderful coming. When the frenzy is over, when the furnace has cooled, what marvel will be left on Manhattan Island" (pp. 53–54)? As Hallet continues ardently, the erstwhile cynic gives way to the helpless idealist:

> What it will be is a new idea of some sort. That's all that ever comes, really. That's what we are all the slaves of, though we don't know it. It's the whip that cracks over us till we drop. Even Merryweather—and that's where the gods have the laugh on him —every firm he crushes to the wall, every deal he puts through, every cocktail he pours down his throat, he does it in the service of this unborn Idea, that he will never know anything about. Some day it will dawn, serene and clear, and your Moloch on the Singer Tower over there will get down and do it Asian obeisance. (P. 54)

So there is a double thrust in the story. The fire, the burning idea, both inspirits and kills. The dream so nobly conceived sacrifices humanity to its realization, but out of that sacrifice can arise the phoenix of its justification. The skyscraper can be a symbol of the upward reach as well as a symbol of ambition and destruction. The Singer Tower cannot boast the symbolic grandeur of the Enchanted Bluff or the rock of Quebec, and it could become another gutted Mont Blanc; but it nevertheless stands as something of a beacon in the night. Cather creates two tower symbols, Mont Blanc to represent the destructive aspects of the metropolitan dream, and the Singer Tower to represent its idealistic capabilities.

One of Cather's few ventures into fully developed social criticism, this story is not simply a pious attack on the city and the machine.[13] It poses very serious questions about a value system that counts common humanity cheaply, but it also admits to some other human need that can be expressed by raising a flock of towers toward the sun. It is Jim Burden's need again, the need to be "dissolved into something complete and great." The Merryweathers, of course, are immune to such compelling inner motives, and so they blunder along on dollar energy, building and destroying, largely untouched by the ugliness and splendor of it all. But the Hallets have a further vision. They know that one must look backward and forward, for the seeds and the fruition of both thrusts, the creative and the destructive, are embedded in the past—in old MacFarlane's dream and in young Caesarino's death, to be released again and again through succeeding generations of dreamers, builders, and unsuspecting martyrs.

NOTES

1. See introduction to Faulkner, *Willa Cather's Collected Short Fiction,* p. xxiii. Unless otherwise noted, all page references to stories through 1912 are from this volume (page references are in parentheses in the text).

2. The exact date of her official resignation from *McClure's* is not known. Apparently, after a trip to Winslow, Arizona, to visit her brother Douglass, she did not again work on a regular basis for the magazine, but struck out for herself, essentially leaving the world of journalism and devoting her energies to the writing of fiction.

3. Putt, *Henry James: A Reader's Guide,* pp. 259, 268.

4. See Slote, *Kingdom of Art,* pp. 50ff. Slote states that even though for the young Cather, "Art includes both the strong and the delicate," greatness is defined chiefly in terms of "strength, power, and passion" (p. 52). Certainly, Gray was deficient in energy. Philip describes Gray's first work (he completed a total of two items) as something which began as a prose drama, grew into an historical novel, and then was reduced to a two-hundred-page psychological study, a "shadowy" thing with only a breath of its former potential and vigor.

5. Cather's use of the rock as a major symbol is commented upon frequently. Of special interest is Gerber, "Willa Cather and the Big Red Rock," pp. 152–57.

6. Cather, *My Ántonia,* p. 158.

7. Giannone (*Music in Willa Cather's Fiction,* p. 58) says that Eric's return "is irrelevant to the action."

8. See Woodress, *Willa Cather: Her Life and Art,* p. 132.

9. Slote (*Kingdom of Art,* pp. 38–39) makes it clear that Cather was no stranger to popular fiction. She read widely, even in popular romance, which was a favorite of her mother's. Slote says, "When Willa spoke of these books in her newspaper column, she knew what she was talking about. If she was often flip or furious about them, it was usually because they were not the highest kind of art, or even art at all—not because she scorned to look at one or even read it. The fact was, she probably read everything, and she knew very well what the world was like for both writer and reader; she could afford to be passionate about her own choices." Nothing in Cather's letters to Jewett, however, indicate that she intended the story as a parody.

10. See particularly her praise for Stevenson in a *Journal* column, 23 December 1894 (Curtin, *World and the Parish,* pp. 136–37), and for Poe in a *Courier* column, 12 October 1895 (Curtin, pp. 157–63). She even urges Kipling, in that same *Journal* article, to get out of America and return to writing romance (pp. 138–39). Her opinions on Howells's brand of realism are mentioned numerous times in columns reprinted in Curtin and Slote. For some typical comments on Zola, see Curtin, pp. 140–42, where Cather contends that he is conscious only of evil. Slote, *Kingdom of Art,* p. 31, accurately describes the young Cather as "primarily a romantic and a primitive," and details Cather's position in the war between romance and realism (see pp. 62–64). It becomes clear, however, that Cather could also see that art, to some degree at least, transcends traditional distinctions between realism and romanticism. Even as early as 1894 she admitted in a *Journal* review of the play *Brother John* that there is a "realism of good" to "remind one that realism after all may not be an absolute synonym for evil" (Curtin, p. 78).

11. "Behind the Singer Tower" is one of the overlooked gems among Cather's short stories. Brown, *Willa Cather: A Critical Biography,* does not mention it, and Woodress, *Willa Cather: Her Life and Art,* only remarks on it in another connection. It is one of the stories that Giannone also passes over in his *Music in Willa Cather's Fiction.* Bradford, however, describes it as "a powerful tale" which is "perhaps the most interesting of the uncollected stories" ("Willa Cather's Uncollected Short Fiction," p. 547). The burning of the Mont Blanc Hotel in the story is probably based on the Windsor Hotel fire in 1899, just as *Alexander's Bridge* draws upon the collapse of the Quebec Bridge in 1907. Mildred Bennett discovered this connection.

12. Cather's acquaintance with numerous immigrants on the Nebraska prairies probably made her keenly sensitive to the plight of city immigrants. Then too, in Pittsburgh she must have taught immigrant children and known some of their parents. That immigrant workers could be regarded as ready candidates for sacrifice seems to have angered her.

13. Bradford would disagree. He sees "Singer Tower" as a "rejection of the American metropolis," and regards it as evidence "that Miss Cather had taken in more of the muckraking attitude . . . at *McClure's* than is generally supposed." He says, "There was much of the social critic in Willa Cather, but save in a few instances she was critical by implication rather than by direct statement." He says further that it was probably "her romantic aesthetic, her belief that art is the creation of beauty," that kept her from "direct social criticism," though this one story certainly "indicates that she would have succeeded as a social critic had she wished to." See Bradford, "Willa Cather's Uncollected Short Stories," pp. 546–47.

FOUR

The City as Landscape: The Teens and Twenties

I. NONARTISTS IN NEW YORK CITY

After the appearance of "The Bohemian Girl" in 1912, Cather did not publish another piece of short fiction until 1915. She did, however, publish three novels in those years, years she devoted almost exclusively to the writing of fiction (and to fulfilling a promise to ghostwrite S.S. McClure's autobiography). Following *Alexander's Bridge,* Cather looked to the Midwest and the desert for the principal settings of her next four novels, *O Pioneers!* (1913), *The Song of the Lark* (1915), *My Ántonia* (1918), and *One of Ours* (1922), and several subsequent novels. It is no surprise, however, that she would continue to use city settings in some of her work, for even though she visited the West during those years, her home was still New York City. Her short fiction through 1920 draws mainly on her city experiences, depicting executives, working-class people, socialites, artists, and other city dwellers.

A. AN UNUSUAL GHOST STORY

Cather's first story to appear after 1912 is an unexpectedly urbane piece called "Consequences" (*McClure's,* November 1915), the tale of a ruddy-complexioned, boyishly agreeable, if prodigal, socialite named Kier Cavenaugh. A stiffly proper lawyer named Henry Eastman, who rents a bachelor apartment upstairs from Cavenaugh's, is essentially the point-of-view character, so his somewhat staid perceptions influence every incident reported in the story. One New Year's Eve Cavenaugh confesses to Eastman that he is apparently haunted by an old fellow garishly attired in tattered evening clothes, complete with top hat and soiled white gloves. Eastman, though doubting the younger man's story, suggests that he go west to escape the old fellow. Cavenaugh is reluctant at first, but when Eastman returns from a business trip, he finds the hall full of traveling trunks and Cavenaugh buzzing with plans for a morning depar-

ture. The next morning, however, Cavenaugh's chauffeur finds his
employer dead in his bed. Sometime during the night the lively
young bachelor had shot himself.

The old man who haunts Cavenaugh, whether fancy, apparition,
or flesh, is a common literary type, the alter ego or double. Certainly, Cather had no dearth of literary models for her character. Preced-
ing her are works like Wilde's *The Picture of Dorian Gray* and Poe's
"William Wilson," and the type has proliferated in modern and contemporary fiction. In many of Cather's works, as has been noted, the
"double" is within rather than outside the character. The two sides
of Jim Laird's nature were mentioned earlier, and nearly all the novels describe a character's sense of self-division. Cather's most obvious model for "Consequences," however, is Henry James's "The Jolly
Corner." But while Cather represents Cavenaugh's old man as a
ghost from the future, frightening the young man with a glimpse of
what he will become, James shows Spencer Brydon what he might
have been if he had not abandoned his home and gone to Europe to
live. Brydon's ghost never takes clear fleshy form, though his apparent old age, vulgarity, colorless hands, and odd evening attire are
mentioned—details in which he clearly resembles Cather's later
ghostly portrait. Unlike Cavenaugh, whose only thought is to run
from his apparition, Brydon stalks and confronts his. And unlike
Cavenaugh, Brydon survives the encounter to recognize that as a result of it he can safely say that the ghost is indeed a stranger and not
himself. Thus, Brydon is triumphant over his double while Cavenaugh is destroyed by his.[1]

For most people, the future can be faced only because it is not
known, and when Cavenaugh discovers what his future holds, he
kills himself to avoid it. So convinced is Cavenaugh that he is haunted by his future self that he continually identifies himself with the
old man, noting similarities in physical attributes, in tastes, and
even in virtues, limited though they be. What is particularly disturbing is that the old man is basically the image of all the worst in
Cavenaugh, projected bizarrely into the future, grown tattered with
reckless living and age.

The real horror of the story is that Cavenaugh is suddenly faced
with the personified consequences of the way he has thought and
spoken and acted and will continue to think and speak and act his
whole life. Who could bear such a revelation? Who could face the
prospect of being overtaken by his own moral and physical and intel-

lectual shabbiness? Cavenaugh must have realized in the end that there is no way to run from the future because every step, every passing minute, only takes one more surely toward it. Cavenaugh does not kill the man he is now; he kills the man he believes he would have become. Eastman, deliberately obtuse through much of the story, is capable of one perceptive comment near the end: "Well, at any rate, he's seen to it that the old man can't establish identity" (p. 84).

Cavenaugh's suicide must be considered in conjunction with three other suicides that are described and discussed by Cavenaugh and Eastman in the story. The two men differ substantially in their views about why suicides occur, and it is this essential difference that explains why Eastman would never commit suicide and why Cavenaugh would. Eastman contends that some suicides are simply motiveless "desperate acts" (p. 76) and are inexplicable. Cavenaugh, on the other hand, believes that "every suicide is logical and reasonable, if one knew all the facts" (p. 75). Cavenaugh is not talking about evidence that would stand up in a courtroom. He is talking about "a draft from outside, somewhere," a draft that can "chill" people. A vision from the future might be just such a suicide-inducing chill; a person "may accidentally have come to a place where he saw himself in too unpleasant a light" and could not bear the revelation (pp. 77–78).

That is the sort of thing the literal-minded Eastman cannot and will not understand. Further, he refuses to verify having seen the ghostly old man, thus unconsciously refusing to acknowledge his own possible fate, to open the door on his own future. Eastman does not ask big questions; in fact, his questions are largely rhetorical; "Had Cavenaugh entertained his visitor last night, and had the old man been more convincing than usual?" With a note of superiority in his voice, the lawyer deftly dismisses the likes of Cavenaugh: "What a soft lot they are, fellows like poor Cavenaugh!" The next sentence, the last of the story, is a fittingly ironic conclusion to a gravely mysterious event, an event observed largely by a man who had neither eyes to see it nor ears to hear it. The whole experience has rolled right over Eastman for whom secrets do not exist, for whom empirical facts constitute the only truths. Eastman's concluding thought is that his own office is "a delightful place" (p. 84). A series of uneventful days in his office is the only future Eastman cares (or dares) to contemplate.

B. Two Business Stories

Cather's next story, "The Bookkeeper's Wife" (*Century,* May 1916), is one of three in the *Uncle Valentine* collection that focus on ordinary people in the business world. It is a rather dull tale about a hapless bookkeeper who makes too little money to satisfy an attractive, if somewhat coarse, wife whose tastes and lifestyle demand a liberal pocketbook. This story is significant perhaps only because it describes one more marriage relationship in Cather's work in which a rather sensitive man is married to an insensitive woman. There are a multitude of such men—Doctor Archie, Jim Burden, Claude Wheeler, and Valentine Ramsay, to name a few. Unlike most of his counterparts in Cather's other works, however, Percy Bixby, the bookkeeper, is additionally cursed by a weak character; he has little to recommend him but his sweet tidiness.

It is tempting to read the story in total sympathy with Percy, to see him as a victim not only of his wife's shallowness, but also of a dead-end job in a city which daily eats up thousands of little people just like him. But Stella raises a very fair question when she asks, "What made you rush me anyway, Percy? What did you go and pretend to be a spender and get tied up with me for" (p. 97)? Percy knew how Stella had been pampered, he knew Stella's mother was a fortune hunter, he knew he could never satisfy either of them on his salary. But he had to go for Stella, the dazzling princess the other fellows dated for a whirl "before they settled down to one of her sisters" because "she came too high for them" (p. 88). Percy won out by misrepresenting his salary and embezzling from his company. As in "The Profile" and "The Willing Muse," Cather is not ready to lay the blame for a man's unhappiness entirely on the seemingly insensitive woman he married.

Cather's next business story, "Ardessa" (*Century,* May 1918), is not a strong story either, though it is better than "The Bookkeeper's Wife." It is of interest chiefly because Cather uses her experience at *McClure's* for some of her materials.[2] Ardessa's boss, O'Mally, the dynamic, hard-swinging, impulsive editor-owner of "The Outcry," can be recognized as a fictional portrayal of S.S. McClure, Cather's boss, though Ardessa bears no resemblance to Cather. If Cather is present, it is probably as the capable but humane Rena Kalski. The story describes a supremacy contest between O'Mally and the forever ladylike Ardessa whom O'Mally inherited from the magazine's previous owner. In the final skirmish Ardessa's own maneuvering leads to her defeat.

Although Ardessa would not understand this, she and O'Mally were in conflict before they ever met, for they represent two different orders. O'Mally, though he is the "grand old man," is brimming over with new methods and new ideas while Ardessa still lives in the old century, a vestige of a sterile brand of gentility that can leave character virtually unimproved over an entire lifetime. This is the story of her displacement from all she holds dear. She is a "lady" forced to live in a changed world where no one cares any longer about sheltering ladies. There is something pitiable about that fact, something sad about the scrapping of the old order, but Cather's concern is only for Ardessa as a human being. She sheds no tears over the demise of a set of empty rituals and gestures which are never the true values of the past. Thus, Cather is saying the same thing here that she was to say later in "The Old Beauty." She feels sorry for Ardessa who has perpetuated a caste system that had to topple eventually and take her with it. Cather contemplates Ardessa's loss, but hints that in her destruction are the seeds of her salvation. Unlike "the old beauty," Gabrielle Longstreet, Ardessa may learn to live in the present.

C. THE INVISIBLE MAN

Cather's next story about business life also portrays the working woman, particularly the exploited, overworked, underpaid young woman of somewhat spare background and opportunities. "Her Boss" (*Smart Set*, October 1919), the best of the three business-centered stories reprinted in *Uncle Valentine*, introduces several characters who appear later in *The Professor's House*. Although Paul Wanning, partner in a New York law firm, has few of Professor Godfrey St. Peter's extraordinary personal qualities, some aspects of his family circumstances are repeated in the novel. The plots of the two works are quite different, however.

Wanning learns that because of malfunctioning kidneys, he will die in a matter of months. His family and associates summarily dismiss the medical verdict, leaving him alone with his strange new grief. His wife, who prefigures Lillian St. Peter, will not even entertain the possibility of his dying; and his daughters, Roma and Florence, grotesque previews of St. Peter's daughters, are even less sympathetic than she. Wanning is valued as a provider, but as a

husband and father with human needs and bad kidneys, he is almost a nonentity. And when Wanning stops off at his son's place,
Harold only smiles from behind a polite but impregnable shield, his
sympathy "fluent," his tolerance practiced. Faring no better among
his colleagues and his partners, the doomed man finally unloads his
burden in a long letter to a former college friend who "couldn't defend himself, couldn't slap Wanning on the back and tell him to
gather up the sunbeams" (p. 127).

Only the little office copyist, Annie Wooley, who has generously
stayed late to do Wanning's letter, is touched by his story. She reluc-
tantly agrees to take dictation after hours and on Saturdays so that
he can complete his autobiography. But by giving him the sympathy
he had been denied everywhere else, she earns herself the suspicious
disfavor of Wanning's partners. Thus, when Wanning dies, she is
left at the mercy of those who despise her. She loses both the one
thousand dollar inheritance he had promised her and her job, a bitter blow indeed after her sacrifice.

Annie and her people serve as a revealing contrast to members of
the professional class. Having no skill in the marketplace, they can
nevertheless handle illness and death without embarrassment.
They can allow a man to be dying. Still, Cather is not simply praising the poor and condemning the rich. She indicts the material cal-
lousness and the emotional aloofness of Wanning's family and associates, but she also realizes that no one can experience the dying of
another—and no one wants to, or should be condemned for not wanting to. Even Wanning, wrapped up in his own need for sympathy,
"could not feel interested" in the ailments of his business associates.

Aside from his relationship with Annie, something important
happens in the mind of the dying man. Late in the story he grows in-
trospective and thus begins to resemble the full-blown character he
would become in *The Professor's House.* Just as disturbing to Wanning as his altered perceptions of his home and his sense of
alienation from his family is his awakened sense of the frailty of human life, the paradoxical destructibility of human flesh compared
with the things which adorn it, or which it creates. Gazing at the
crowded streets and the harbor from his office window, he reflects,

> How had a short-lived race of beings the energy and courage val-
> iantly to begin enterprises which they could follow for only a few
> years; to throw up towers and build sea-monsters and found great
> businesses, when the frailest of the materials with which they

worked, the paper upon which they wrote, the ink upon their pens, had more permanence in this world than they? All this material rubbish lasted. The linen clothing and cosmetics of the Egyptians had lasted. It was only the human flame that certainly, certainly went out. Other things had a fighting chance; they might meet with mishap and be destroyed, they might not. But the human creature who gathered and shaped and hoarded and foolishly loved these things, he had no chance—absolutely none. Wanning's cane, his hat, his top-coat, might go from beggar to beggar and knock about in this world for another fifty years or so; but not he. (Pp. 130–31)

St. Peter, too, is troubled, by large philosophical questions and by the growing distance between himself and his family. But while Wanning is isolated mainly by his family's lack of sympathy, St. Peter is isolated by his family's increasing materialism and petty jealousies. Wanning does not understand the rupture with his family so well as St. Peter understands the rupture with his, but Wanning's responses to it are similar to St. Peter's. Not only do both men *accept* solitude, but in the end they turn to it gratefully. Both are left alone for the summer season, their families having rushed off on vacations. Wanning enjoys spending long hours at his office just as St. Peter enjoys basking indolently in the privacy of the old house or the old garden. Some passages in these sections of the two works could almost be interchanged. For Wanning, that summer "was like living his life over again." He realizes, almost guiltily, that "he did not miss his wife or his daughters. He had become again the mild, contemplative youth he was in college, before he had a profession and a family to grind for, before the two needs which shape our destiny had made of him pretty much what they make of every man" (pp. 132–33). His family gone, St. Peter also entertains a shadow of his younger self—not his college self, however, but his primitive youth self, the nonsocial being who never married and never had a family. That summer, St. Peter realizes that "life with this Kansas boy, little as there had been of it, was the realest of his lives. . . . His career, his wife, his family, were not his life at all, but a chain of events that had happened to him. All these things had nothing to do with the person he was in the beginning.[3]

In spite of the similarities noted between Wanning and the professor, the story and the novel are basically very different. "Her Boss" is not powerfully value-centered like *The Professor's House;*

and Paul Wanning is weak and indecisive, even comic, while St. Peter is strong and impressive. St. Peter's family are also clearly drawn and individual while Wanning's wife and children fall into a rather undistinguished lump. Still, it is instructive to see Cather working with materials in a short story that would later take more meaningful form in a novel.

II. ARTISTS IN NEW YORK CITY

A. THE SINGER AND SOCIETY

In the five years following the publication of *The Song of the Lark* in 1915, at the same time that Cather was publishing the business-centered city stories just discussed, she was also writing stories about successful artists who lived in New York, female singers of no small fame and talent. These stories—"The Diamond Mine" (*Mc-Clure's*, October 1916), "A Gold Slipper" (*Harper's*, January 1917), and "Scandal" (*Century*, August 1919)—were collected, along with "Coming, Aphrodite!" and four stories from *The Troll Garden*, into *Youth and the Bright Medusa* in 1920. These stories, like *The Song of the Lark*, probably have their genesis in Cather's meeting and subsequent friendship with Olive Fremstad, a Swedish-born opera singer of great vitality and presence who reminded Cather of the strong immigrant women she had known in Nebraska. It was Cather's acquaintance with Fremstad that generated the character of Thea Kronborg and gave shape to the last section of the novel which deals with the performing artist.[4] There are two protagonists in the three stories. Cressida Garnet, who resembles Fremstad and the older Thea, appears in one; Kitty Ayrshire, who is perhaps more like Mary Garden than she is like Fremstad, appears in two. Both are lively, generous, attractive, flamboyant, almost naively trusting, and capable of preposterous attachments.

Cather's title for this collection indicates a shift from the troll garden metaphor to the Medusa myth, which she translates as the quest for art—a lifelong subject for her. The problem is, of course, that anyone who looked upon the Medusa, the Gorgon, would be turned to stone. Anyone who pursues art will become its captive.[5] As was mentioned earlier in the discussion of "Nanette: An Aside" and "A Singer's Romance," for Willa Cather the choice for art, the pursuit of the bright prize, is not only perilous, but lonely. It often precludes marriage, at least happy marriage. Cather herself apparently elected to marry only her art, and the artists she portrays almost invariably find marriage difficult, if not impossible. This concern surfaces again in "The Diamond Mine" where Cressida Garnet, who had a happy first marriage, suffers through three more unsuccessful ones. Like Cather, Kitty Ayrshire does not marry; but many of Cather's artists do. We recall, for example, that the actresses whom Paul admired in "Paul's Case" were typically supporting shiftless husbands. James Woodress notes that Cather's conviction on this point was so strong that when she used musician Ethelbert Nevin for her portrait of Valentine Ramsay, she turned the happy Nevin marriage into a disaster. And, as Woodress observes, it is a rare novel in which an unhappy marriage does not appear.[6]

The principal conflicts in these stories, however, arise less from marriages than from the artists' being victimized in an uncomprehending, unappreciative environment. Much as Cather had written about artists already, only Cressida and Kitty, with the possible exception of Kenneth Gray ("The Willing Muse"), are shown in the midst of rather traditional quarrels between the working artist and society. In her longer fiction Cather had been writing, and was still to write, of the materialistic world view that regarded the land as something to be exploited and even destroyed for personal gain. In these three short stories the same attitude prevails toward people. A person who has resources that can be turned to profit is the property of any who can file a legitimate claim. In "The Diamond Mine" the parasites in Cressida Garnet's life, her family mainly, and to some extent her teacher-accompanist, extract every possible penny from her while she lives and then contend for every last scrap of her clothing and jewelry after she dies. The narrator, whom Woodress suggests "bears somewhat the same relationship to her that Willa Cather did to Fremstad,"[7] observes, "It never seemed to occur to them that the golden stream, whether it rushed or whether it trickled, came out of the industry, out of the mortal body of a woman. They regarded her as a natural source of wealth; a copper vein, a diamond mine."[8] Kitty Ayrshire, who figures in both "A Gold Slipper" and "Scandal," is similarly regarded by her family and others. She is currently "supporting just eight people" in addition to those she hires, and she assists talented students with "money and time and effort," with the light and desire that are "one's blood." Her only resource, she points out, is one small body; she had "only this to do it with" (pp. 140–41).

Cressida Garnet's rather modest wealth was no factor with her first husband, the love of her youth who died after three years; or with her second, a business executive who forced a choice between himself and her singing teacher, Miletus Poppas. Her third, however, Balsius Bouchalka, is corrupted by her money; and her fourth, Jerome Brown, manages to lose most of her money in financial speculation. Also trailing behind the Garnet paywagon are Cressida's foppish son, her brother, and her sisters, who "reminded one of two sombre, bumping electrics, rolling about with no visible means of locomotion, always running out of power and lying beached in some inconvenient spot until they received a check or suggestion from Cressy" (p. 76).

But the greed of Cressida's family goes beyond a simple desire for financial support. Coveting the qualities which had made her success, as well as the benefits that came from it, they apparently feel that Cressida has depleted the success allotment for the entire Garnet family, and that she therefore has an obligation to share the wealth with them. The story is full of the language of financial and emotional exploitation. Even a casual bystander notes that Jerome Brown's credit rating went up when his engagement to the "diamond mine" was announced, and the narrator is sorry to learn "that mining operations were to be begun again" (p. 68). Cressida's son and sisters derive their only spirit and motivation secondhand from Cressida. And even Poppas, so necessary to Cressida's art, so much a factor in her success, is characterized by the narrator as "a vulture" (p. 75).

Perhaps by allowing her family and husbands to exploit her, Cressida has innocently contributed to their corruption. Perhaps the person hurt most by Cressida's generosity is Bouchalka, the ill-clothed, ill-fed immigrant fiddler and songwriter whom Cressida discovered by accident, sponsored in the right circles, and finally married. Fiery and productive in the clutches of want and deprivation, he became fat and lethargic in the warmth and plenty of Cressida's household.

Cressida is essentially defenseless against exploitation because of her emotional needs and dependencies. Her love for her family makes her a ready victim of their greed, and she had thrived on Bouchalka's admiration. In fact, it is her need for emotional support that drives her to a final marriage with Jerome Brown, the weakest of her husbands. But, of course, Brown's dependence is much greater than hers, and he only lengthens the list of shareholders in the Cressida Garnet diamond mine, becoming another unstoppable drain on her wealth and energy. A passenger on the *Titanic* when it goes down, Cressida apparently never makes even a feeble attempt to save herself. She simply lets the waters rush over her and free her from an ever-increasing tangle of demands.

Cressida is certainly one of those Cather characters who, like Thea Kronborg, are blessed or cursed by a driving life-force. Rich or poor, Cressida would have made it in the art world. Bouchalka, on the other hand, had a gift, but his character was too weak to handle prosperity. Unfortunately, the only person in the story who fully appreciates Cressida is the narrator, and she is as blind to the singer's faults as Cressida's family is to her virtues. To the reader, Kitty Ayrshire is somehow more real, partly because she speaks for herself rather than through a protective narrator. The two stories about Kitty actually form a trilogy of tales, the first dramatized as the story called "A Gold Slipper," the second told by a visitor to Kitty's home, and the third told by Kitty herself. The latter two tales are encased in the frame story, "Scandal." All three, however, like "The Diamond Mine," treat incidents in which the artist is at the mercy of minds more interested in capital or social gains than in art. Kitty is clearly a victim of ruthless exploitation in both "Scandal" stories; her name and image are used to enhance another's social credibility.

In "A Gold Slipper" Kitty is less obviously, but perhaps just as surely, victimized. The main part of the story takes place on the New York Express where Kitty, after an evening concert, converses with a stodgy, self-satisfied businessman named Marshall McKann, who by chance, and against his will, had attended Kitty's concert that evening and had scowled unremittingly throughout her performance. Since he had unhappily occupied a chair on the stage along with other overflow patrons, she had to walk past his scowl several times. At the end of his discussion with Kitty, McKann retires, grateful not to have changed his views about the shallowness of artists and the uselessness of their lives and contributions. But Kitty has her little joke. First, she leaves him with a naughty dare, " . . . by the way, dream of me tonight, and not of either of those ladies who sat beside you" (p. 146); and sometime before morning she tucks one of her gold slippers into the hammock above his bed. Years later,

in the throes of a long, unexplained, debilitating illness, a much diminished McKann pulls the slipper from his office strong box and
stares at it.

Cather's main point in the dialogue between Kitty and McKann
is that among people who regard the artist as a commodity rather
than a human being, the artist becomes a victim. Cressida's family
are the particular instruments of her victimization, while Kitty is
victimized by two different segments of society at large, one represented by Marshall McKann in "A Gold Slipper," the other represented by a treacherous social climber in "Scandal." What McKann
argues is that Kitty and others like her are purchased and support-
ed by Philistinian, soulless culture buffs who patronize the arts to
achieve the veneer of social respectability. He is disgusted by such
pretense. Art is unimportant and she is not a person; she is only a
performer, a parasite allowed to thrive by the dubious grace of social
whim. While he plods through his argument, making low-minded
capsulizing statements like, "With a woman, everything comes back
to one thing" (p. 143), she dodges about, now chiding him for being
unimaginative in his criticism of her, now teasing him with para-
doxes from Tolstoy, now earnestly throwing her record of generosity
at him—lecturing him, classifying him, accusing him of having a
real self somewhere beneath his "custom-made prejudices" (p. 144).
She even blames him because his attitudes and the attitudes of people like him have conditioned her too. She sometimes finds herself
believing, like him, that stenographers and shop girls are worthier
than she. Kitty speaks of herself as "a victim of these ineradicable
prejudices" that make her think ill of herself.

It is easy to condemn McKann for the stolid self-satisfaction that
will not let him even consider that art has meaning beyond frills and
frosting. It is tempting to damn him for viewing women, even highly
gifted women, as little more than sex objects. It is satisfying to gloat
over his delayed defeat by a woman so slender he "could almost have
broken [her] in two with his bare hands" (p. 141). But it is instructive to remember that Kitty has her own set of "custom-made prejudices." She speaks sneeringly of "his kind" who "always say the
same thing," and by implication she accuses him of "lazy, obese cow-
ardice" (p. 146). With sarcasm bred over years of countering anti-art
reproaches, she calls him "Mr. Worldly Wiseman" and one of the
"prudent people" (p. 141). Though his pragmatic generalizations and
stereotyped labels are more numerous and more damaging than
hers, she too begins treating another human being with

dehumanizing contempt. As they talk, the two keep adding stones to the growing wall between them, and any hope for reconciliation or understanding steadily fades. Their argument becomes a personal as well as a philosophical contest, and Kitty finally wins by throwing a punch after the bell. The human in both Kitty and McKann has suffered.

Kitty's victimization is more obvious in the two episodes described in "Scandal." In "A Gold Slipper" she is actively defending herself, dealing face-to-face with an antagonist for whom she is a fair match, except for the weight of the group he symbolizes ("there are a great many more at home like you," p. 144). But in "Scandal," Kitty's assailants work deviously, using her without her knowledge, tricking her into serving their interests. Here she is the exploited victim with no chance at self-defense, much less counterattack. Ill with a serious cold and throat infection, Kitty has been sealed up at home for nearly two months while stand-in singers collect her pay and her applause. When her sole visitor (she has strict orders from the doctor), Pierce Tevis, arrives, he confirms that her prolonged absence from the stage has triggered speculation about her. Such talk leads Tevis to recall a less friendly rumor that was deliberately staged and produced by an unprincipled clothing manufacturer, a millionaire named Sigmund Stein whom Tevis describes as "one of the most hideous men in New York" (p. 166). Cather's uncomplimentary, anti-Semitic portrait of Stein is generally regarded as growing out of her supposed initial distaste for Jan Hambourg, whom Isabelle McClung was planning to marry at about this time. Stein is uglier than Miletus Poppas in "The Diamond Mine," and even more despicable.[9] The shrewd and enterprising Stein had somewhere found a young woman who bore a strong resemblance to Kitty. Dressing her like Kitty, he began making appearances with her, always managing to keep her face shadowed or partially hidden. When Kitty was performing, he would appear in a box unaccompanied; when Kitty was not, he would appear elsewhere with the imposter, all the time enhancing his reputation and social stature at Kitty's expense. Stein, faultless in his sense of timing, carried on the masquerade for two years, just long enough. Then he married an heiress. Where McKann is merely stupid and callous, Stein is calculating and evil.

It is a night for revelations. After Tevis finishes his tale, Kitty provides the sequel to it, recounting an incident that until now had never been explained for her. It, too, is a tale of exploitation with

Stein again using Kitty as if she were some piece of expendable mer-
chandise. With the understanding that Kitty's friend, Peppo Amo-
retti, would be allowed to perform, Kitty agreed to attend the
Steins's housewarming party. To her dismay, a week later *The
American Gentleman* ran pictures of Kitty with the Steins at the
event. Peppo was not even mentioned. Inclined to be open and trusting, Kitty was sure "to fall for such a plot." The artist of Kitty's or
Cressida's inclination has little built-in protection against the
money-monitored mind or the socially ambitious disposition. As Kitty says, if they want you, "they'll get you in the end" (p. 177).

Marshall McKann and Sigmund Stein, then, represent segments
of a society inimical to art. Such a society uses the artist like a
cheap, paste-over jewel to mask its wholly commercial nature. Every
bank opening features some piece of art; every massive corporation
gives some bit of cash to support the performing arts. Society makes
its gestures to art, Cather says, but such gestures confirm that art is
merely decorative, and its moral force is blunted. Kitty, in person, a
living human being, cannot make McKann even admit that she is
real. To institutionalize art into a set of formalities which we pretend to value, but in fact do not, is to rob the artist of spiritual and
moral validity. Kitty is the particular instance of this kind of dehumanization and demoralization, but she represents the entire world
of genuine art. She (hence, all of art) is the victim of society's lust for
material and social power. She is used, but she is not valued. She is
dispensable, like any commodity in the marketplace. And as Cressida Garnet knows too well, even one's family cannot be counted on for
sympathy. Even another artist cannot, as Cather so clearly demonstrates in her next story, "Coming, Aphrodite!"

B. ELEMENTAL WOMAN

The last of the New York stories in *Uncle Valentine,* and the first
of the stories in *Youth and the Bright Medusa,* "Coming, Aphrodite!"
or "Coming, Eden Bower!" is quite different from the three business-
centered stories and the three artist-versus-society stories which
precede it. Maybe "nifty" is the best word to describe this piece, so
cleverly conceived and ingeniously tailored is it. This story about
the love affair of a singer and a painter is a superb display of Cather's technical craftsmanship, but it lacks the personal emotion and
warmth we have come to expect in stories that command so much of
her artistic energy. Nevertheless, it is a major achievement in the

Cather canon and deserves much more critical attention than it has received.

"Coming, Eden Bower!" was published in *Smart Set* in August 1920, just weeks before it appeared in *Youth and the Bright Medusa* in its original form, as "Coming, Aphrodite!" For its magazine printing the story underwent some changes, several of them calculated to make it more palatable to squeamish readers.[10] The most significant changes in the story reduce the more explicit sexuality of some passages to implicit, but no less obvious, suggestion. Simple references to Eden's thigh and breast are omitted, and the phrase "a woman's body" is transmuted into " a human body." And while Eden Bower performs her exercises in the nude in "Coming, Aphrodite!" she is "clad in a pink chiffon cloud of some sort" in "Coming, Eden Bower!" In spite of the changes, most of them stylistic, the stories are essentially the same, and no change of title can obscure the fact that young Eden Bower is Aphrodite, the goddess of love.

Unlike her female predecessors in Cather's fiction, Eden Bower is multidimensional. She represents whatever is meant by the term Woman; she is elemental, she is sexual, and she is an artist. Eden's similarity to several of Cather's female characters is readily apparent, however, in spite of her additional complexity. Characters with a mythic dimension—Alexandra Bergson, Thea Kronborg, Ántonia Shimerda, and Lucy Gayheart—are all suggested in the figure of Eden Bower. All four of them have, like Eden, close association with elemental things; they are primitives with strong ties to earth's natural rhythms. Alexandra and Ántonia have even been described as earth mothers. And although they are not explicitly love goddesses, as Eden is, they are not immune to romantic passion. Alexandra's yearning is expressed in the giant figure who appears in her dreams and carries her off in his arms. Ántonia's sexuality is expressed in her generous fertility, her motherhood, and her oneness with all growing things. Thea's is expressed not only in her link with the earth, but also in her love for Fred Ottenburg. And finally, Lucy, who is taken into the earth's bosom in her drowning and death, conceives a great love for Clement Sebastian. No less important, in her desire for art Eden also resembles Thea and Lucy.

In this story Cather describes primitive passion, the mystery of innate feeling between men and women, objectively and sensitively. Like the heroic women in Cather's novels, Eden also has her male admirer, but his role differs somewhat from that of Carl Linstrum,

Doctor Archie (or Fred Ottenburg), Jim Burden, and Harry Gordon. Unlike the others, Don Hedger has a relationship with his "goddess" that is overtly sexual. Hedger first takes notice of Eden Bower when quite by accident he discovers a knothole in his closet which offers a view into her adjoining room in an old rooming house on New York's Washington Square.[11] Reflexively, he stoops to look and is stunned by the breathtaking sight of her young body in motion. She is performing exercises before a mirror, quite unaware that she has an audience. But to Hedger, "the spot seemed enchanted; as if a vision out of Alexandria, out of the remote pagan past, had bathed itself there in Helianthine fire" (p. 151). Agitated to the point of distraction by this bright figure "enveloped . . . in a luminous mist" (p. 152), Hedger thereafter watches her routine daily.

Hedger perceives that Eden has another identity, but for a time, he is content to know her only as the figure who moves magnificently in a flood of sunlight, showered like Danaë by Zeus's golden rain. Just as Jim Burden cannot bear to know anything about Ántonia that might tarnish his image of her, so Hedger wants none of the everday Eden Bower, the woman who "wore shirtwaists and got letters from Chicago." He wants only the woman he has seen "in a room full of sun, before an old mirror, on a little enchanted rug of sleeping colours." This woman "had no geographical associations. . . . She was the immortal conception, the perennial theme" (p. 153). Her exercising is a ritual, ancient, timeless; she is the basis for all things, immense, "older than art" (p. 172).

Discomposed and jealous of Eden's friendships with other men, Hedger takes Eden to watch his model, Molly Welch, perform in a hot air balloon. He is furious when Eden switches places with Molly and executes her routine high in the sky. Later, in a resurge of anger, he tells Eden an Aztec legend about a Rain Princess whose lust cost her her life,[12] then leaves her with "a harsh, threatening glance" (p. 168). Unable to sleep, she climbs to the roof, only to find Hedger and his dog Caesar already there. Once the skeptical Caesar is dismissed, Eden and Hedger converge in an ageless magnetism that is expressed ineluctably in the physical act of love.

Perhaps just as inevitable as their union is the quarrel that splits them apart. She, ambitious for her own career, never really understands about his art which takes no account of commercial considerations. Eighteen years later, "after years of spectacular success in Paris" (p. 174), Eden returns for a New York engagement. Deliberately, if somewhat disinterestedly, she asks an art dealer about Hedger and is gratified to learn that he has achieved some reputation, if not measurable wealth. For after all, she says, "One doesn't like to have been an utter fool, even at twenty" (p. 176).

This story is more packed, more loaded with details than most of Cather's fiction. It is basically a love story, but in "Coming, Aphrodite!" Cather avoids sentimentality by anchoring the love relationship in the primitive, and by describing it in impersonal, mythic terms. Drawn together by forces neither of them can resist, Hedger and Eden Bower for a time play their respective roles in the great, but somehow formal, primeval drama ordered from the foundations of the world. They become Everyman and Everywoman. We sense the rudimentary nature of their relationship when Eden's experience with Hedger on Coney Island and his telling of the Aztec legend leave her too disquieted, too aware of the elemental in herself, to sleep:

> The balloon had been one kind of excitement, the wine another; but the thing that had roused her, as a blow rouses a proud man, was the doubt, the contempt, the sneering hostility with which this violent man had looked at her when he told his savage story. Crowds and balloons were all very well, she reflected, but woman's chief adventure is man. With a mind over-active and a sense of life over-strong, she wanted to walk across the roofs in the starlight; to sail over the sea and face at once a world of which she had never been afraid. (P. 186)

Standing together on the roof that night, "with the sky behind and blue shadows before, they looked like one of Hedger's own paintings of that period; two figures, one white and one dark, and nothing whatever distinguishable about them but that they were male and female. The faces were lost, the contours blurred in shadow, but the figures were a man and a woman, and that was their whole concern and their mysterious beauty. . ." (p. 169).

Cather reinforces the mythic aspects of Eden's nature and of the relationship between Eden and Hedger through the legend of the Rain Princess, for it underscores theme and intensifies the story's emotional climax. The Rain Princess of the legend, like Eden, is both goddess and mortal, gifted with unworldly powers but cursed with worldly desires—desires for power, love and, in Eden's case, success. Hedger uses the savage legend not only to vent his anger over the balloon incident, but also to declare his love for Eden, a declaration that leads to their first sexual union. Even though that night they descend from the roof in order to make love, and the goddess of love seems to consent, for a moment, to mortality, Eden's mythic dimension is still predominant in the description of the two of them as "male and female," as "man and woman." Instead of making Eden "mortal," Cather stresses her remoteness and primitiveness, and makes Hedger a part of the larger design. Eden is associated with cosmic principles of light—stars, moon, and sun, raised high in the heavens. Like Lucy Gayheart and Alexandra, she is given to contemplating the stars, and like Lucy and Thea, she is associated with light and the moon. The moon, which in Cather's major works is nearly always a symbol for desire, serves here to signify Hedger's desire for Eden as well as Eden's desire for achievement in the world of art. Whether consciously or unconsciously, Hedger is yearning for her whenever he contemplates the moon or stars. At night, on the roof, he and his dog become "quite lost in watching the glittering game." When her song breaks through his rooftop revery, it almost seems an answer to his contemplation of the "slender, girlish-looking young moon in the west" which was "playing with a whole company of silver stars" (pp. 147–48). In her excursions to the roof, she too gazes long and far at the stars. And much later, after Hedger's impulsive departure, the moon prompts him home to her. "The first stars and the first lights were growing silver against the gradual darkening" (pp. 172–73) when he enters the house, but Eden is gone. Hedger turns off the light and looks out the window at the stars.

This imagery of heavenly orbs and light underscores Eden's immortal and primordial condition before worldly struggle and success exact their onerous toll. And when Eden returns to New York eighteen years later, Cather uses light imagery to indicate the terrible, but perhaps necessary, price the singer has paid. Once again on Washington Square, Eden seems momentarily blinded by the light, forced to blink against the descending sun, but still finding delight in watching the sky. She has achieved what she sought, but finally, it is Hedger, "original, erratic, and . . . changing all the time," who has lost very little over the years while Eden Bower's pursuit of success has made her hard and inflexible, capable of elasticity only in those brief wonderful moments when she is transformed behind the stage lights, when she is undeniably the artist. In this, too, Eden resembles Thea Kronborg, for Doctor Archie observes just such a transformation in Thea, from a bedraggled singer into a glowing artist.[13] Slote accurately describes the older Eden as "dead in life and alive in art."[14] Cather conveys that idea through still further references to light. When Eden emerges from the art dealer's offices, the sun which had long ago bathed her plastic features with glorious light has set. Now only "the street lamps flashed their ugly orange light" on her face, a face that has become "hard and settled, like a plaster cast" (p. 176). In our last view of Eden, her once splendidly mobile image is ossified by a grotesque and unnatural light. Hence, it is somewhat ironic that the opera house entrance blazes out the news that Aphrodite, the goddess of love, is coming. That figure has been mostly buried in the success of Eden Bower.[15]

If the young Eden is light, then Hedger is surely the complementary dark principle. His rooms, always dark and dingy, are never blessed by the sun, and even his musty closet is full of laundry tied in dirty gray sheets. Conversely, her rooms on the other side of the house receive the sun directly and seem filled with perennial light. In other ways, too, Eden Bower and Don Hedger are complementary opposites. She looks to the cosmos, aspires skyward, while he ventures no higher than the roof. Even the word "bower" suggests flowering growth suspended in air, while "hedge" suggests something less luxuriant and closer to the ground. In her visits to Washington Square, Eden instinctively rises when a flock of pigeons appear overhead. With a "kind of defiant delight in her face," she follows their flight as they go "wheeling rapidly up through the morning air, soaring and dropping, scattering and coming together, now gray, now white as silver, as they caught or intercepted the sunlight" (p. 154). The earth-sprung pigeons become an important symbol of Eden's aspiration, of her desire. There will be no holding her back, and she knows it. Here, too, Eden is like Cather's other aspiring artists, Thea Kronborg and Lucy Gayheart. Lucy is described as seeming to have wings, and she yearns to float with the airborne gulls. And it is an eagle steeped in light that becomes the primary symbol for Thea's artistic striving. Watching the pigeons from her music room couch, Eden sees "only the sky itself," and "the birds that crossed and re-crossed her field of vision." Limited though her knowledge might be at age twenty, "one thing she knew; that she was to be Eden Bower. She was like someone standing before a great show window full of beautiful and costly things, deciding which she will order" (p. 157).

Just as she is attracted to the high-flying pigeons, so is Eden Bower attracted to other things that fly, so she must ride in the big balloon high above the earth and the crowds. Not Hedger. Eden asks the painter if he would not like to go up with Molly, and he replies without hesitation, "Of course not." But the balloon soaring "in the brilliant light . . . like a big silver-gray bat, with its wings folded" (p. 161) is a temptation Eden cannot resist. In language that deliberately picks up the principal images of Eden and her desire, Cather portrays her flying high, catching the light on the silver slippers, scouring the sky in a balloon that is at once a "slowly falling silver star" and a "great bird" (p. 163). In the end, after Eden returns many years later to sing in the United States, she remembers and is still captivated by the pigeons on Washington Square. As they spiral "quickly upward into the brilliant blue sky," she throws her head back and watches them "with a smile of amazement and delight." She is astonished that "they still rose, out of all that dirt and noise and squalor, fleet and silvery, just as they used to rise that summer when she was twenty and went up in a balloon on Coney Island!" And "all the way down town her mind wandered . . . and she kept smiling and looking up at the sky" (p. 175).

Thus, even in the nature of their artistic desire Eden and Hedger are complementary, opposites that attract with polar energy. And Cather insists that somehow human aspirations toward art and self-realization can be circumscribed by the primeval drive that brings Eden and Hedger together in the first place. Eden's desire is written in the sky, in the light; Hedger's is written in the dark:

> While Eden Bower watched the pigeons, Don Hedger sat on the other side of the bolted doors, looking into a pool of dark turpentine at his idle brushes, wondering why a woman could do this to him. He, too, was sure of his future and knew that he was a chosen man. . . . Each of these two young people sensed the future, but not completely. Don Hedger knew that nothing much would ever happen to him. Eden Bower understood that to her a great deal would happen. But she did not guess that her neighbour would have more tempestuous adventures sitting in his dark studio than she would find in all the capitals of Europe. . . . (Pp. 158–59)

Eden's aspirations, however, draw her away from Hedger, and this story chronicles the loss of Eden, the Garden, as well as Eden, the woman. The pair fall from Garden primitivism into the world, and it is the woman who shatters the dream.[16] However it happens, the innocents, the prototypical man and woman, lose paradise. He, born of the dark and the earth, she, born of the sky and the light, are in that sense complementary. But, like so many of Cather's admiring males, he is only mortal, and she has immortal longings. Much as she understands artistic necessity, Cather seems to regret the sometimes inevitable sacrifice of basic humanness and sexuality to it.

III. PITTSBURGH AND THE CONFLICT OF VALUES

A. MIXED MELODY

Three major novels occupied Cather's time between the publication of "Coming, Aphrodite!" and "Uncle Valentine" (*Woman's Home Companion,* February, March 1925). They are *One of Ours* (1922), *A Lost Lady* (1923), and *The Professor's House* (1925). "Uncle Valentine," as will be seen later, has an important thematic relationship to these novels. Busy as Cather was with longer fiction at this time, she still continued to produce occasional short fiction, much of it of a very high quality. "Uncle Valentine" is one of her richest, most satisfying stories, perhaps because she gives herself to it so completely. She is present in every feeling, setting, mood, and incident.

Cather was not one to forget, and in "Uncle Valentine" she calls up the figure of Ethelbert Nevin, a musician and songwriter whom she had many years earlier described with loving superlatives in several newspaper columns. She knew him well, regarded him as her first bonafide artist friend in Pittsburgh, and spent many happy hours with him and his family at Vineacre in the country outside Pittsburgh. Vineacre (called "Greenacre" in the story) is the setting for "Uncle Valentine," and Valentine Ramsay is drawn from Nevin, who died at age thirty-eight in 1901.[17] Cather's description of Nevin, published in the *Journal,* 24 March 1901, is, to the letter, a portrait of Valentine Ramsay whom Cather created fictionally in the middle 1920s:

His personality had preserved all the waywardness, freshness, enthusiasm and painful susceptibility of youth, and he had never become accustomed to the routine processes of living, but found life always as new, as perplexing, as untried, as violent and as full of penetrating experiences as he had found it at eighteen. He had never developed the fortifying calm which usually comes to a man of genius in his thirties, the interior life which goes on undisturbed by external mischances. . . . He had been unable to place any sort of non-conducting medium between the world and himself, no sort of protection to break the jar of things. . . . Every day that he lived he got up to meet life as barehanded and raw to the weather, disturbed by the roughness of the machinery of life, oppressed by the slightest neglect from anyone near him, sensitive to the criticism of strangers, enervated by the gloom of an overcast sky, like a weathervane at the mercy of the uncomprehending and unheeding universe.[18]

"Uncle Valentine" is about the people who lived near Greenacre, Pennsylvania, at the turn of the century, in old country homes as yet untouched by the industrial machine that was steadily snarling toward them. It is about one particular year, one "golden year" (p. 31), in the lives of these people, the year Valentine came home. Having no head for practical matters, as a young man Valentine had allowed himself to be pursued and shackled by the wealthy Janet Oglethorpe, a woman so caught up with spending and owning that he suspects she "bargains in her sleep." After being "dragged about the world for five years in an atmosphere of commonness and meanness and coarseness," he finally ran off with another woman, deliberately creating a scandal, damaging Janet's "pride so openly that she'd have to take action" (p. 13). Valentine's ill-advised and unhappy marriage to a woman of impossible selfishness and stupidity recalls again the similar unfortunate marriages that seem to prevail in Cather's fiction.

One day Valentine comes home to live at Bonnie Brae with the three old men who are quietly wearing out their lives there—his father, the aging but gracious Jonathan; his much older brother, the kindly but somewhat feeble-minded Morton; and his uncle, Jonathan's younger brother, Roland, the child prodigy who came home broken at age twenty-eight and never left again. Next door at Fox Hill are Charlotte Waterford and her husband, Harry, her own four daughters, and two orphaned nieces.

Charlotte, who resembles Mrs. Harling in *My Ántonia,* is one of two remarkable women in the story, and she enjoys an extraordinary friendship with Valentine, a friendship enhanced by her musical background and sensitivity. The other is Louise Ireland, the singer who accommodated Valentine's need to create a scandal in order to free himself from Janet Oglethorpe. Ireland, who combines some qualities of Thea Kronborg, Lucy Gayheart, and Marian Forrester (*A Lost Lady*), appears only in snatches, mainly in Valentine's admiring remarks about her, although the frame story is set in her Paris studio many years after the Valentine story takes place. Ireland's reputation is far from spotless—she had run off with desperate men before—but reputation is often a poor index to personal worth. Valentine describes her as "a glorious creature," insisting that "everything she does is lovely, somehow or other, just as every song she sings is more beautiful than it ever was before." He compares her with Janet: "A woman's behavior may be irreproachable and she herself may be gross—just gross. She may do her duty, and defile everything she touches. And another woman may be erratic, imprudent, self-indulgent if you like, and all the while be—what is it the Bible says? Pure in heart" (p. 14).

To establish the plot line Cather works chronologically through the seasons, as she had done in novels like *O Pioneers!* and *My Ántonia,* letting them set the structural pattern as well as the tone for the story. The year's events, having begun somewhat tentatively in late fall with Valentine's homecoming party, burst into wondrous excursions through forests and over hills with the coming of spring. The experiences of Valentine and his friends next door grow lovelier with the deepening of summer, and Valentine even decides that he just might stay at Bonnie Brae forever. But with the dying summer comes the news that the Wakely property which takes in his beloved woods and meadows has been sold. Worse still, it has been sold to Janet Oglethorpe and her second husband. With Janet closing in on him once more, Valentine cannot stay. After several painful delays, he sails for Europe, and that one glorious year comes to an end. Before two years have passed he is killed by a motor truck outside Louise Ireland's studio.

In one sense, the story's principal character is the narrator, Charlotte's niece Marjorie, because the story chronicles the sixteenth year in Marjorie's life, the year she stands on the borderline between

childhood and adulthood. In that crucial year she lives next door to
Uncle Valentine, and she will always bear the stamp of that experience. Whether Marjorie's own musical gift flowers is never explicitly
stated, but unquestionably her presence in Ireland's studio in the
frame story—whether as friend, student, disciple, or casual visitor—
is at Valentine's unspoken behest. All those years ago he planted the
seed that would one day take Marjorie to Louise Ireland.

Marjorie habitually speaks of "that year" or "that winter" or
spring or summer in a way that attaches special significance to it.
That year she and Valentine together fend off adulthood, clasp
youth and wonder, recreate the Golden Age in their own Arcadian
fields. What Cather says of Ethelbert Nevin is true for Valentine:
"Indeed it was almost impossible to conceive of his outliving youth,
or that there should ever come a winter in his Arcady."[19] Cather
had sentimentalized the desire for youth and the Golden Age in early stories like "Jack-a-Boy" and "The Treasure of Far Island," but she
avoids sentimentality here because Marjorie and Valentine are
aware that the world lies just outside their enchanted gates. It is
during that year, too, that Valentine composes his most memorable
songs. Marjorie remembers summer as particularly joyous, recalling
that she "expected life to be like that forever. The golden year, Aunt
Charlotte called it, when I visited her at Fox Hill years afterward"
(p. 31).

Clinging to childhood but facing adulthood, Marjorie learns in
that year what she will need to know her whole life through. That is
the year through which all her sensibilities will filter experience as
long as she lives. It sets the standards for sensitivity, for sympathy,
for wonder, for pain, for desire, for values that last a lifetime. From
Charlotte and Valentine, individually and in combination, she
learns the validity of mystery and beauty, and about the importance
of place; she learns also about freedom and bondage, and she learns
about the essential aloneness of every person. Observing Charlotte
and Valentine together, Marjorie comes to understand the meaning
of their affection, to understand why Valentine regards Charlotte
and Louise Ireland, two women so different from each other, as his
best friends. It is because the deepest human attachments are aesthetic; a mutual appreciation of the beautiful is the strongest bond
possible. Janet Oglethorpe has to be rejected on the same grounds
that Charlotte and Ireland are accepted—aesthetic grounds.

The essential oneness of Charlotte and Valentine is further stressed in their mutual love for the countryside around Greenacre and the houses at Bonnie Brae and Fox Hill, a feeling that is not lost on the perceptive and impressionable Marjorie. Valentine's year in his own place is the most productive year of his creative life, and he is forced to agree with Charlotte when she says, "It's the valley you're tied to. The place is necessary to you, Valentine." Marjorie knows too that "the place was vocal to him. . . . Some artists profit by exile. He was one of those who do not. And his country was not a continent, but a few wooded hills in a river valley, a few old houses and gardens that were home" (p. 31).[20]

Marjorie's lesson on the importance of place is underscored by the almost frantic reactions of the Ramsay and Waterford households to the news that the Wakely place has been sold. She knows that the loss of the creeks and woods means "the end for us" (p. 37). Perhaps nearly as tragic as the loss of place are the terms on which it is lost. Valentine can only interpret it as a loss of freedom and a return to bondage, and Marjorie learns that money in the hands of the stupid or unscrupulous can enslave as surely as any set of chains. Valentine understands Janet's purchase of the Wakely property to be an attempt to gain control over him once more. In despair he cries, "She's Scotch; she couldn't let anything get away—not even me. . . . Everything about her's bunk, except her damned money. That's a fact, and it's got me—it's got me. . . . That was her creek we were playing along this afternoon. . . . I can't get in or out" (p. 36). Thus Valentine is forced to flee again from Janet whose callous presence is enough to paralyze him. With Greenacre lost, he has little to live for, and in less than two years he is dead.

Crassly materialistic as she is, Janet Oglethorpe is only symbolic of a still larger threat to Greenacre, and even to art itself. The Ramsays have never been taught how to compete in a world run by machines and money, and their fate has been predestined from the time Roland withdrew from the world and came home. The defeat of the Ramsays is assured in the inevitable industrial takeover of their air and lands and streams. Though in the particular year of the story, the characters see the city's industrial smoke as a distant threat at most ("that smoke did not come down to us; our evenings were pure and silvery" p. 25), Marjorie reports years later that life at Bonnie Brae as Valentine had conceived it could have lasted only a moment anyway. It was just one weak and ineffectual stay against impossible economic odds. The Hartwell home in "The Namesake" was similarly doomed.[21] Finally, the only thing that remains of Bonnie Brae and Fox Hill is the song Valentine had written about Uncle Harry's retaining wall and the profusion of blood red roses that covered it.

Thus, here too, as she does in so many stories and novels, Cather decries the exploitive materialism that scores lives and destroys landscapes. The settings may be different, but in this thematic concern "Uncle Valentine" bears a special relationship to the three novels of the same period mentioned earlier. In *One of Ours*, Claude Wheeler's love for the land and growing things is posed against his father's lack of feeling for it and his brothers' inordinate interest in profitable business ventures. Nat Wheeler is the kind of man who cuts down a beautiful cherry tree for a joke. Ivy Peters in *A Lost Lady* is almost a male incarnation of Janet Oglethorpe. He takes special pleasure in gaining control of the Forrester property and the woman who had lived there with a style he had no capacity to appreciate. His only concern is to make money off the land. He has no feeling for it. And his kind are on the ascendance; in the wake of their onslaught the land is sucked up, and the old values and beauties crumble. It is detecting the same impulse in his family that finally breaks the spirit of Godfrey St. Peter in *The Professor's House*. In their increasing desire for money and material things, people like Janet Oglethorpe and Ivy Peters participate in the destruction of life's true valuables just as surely as does the collector who carries off Tom Outland's mesa relics.

Another of Cather's favorite themes, individual freedom, also figures in this story. She has always insisted that the freedom to be oneself, to pursue one's loves, to have one's place, unfettered by ugliness or meanness or greed, is one of life's highest values. In "Uncle Valentine" Marjorie learns the importance of freedom very early from Charlotte, and realizes it more fully through Valentine. Charlotte, she remembers, "allowed us a great deal of liberty and demanded her own in return. We were permitted to have our own thoughts and feelings" (p. 9). Marjorie comes to realize that the contempt with which city people viewed Valentine after his scandalous behavior and his inauspicious homecoming was actually envy, "because everything about him told how free he was. And up there, nobody was free. They were imprisoned in their harsh Calvinism, or in

their merciless business grind, or in mere apathy—a mortal dull-
ness" (pp. 15–16). Perhaps the dominant image in the story, in terms
of sheer numbers, is the image of a window, a symbol of freedom.

The kind of privacy and personal freedom so essential to the sensitive human being carries something of a dark corollary, however—
the indisputable fact that every human creature on this earth is,
finally and essentially, alone. It is a fact which many Cather characters confront: Godfrey St. Peter, Myra Henshawe, Bishop Jean Latour, Sapphira Colbert, to name a few; and it is another of the vital
things Marjorie learns in her crucial sixteenth year. One evening
after a hike with Valentine she feels intensely aware of the night
and "vaguely afraid to be alone" (p. 29). She seeks out Charlotte, but
Charlotte sends her off to bed, pleading a headache and a need for
solitude. Uncle Harry also puts her off, as does Valentine when she
discovers him lying in the study in the moonlight. Walking in the
garden alone, still disinclined to sleep, Marjorie hears from the Jap-
anese summerhouse "a groan, not loud, but long, long, as if the unhappiness of a whole lifetime were coming out in one despairing
breath." Looking inside, she sees "Roland, his head in his hands, the
moonlight on his silver hair." She steals away, realizing that "tonight everyone wanted to be alone with his ghost" (pp. 29–30).

Roland is the symbol of that basic human aloneness Cather is describing, and his anguish is a dark tonal thread which runs through
the story, muting the happy days, breathing the reality of past sorrow and the threat of future sorrow into the carefree winds of the
golden year. Wherever there is music, there is Roland—a shadow at
the window, a groan behind the wall, a figure in the doorway, a
waxen face at a concert. He had been a prodigy, and now he is lost.

Symbolizing the aloneness of all the characters and their inevitable lostness in the grips of an encroaching materialism they will not
be able to withstand, and symbolizing as well the defeat of the artistic sensibility, Roland in a very particular way also spells out Valentine's fate. Returning with mature subtlety to the device she had
used ten years earlier in "Consequences," Cather makes Roland the
ghost of Valentine's future self. Like Kier Cavenaugh, Valentine is
haunted by the self he could become, and the realization is intolerable to him. When Valentine runs from Bonnie Brae to Europe, he is
running from his future self, projected before him in Roland, as well
as from Janet Oglethorpe. Valentine senses a special relationship
between Roland and himself. Commenting on Roland's condition on

the night described earlier, Valentine asks a rhetorical question: "Do you suppose that's the way I'll be keeping Christmas ten years from now, Charlotte" (p. 20)? Returning from several days in the city, having decided to remain at Bonnie Brae, Valentine says, "Likely I'm here forever, like Roland and the oak trees" (p. 30). On one occasion he makes an explicit reference to himself and Roland that clearly indicates he is reading his own future whenever he looks at Roland. Valentine says, "What haunts me about Roland is the feeling of kinship. So often it flashes into my mind: 'Yes, I might be struck dumb some day, just like that'" (p. 26). The descriptions of Roland picture a living ghost, a walking corpse, and hence a threat to Valentine in the same way that the old man in the top hat and soiled gloves was a threat to Kier Cavenaugh. Roland has a "waxy, frozen face," motionless features and eyes set in "deep hollows" (p. 23), "just a coffin of a man," Valentine observes. Just as the old man kept appearing in Cavenaugh's quarters, so does Roland keep dogging Valentine's steps. It is not uncommon, Valentine says, for Roland to "come drifting in through the wing and settle himself in my study and sit there half the night without opening his head" (p. 26).

Roland, Valentine, Charlotte, indeed all of them at Bonnie Brae and Fox Hill that year, are particular instruments for Marjorie's education. In creating a legend about Uncle Valentine she learns how important place is, and what freedom means, and what beauty and loneliness are, and what holds people together. Apparently she takes what she has learned to Louise Ireland, the only living being, once life has vanished at Greenacre, whose own schooling guarantees an instant sympathy. Only she and Louise Ireland, in this whole earth, know the meaning of the song casually picked up and casually sung by the young student in Ireland's studio so many years later, the song that begins, "I know a wall where red roses grow. . . ."

B. Restoration

Chronologically, "Double Birthday" (*Forum,* February 1929), the latest story reprinted in the *Uncle Valentine* collection, comes four years after "Uncle Valentine." Less passionate than "Uncle Valentine," "Double Birthday" is still a good story, and it affirms recovery even while recounting loss. Cather's writing was taking some interesting turns in this period, moving from almost soul-rocking pessimism in *The Professor's House* (1925) and *My Mortal Enemy* (1926)

to solid spiritual optimism in *Death Comes for the Archbishop*
(1927), "Neighbour Rosicky" (1928), and *Shadows on the Rock*
(1931). It is perhaps significant that "Double Birthday" was published immediately after "Neighbour Rosicky" and midway between
the two novels which take their essential flavor from religious characters, themes, and practices. In the values it emphasizes, "Double
Birthday" is very close to "Neighbour Rosicky" and the two novels.

The characters in the story are inspired to some degree by people
Cather knew, and are portrayed with special sympathy. Bernice
Slote suggests that old Albert Engelhardt is probably drawn from
Dr. Julius Tyndale of Lincoln, Cather's own would-be mentor, while
the characters of Margaret Parmenter and her father, Judge Hammersley, are drawn from Isabelle and Judge McClung.[22] The story
is about the birthday celebration of two Albert Engelhardts, uncle
and nephew, born on the same day twenty-five years apart. Both
bachelors, they share the upper story of an old house in a rather dingy section of Pittsburgh, a piece of property that had somehow been
overlooked when the younger Albert and his brothers were
liquidating the assets they had inherited from their industrious father, August Engelhardt. In spite of straitened circumstances, however, they do not live meanly; they have retained their pride, their
taste for fineness, and their appreciation for humanity and the arts.
After the younger Albert's chance meeting with Judge Hammersley,
he and his uncle are reunited in their birthday supper with the widowed Margaret Parmenter whom they had known in the prosperous
days when her father and old August Engelhardt were friends.

This story about a double birthday also has a distinctly double focus, on the eighty-year-old Albert Engelhardt, a retired physician
who had specialized in treating the throats of singers, and on the
fifty-five-year-old Albert Engelhardt who, given the choice, would
still have squandered his means on the pleasures of youth. The most
consequential experience of the doctor's life was his discovery of a
singer, a young German girl named Marguerite Thiesinger. Like
several other singers in Cather's stories, she is patterned after Thea
Kronborg; and like Thea, she was encouraged in her music by a doctor older than she who had an appreciation for her gift. And she, too,
had a strong, natural artistic personality—vital, alive, almost primitive. Coarse, less intelligent than Thea, and not particularly interested in training her voice, Marguerite nevertheless was persuaded
to become a singer, and the doctor invested his life and strength in

her. His dream, however, was destined to crumble. She developed an inoperable cancer and wasted to death while he watched helplessly.

In describing her death, Cather quite deliberately, if unexpectedly, invokes Gethsemane, and portrays the doctor actually taking up the burden of Marguerite's suffering and bearing it for her through the death passage. Years later he tries to explain how it was to Albert, concluding, "Anyway, I died for her; that was given to me. She never knew a death-struggle—she went to sleep. That struggle took place in my body. Her dissolution occurred within me" (p. 53). The account of his struggle and his explanation of its meaning come structurally at the very center of the story, at the end of the third of six sections. The meaning of that experience seems also to be at the thematic heart of the story, just as Christ's suffering in Gethsemane is at the heart of the Christian Gospel. Cather is not one to stretch this kind of analogy, but she opens section 4 with references to the doctor's occasional streetcar trips to "the hills beyond Mount Oliver" (Gethsemane is on the western side of the Mount of Olives) and to the three trees that grow in the Engelhardts' courtyard. Thus the loss of Marguerite Thiesinger was a gain for the doctor as well as a loss, for through his suffering he was spiritually strengthened and ennobled.

Cather seems to suggest that the old man's loss, its reality, its validity, provides a standard against which the magnitude of almost any significant loss might be measured. And it is that standard that provides a bridge between the doctor's story and that of his nephew. Albert's loss of money, property, and social position might seem a terrible tragedy; but set against his uncle's very personal loss, Albert's deserves no more tears than he accords it. He has lost most of the trappings of life but retained most of the essentials. He has lost nearly all of the outward signs of prosperity, but retained a prosperity of spirit. Indulged by their father, the Engelhardt boys lived freely and frankly, enjoying life wholeheartedly in their youth, ignoring social distinctions, avoiding the business world, and hence running through their father's fortune with scarcely a second thought. His wealth gone and his brothers dead, Albert has made do with whatever fate handed him, grateful to have a roof over his head and some of his cherished personal effects about him, his books, his desk, his mother's fine linen, and a few art pieces.

Margaret Parmenter remembers warmly that the Engelhardt boys were different from the other boys in her set, boys who scorned all girls and then "grabbed . . . brutally" the one they wanted. But she sensed that "the Engelhardt boys . . . enjoyed her aesthetically, so to speak, and it pleased her to be liked in that way" (p. 57). The Engelhardts recall the Erlichs whom Claude Wheeler admired so much in *One of Ours*. Claude enjoyed going to their home because they managed to live graciously even without a great deal of money. They knew books and art and music, all the things Claude felt he was missing. The Erlichs were drawn from the Westermann family with whom Cather became friendly while she was at the university in Lincoln.

Even though Albert is not so strong a character as Godfrey St. Peter or Jean Latour or Neighbour Rosicky, he has their natural fineness and taste. And he has few regrets about the almost unconscious choice he and his brothers made to spend their youths generously and let the future take care of itself. In fact, considering the kinds of things that use up the lives of his old school chums, things like making frequent trips to the doctor, paying "the bills of incorrigible sons," and living discontentedly in "massive houses," he rather thinks that "he had had the best of it; he had gone a-Maying while it was May. . . . Money? O, yes, he would like to have some, but not what went with it" (pp. 54–55). Much as Cather valued fine art objects and civilized surroundings, she hated ostentation and gaudiness. And she was always keenly aware of the capacity of material things to encumber the spirit. This is certainly a central concern in "Neighbour Rosicky," and it is at least a minor theme in nearly all her novels. Cather much preferred generous, irresponsible youth to pinched, acquisitive age.

In the toasts that the old man and Albert propose at the conclusion of the birthday supper, it is clear what they have cared for, what they have spent their lives for—one for a woman and her voice, the other for a richly lived youth. And it is clear that Cather thinks they bargained well. A "beautiful, wonderful look" comes over the old man's face and he drinks "to a memory; to the lost Lenore." Albert softly voices his toast "to my youth, to my beautiful youth" (p. 63)! Through the lives and tempers of the two surviving Engelhardts, then, Cather asserts that the mean life is not the life bereft of things or money, not the life squandered on the glories of youth or sacrificed to a fated singer, but the life in which one has not cared enough about anything to give everything for it. The rich life is the one which has contained something worth spending everything for. Judged by this standard, the Engelhardts are rich indeed. They have had something to prize.

NOTES

1. For a brief comparison of the two stories, see Slote's introduction to
Uncle Valentine and Other Stories, p. x. All citations from the previously uncollected stories in this chapter are from this volume as previously
documented (page numbers are in parentheses in the text). For a lengthy
treatment of character duality in Cather's novels, see my doctoral thesis,
"Self-division and Self-unity in the Novels of Willa Cather" (University of
Wisconsin, 1968).

2. In the meantime, Cather had published two stories about artists,
"The Diamond Mine" and "A Gold Slipper," which she later collected in
Youth and the Bright Medusa. A third, "Scandal," appeared in August 1919,
just two months before "Her Boss." They are discussed later in this chapter.

3. Cather, *The Professor's House,* p. 264. See also my discussion on the
conflict between solitude and society in this novel in "Function of Structure
in Cather's *The Professor's House,*" pp. 169–78.

4. Cather wrote a piece on three opera singers for *McClure's* (she had
earlier written on three actresses), and had always had a strong interest in
women in the theater and the opera. She chose to write on Louise Homer,
Geraldine Farrar, and Olive Fremstad who was then, according to Woodress
(*Willa Cather: Her Life and Art,* p. 163), "reigning Wagnerian soprano at
the Met."

5. While Woodress (Ibid. p. 186) assumes that for Cather art *is* the Medusa, Stouck (*Willa Cather's Imagination,* p. 200) suggests that the Medusa
is rather the symbol of "commercial success" and that the artist triumphs
over her "only by contemplating the Gorgon in the reflection of art (like Per-
seus with Athena's shield)."

6. Woodress, *Willa Cather: Her Life and Art,* pp. 87–88. Also prominent
in Cather's work, however, are the happy marriages based on solid value
systems, marriages like that of Mary and Anton Rosicky. There are also apparently harmonious marriages that receive no comment.

7. Ibid., p. 187.

8. Cather, *Youth and the Bright Medusa,* p. 119. All citations from the
three singer stories are from this source as previously documented (page
numbers are in parentheses in the text).

9. See Woodress (*Willa Cather: Her Life and Art,* pp. 188–89) for a
discussion of Cather's reaction to Isabelle's engagement and marriage, and
its relationship to the stories in this section. As Woodress attests, Cather's
novels and letters show none of the anti-Semitism present in the stories of
this period. Cather and Jan Hambourg later became good friends.

10. See Slote's introduction to *Uncle Valentine and Other Stories,* pp.
xvi–xxii, for a discussion on censorship problems of the time which probably

led to certain modifications in the text, and for a useful discussion of the story itself. The appendix to *Uncle Valentine and Other Stories* lists the many variants in the two stories, page by page. For consistency and convenience, quotations, unless otherwise noted, will be from "Coming, Eden Bower!" as it is reprinted in *Uncle Valentine and Other Stories*. The quotation just cited is found on p. 151.

11. Cather also lived for a time on Washington Square.

12. A letter written to Elizabeth Sergeant from the Grand Canyon dated 21 May 1912 tells where Cather got the story. She apparently heard it from a handsome Mexican named Julio whom she found incredibly fascinating. The Aztec princess of the tale she likens to Cleopatra, and tells "Elsie" that she plans to write the story herself once she can visit the supposed site. (Letter at University of Virginia Library, Charlottesville.)

13. According to Edith Lewis, Cather had apparently observed a similar phenomenon in singer Olive Fremstad. Preparatory to writing an article for *McClure's*, Cather went to interview Fremstad and found her worn and depleted, scarcely able to speak. But called upon to substitute for an ailing soprano that very night, Fremstad appeared on stage radiantly beautiful, singing as if she had never known weariness. Lewis, who reports having attended the performance with Cather, says Cather was absolutely astonished. See *Willa Cather Living*, pp. 90–92. Slote, in her introduction to *Uncle Valentine and Other Stories*, p. xxi, notes that a Cather visit to actress Minnie Maddern Fiske produced a similar observation about artists. Cather wrote about her visit with Fiske in a column published in the *Courier*, 14 January 1899, and reprinted in Curtin, *World and the Parish*, pp. 660–61.

14. Slote, introduction to *Uncle Valentine and Other Stories*, p. xxx.

15. Eden's identification with Aphrodite is stressed particularly when on her return to New York after eighteen years in Europe the lights on the opera house blaze out the news that Aphrodite, the goddess of love, is coming. Although the Aphrodite reference on the marquee is to an opera, or possibly a pageant, its intended application to Eden Bower is obvious. Aphrodite, or Venus, like Eden Bower, has a dual nature. As the goddess of love and beauty she is wonderfully spirited and lovely, simply irresistible; but in later characterizations Aphrodite is more like the primitive Rain Princess of Hedger's legend, given to treachery and maliciousness, and to exercising destructive and deadly power over men.

In the *Smart Set* version of the story Eden is to play the role of Clytemnestra, the faithless but courageous wife of Agamemnon. For either role, Eden Bower is particularly well-suited.

16. Slote suggests that Dante Gabriel Rossetti's poem about Adam's legendary first wife, Lilith, may have been Cather's source for the name Eden Bower and for some of Eden's character traits. Lilith bears resemblance to the Rain Princess, too, for it is Lilith who is said to have plotted with the

serpent to destroy humanity. The critical verse of the Rossetti poem reads:

> It was Lilith the wife of Adam:
> (Eden's bower's in flower.)
> Not a drop of her blood was human,
> But she was made like a soft sweet woman.

Slote says, "Willa Cather's Eden Bower is both Lilith and Eve, the female principle of beauty and evil without love (or for whom love is a momentary delight)." See the introduction to *Uncle Valentine and Other Stories,* p. xix.

17. See *Courier* and *Journal* articles in 1898, 1900, and 1901, reprinted in Curtin, *World and the Parish,* pp. 532–38, 627–42, 650–55, for Cather's tributes to the musician, and for her accounts of personal experiences with him and his family. She wrote in a particularly moving way after his death and funeral. See Slote, introduction to *Uncle Valentine and Other Stories,* p. xxiii; Woodress, *Willa Cather: Her Life and Art,* p. 89; and Brown, *Willa Cather: A Critical Biography,* p. 82, for brief commentary on the relationship between Nevin and Valentine. It has also been suggested that Adriance Hilgarde, the absent musician of "A Death in the Desert," is at least partially drawn from Nevin. As was noted earlier, Valentine differs from Nevin in one important regard: Nevin's marriage was a very happy one, Valentine's a very unhappy one.

18. Curtin, *World and the Parish,* p. 638.

19. *Journal,* 24 March 1901. See Curtin, *World and the Parish,* p. 638.

20. In her feeling for place, Cather is like Valentine. Her personal letters to friends are full of comments about her inability to work except at certain places under certain conditions.

21. The Hartwell estate to which Lyon Hartwell returned in "The Namesake" is in the same Pennsylvania countryside as Fox Hill and Bonnie Brae.

22. See Slote's introduction to *Uncle Valentine,* pp. xxvii–xxix.

FIVE

The Last Fifteen Years: The Encompassing Vision

I. THE MEANING OF NEBRASKA: OBSCURE DESTINIES

Given the circumstances in the Cather family during the composition of the stories in *Obscure Destinies* (1932), it is no wonder that the book seems to have special significance for the writer. Cather's father suffered a heart attack sometime in the latter half of 1927 and a subsequent fatal attack the following March.[1] Cather's mother went to stay with Douglass in California, but before the year was out she suffered a paralytic stroke and had to be confined to institutional care. During the next two and a half years, until her mother finally passed away, Cather made wearying journeys across the continent and spent many long days and weeks with her mother in Pasadena. All three stories in *Obscure Destinies*—"Neighbour Rosicky," "Old Mrs. Harris," and "Two Friends"—show the influence of what must have been for Cather a poignant surfacing of home and family memories.[2] Hoping against hope for her mother's recovery, Cather even refurbished the most recent family home in Red Cloud, but as the months dragged on, it became apparent that there would never again be a real home there for her. Her mother died in August 1931, and Cather traveled west at Christmastime for a family reunion. That was the last time she ever went to Red Cloud. With her parents gone, the essential ties were broken.[3] Thus, when she wrote the stories in *Obscure Destinies,* Cather was at a pivotal juncture in her life and art. Speaking of the effect on Cather of watching her mother's life ebb away, Edith Lewis says, "It was one of those experiences that make a lasting change in the climate of one's mind."[4] Indeed, times of disturbing change and loss force us to look at the creeds we have lived by and to reaffirm those that seem worthy. This was the end of an era for Cather, and *Obscure Destinies* is her pause, her private meditation over what the Nebraska experience has meant and means.

At the suggestion of Virginia Faulkner, David Stouck comments on Cather's title allusion to Thomas Gray's "Elegy Written in a Country Churchyard." The pertinent lines are these: "Let not Ambition mock their useful toil, / Their homely joys, and destiny obscure; / Nor Grandeur hear with a disdainful smile / The short and simple annals of the poor." Stouk says that with *Obscure Destinies* Cather turned her interest toward the simple, ordinary people she had known as a youngster.[5] There is a pleasing unity about *Obscure Destinies,* a sense of wholeness among the stories that deal first with the farm folk, then with the family, then with the town folk. The craft is sure; the mood is perfectly rendered to evoke Nebraska as it seems to the writer that it must have been. Still aware of small town pettiness and the craving for material things, Cather nevertheless emphasizes the largeness, the generosity, the sacrifice, and the human caring that now seem to dominate her memories of that particular landscape.

Richard Giannone makes an excellent observation about Cather's use of one particular symbolic event to tie all three stories together in a repeated structural and thematic pattern. He refers to the occultation of Venus described in "Two Friends." In this story as the two older men and the young narrator watch the night sky, Venus and the moon cross paths. But instead of merely crossing, they appear actually to meet. Closing off what had once been a considerable distance between the two orbs, the planet seems to pass into the center of the moon. After what the narrator judges to be "about fifteen minutes," the watchers see "a bright wart on the other edge of the moon, but for a second only." Then, "the planet swung clear of the golden disk, a rift of blue came between them and widened very fast. The planet did not seem to move, but that inky blue space between it and the moon seemed to spread. The thing was over."[6] As Giannone points out, the closing of space for a time, and then the widening, has sure significance in the story about two friends who find great pleasure in a mutually satisfying association until the day they are split by an argument that is never mended. And the cosmic event described is applicable to relationships in the other two stories as well. Rosicky and his daughter-in-law, Polly, find a moment of closeness and understanding only to be separated almost immediately by his death. Mrs. Harris and Mrs. Rosen take one brief opportunity to express their mutual caring, and then Mrs. Harris dies. As with Venus and the moon, such crossings may happen only once in a lifetime.[7]

A. The Complete Life

The first story in the collection, "Neighbour Rosicky" may have been written as E. K. Brown believes, in "the early months of 1928, when her [Cather's] feelings were so deeply engaged by her father's illness and death."[8] It is generally agreed that the portrait of Anton Rosicky is a composite picture of both Ántonia's (Annie Pavelka's) husband and Charles Cather, Willa's father. Excruciating though the loss of her father must have been, Cather does not use "Neighbour Rosicky" to vent bitter feelings about death and loss. Rather, she makes the story an expression of acceptance and faith. In "Neighbour Rosicky" death is not a confinement, nor is it a rupture with life; it is, instead, a final liberating union of a human being with the earth. As a rule, Cather took death hard; yet, Rosicky's death seems somehow more a continuation than a severance, and nothing to be feared or fretted over. Rosicky has simply gone home, as perhaps Charles Cather had gone home.[9]

There is a quiet perfection about "Neighbour Rosicky" that almost defies comment. Surely, it is one of the stories for which Willa Cather will always be remembered. Nothing is out of place, everything counts, and the tone is maintained consistently. What one senses in reading the story is harmony, unity, and completeness in both life and art. One of the story's thematic accomplishments is a strong sense of acquiescence, of bowing to things that must be, of enjoying the good rather than grieving over the ill. No blind idealist, Rosicky has a total understanding of what is worthy and what is not, and his one desire as an old man is to convey that understanding to his children. Through a lifetime of sorting out values he has acquired a sense of balance, a healthy perception of the other side of things, and a great tolerance for variety.

Cather seems to be looking, especially now, for a way to organize experience, not just in art but in life as well. She is using art to generate a comprehensive vision that can reconcile and make whole the vast number of disparate elements that constitute a human life. Particularly with *Obscure Destinies,* she seems to be trying to fit Nebraska into her life's larger scheme, a life spent variously—in Europe, in the American city, and on the prairie. Rosicky is a character who brings together all of those aspects of Cather's experience. In "Neighbour Rosicky" Cather uses memory as an integrative device, and the winter Rosicky spends indoors tailoring and carpentering in deference to his ailing heart is a highly reflective one for him. Rosicky's attitude toward the past, so different from the ambassador's in "On the Gulls' Road" and Harriet Westfield's in "Eleanor's House," is clearly the attitude endorsed by Cather. Rosicky does not look longingly at the past—indeed, he had known loneliness and terrible poverty in the past—but he sets it gently against the present and is grateful.

The picture of Rosicky's past gradually materializes as Cather weaves the various strands of his life and memory into a pattern, moving carefully and repeatedly from present to past and then back to present again, from earth to city and back to earth again. Rosicky's mother died when he was a youngster, and for a time he lived with his grandparents who were poor tenant farmers. On the death of his grandmother, however, he was returned to his father and stepmother. A hard woman, she made his life such an agony that finally his father helped him get away to London. Unfortunately, the cousin whom he sought there had already moved to America, and the young man was stranded penniless in a foreign land.

This was "the only part of his youth he didn't like to remember" (p. 26). But remember it he does, and on the day before Christmas his mind reaches back to the meager, starving years he spent in London, shivering in the wretched home of a poor tailor who took him in off the streets out of pity, but who had little to give him but a corner to sleep in. He was filthy always, and his quarters were infested with bugs and fleas. Rescued almost miraculously by some of his countrymen one bleak Christmas Eve, Rosicky made it to New York and got a job with a tailor.[10] For the most part he remembers the New York years as good years, full of jolly times with friends and frequent exposures to the opera (at standing room prices). For a time "Rosicky thought he wanted to live like that for ever" (p. 29). But gradually he grew restless and began drinking too much, drinking to create the illusion of freedom. Then one day, appropriately the Fourth of July, he discovered the source of his trouble. Not only was the city empty in midsummer, but its "blank buildings" seemed to him "like empty jails" in "an unnatural world" that "built you in from the earth itself" (pp. 30–31). It was then that he decided to go west and reestablish ties with the soil.

Still another piece of Rosicky's past is revealed through the memory of his wife, Mary. She recalls one terribly hot Fourth of July when Rosicky came in early from the fields and asked her to get up a nice supper for the holiday. He took the boys, just little fellows then, and dunked them in the horse tank; then he stripped off his own clothes and climbed in with them, playing and frolicking in a way that made a passing preacher raise his pious eyebrows. It was not until later as they picnicked under the linden trees that Mary noticed how the leaves were all curled up and thought to ask about the corn. He told her it was all gone, roasted by midafternoon, and added, "That's why we're havin' a picnic. We might as well enjoy what we got" (p. 49). So while the neighbors grieved and spent a miserable year, the Rosickys made out and managed to enjoy the little they did have.

Just as in its concern with the unity of experience this story carefully balances past and present, so it also balances life and death. A mood of spiritual equanimity pervades Rosicky's life and death, and death comes *for* him in the same sense that it comes for Jean Latour in *Death Comes for the Archbishop*. Death is neither a great calamity nor a final surrender to despair, but rather, a benign presence, anticipated and even graciously entertained. It is the other side of life, and comes, as Latour says, as a natural consequence of "having lived." It is a reunion with the earth for one like Rosicky who has lived close to the land.[11]

Cather creates this sense of balance between life and death, a balance that lends unity to experience, at least partly through structure and symbolic landscape. The story opens with a consultation in Doctor Ed's office in which Rosicky learns that his heart is going bad. On his way home in the wagon he pauses at the small graveyard which nestles comfortably on the edge of his hay fields, especially cozy in the lightly falling snow. Aside from the Rosicky home itself, the most important setting in the story is that little graveyard. Cather introduces it early, and she ends the story there—bringing both her story and Rosicky's life full circle. Still pondering the news about his heart, Rosicky contemplates the view of his own fields and home from the graveyard. Though he admits that he "wasn't anxious to leave," Rosicky sees death and the graveyard as unifying, completing aspects of life. To him the graveyard is "sort of snug and homelike, not cramped or mournful,—a big sweep all round it." Life continues to hum along nearby, and home is close. "The snow, falling over his barnyard and the graveyard, seemed to draw things together like. And they were all old neighbours in the graveyard, most of them friends; there was nothing to feel awkward or embarrassed about" (pp. 18–19). The winter snow itself is symbolic of death, for it too carries an element of the "mysterious"; it too means "rest for vegetation and men and beasts" (p. 19).

At the conclusion of the story, after Rosicky is dead, Doctor Ed starts one evening for the farm to see the family. He pauses by the graveyard as Rosicky had done some months earlier, remembering that his old friend is there in the moonlight rather than over on the hill in the lamplight. His thoughts echo Rosicky's thoughts the night the old farmer had stopped his horses to watch the snow fall on the headstones and on the long red grass. He, like Rosicky, feels something "open and free" out here with just the "fields running on until they met that sky," and he senses that this particular graveyard, unlike the dismal cemeteries of cities, is not a place where things end, but where they are completed. He sees a mowing machine where one of Rosicky's sons and his horses had been working that very day; he thinks of the "long grass which the wind for ever stirred," and of "Rosicky's own cattle" that "would be eating fodder as winter came on"; and he concludes that "nothing could be more undeathlike than this place." Ed feels a sense of gratitude that this man who had lived in cities, but had finally wanted only the land and growing things, "had got to it at last" and now lay beneath its protective cover. The story's conclusion sums up the man: "Rosicky's life seemed to him complete and beautiful" (pp. 70–71).

In a multitude of other ways Cather achieves a sense of balance and wholeness in the story. Often she does it through contrasting or pairing opposites: city and country, winter and summer, older generation and younger, single life and married life, Bohemians and Americans. Not infrequently opposites are paired in a single sentence through a character's natural thought processes. For example, of herself and Rosicky Mary thinks, "He was city-bred, and she was country-bred. . ." (p. 22). She is aware that their life together "had been a hard life, and a soft life, too" (p. 24). Once the family has been warned about Rosicky's condition, they rush to his aid whenever he starts some manual task. In response, Rosicky sometimes even speaks in balanced rhetoric, complaining that "though he was getting to be an old man, he wasn't an old woman yet" (p. 25). And the narrator mentally balances Rosicky's older self against his younger self, observing that "the old Rosicky could remember as if it were yesterday the day when the young Rosicky found out what was the matter with him" (p. 30). Cather also achieves a marked sense of equilibrium by balancing two halves of sentences against each other. The technique seems quite deliberate because some paragraphs are made up almost wholly of compound sentences. For example, although the first sentence in the following paragraph is not based on structural coordination, the rest are; and the achievement of balanced antithesis is felt in both subject and form:

> On that very day he began to think seriously about the articles he had read in the Bohemian papers, describing prosperous Czech farming communities in the West. He believed he would like to go out there as a farm hand; it was hardly possible that he could ever have land of his own. His people had always been workmen; his father and grandfather had worked in shops. His mother's parents had lived in the country, but they rented their farm and had a hard time to get along. Nobody in his family had ever owned any land,—that belonged to a different station of life altogether. Anton's mother died when he was little, and he was sent into the country to her parents. (P. 31)

The pattern is the same for the concluding sentences in the paragraph.

But finally, perhaps the most important kind of balance in "Neighbour Rosicky" is more abstract, a balance defined in human terms, a wholeness and completeness that derives from human harmony and caring. Probably nowhere else has Cather drawn a more sublime picture of oneness and understanding than in the relationship between Rosicky and Mary, a relationship anchored in mutual love and in a value system that always keeps its priorities straight: "They agreed, without discussion, as to what was most important and what was secondary. They didn't often exchange opinions, even in Czech,—it was as if they had thought the same thought together. A good deal had to be sacrificed and thrown overboard in a hard life like theirs, and they had never disagreed as to the things that could go" (p. 24). When a creamery agent comes to tempt them to sell the cream off the milk they drink, they agree without discussion that their children's health is more important than any profit they might realize from skimming cream. Yes, people like the Rosickys do not get ahead much in worldly terms, Doctor Ed reflects, but "maybe you couldn't enjoy your life and put it into the bank, too" (p. 15). As Rosicky intimates to his favorite clerk in the general store, in a home as harmonious as theirs, "We sleeps easy" (p. 16).

Rosicky's unifying influence extends also into the somewhat troubled lives of his son Rudolph and Rudolph's wife, Polly, a town girl who has found farm life lonely and Bohemians a little strange. Rudolph is ready to leave the land and look for work in the city. Rosicky is worried about Rudolph and Polly, but is finally able to enclose them in the healing warmth of his remarkable capacity for love. Polly learns a little about that capacity when Rosicky slips over one Saturday night with the family car and sends her and Rudolph off to a movie in town while he cleans up their supper dishes. She has just a passing urge then to lay her head on his shoulder and tell him of the lonesomeness a town girl feels when stuck in the country. She learns still more the Christmas Eve he describes his last Christmas in London. Then, finally, the two of them are brought into complete harmony the day he rakes thistles to save his alfalfa field and suffers a heart attack. She leads him into her house and cares for him tenderly, understanding at last his ability to touch another life and make it whole. After hot-packing his chest until the pain subsides, she sits by the bed and holds his "warm, broad, flexible brown hand" (p. 66) in hers. From that hand comes a revelation that is "like an awakening to her. It seemed to her that she had never learned so much about life from anything as from old Rosicky's hand. It brought her to herself; it communicated some direct and untranslatable message" (p. 67). This is the culminating experience of the story, a sacred moment of oneness for both Rosicky and Polly. She really knows now the meaning of love, and he knows that he can count on her. For the first time, she has called him "Father."

Watching the Rosickys over the years, grateful to visit a home where the kitchen is warm and lively and the food plentiful and wholesome—and where the laughter is ready and the comeback easy—Doctor Ed is himself a device for sustaining wholeness in the story. Something of an outsider even though Mary claims him for her own, Ed provides the appreciative eye that encompasses the Rosicky family phenomenon. Standing close enough to feel the radiated warmth, he frames the miracle. Artistically, the story is unified and whole, completing not only itself but in some respects *My Ántonia* as well. Ed understands, perhaps even better than Rosicky's family, the completeness and beauty, as he calls it, of the man's life. Whoever Rosicky touched was graced by that wholeness—from the girl with the funny eyebrows in the general store to Polly, and to Ed himself. A work of art can be like that, restoring a sense of unity to experience. "Neighbour Rosicky" is like that.

B. BARRIERS AND BRIDGES

Less serene, perhaps, but no less rich and wise than "Neighbour Rosicky," is the second story in *Obscure Destinies,* "Old Mrs. Harris." Apparently completed in 1931, this story seems to relate directly to the Cather family's experiences in trying to assimilate themselves and their southern background into the world of Nebraska in the late 1800s. Old Mrs. Harris recalls Cather's Grandma Boak who came west with her daughter and her daughter's family; Victoria Templeton bears some resemblances to Mrs. Cather; and fifteen-year-old Vickie Templeton is, in some respects, the young Willa Cather. The Rosens resemble the Charles Weiners, a cultivated Jewish couple who lived near the Cather home in Red Cloud. The story deals with two basic kinds of conflict, one generational, the other cultural. The generational problems revolve around the sometimes contending perceptions, blindnesses, and needs of three generations living together in one house. Grandma Harris, Victoria Templeton, and Vickie Templeton share the same blood and background, but are sometimes frighteningly separate from each other. The cultural conflict is made apparent principally through the relationships among Grandma Harris, Mrs. Rosen next door, Victoria, and the small western town in which they live. Critical comment has customarily focused on the grandmother-mother-daughter problems in the Templeton household, but structurally, the story revolves around the three adult women—Mrs. Harris, Mrs. Rosen, and Mrs. (Victoria) Templeton—and the conflicts of manners among them. That young Vickie is less important to the story than the older women is suggested by the fact that when the story appeared in the September–November 1932 issues of the *Ladies Home Journal,* it was titled "Three Women."[12]

If the story has a controlling consciousness, it is the cultivated northern city consciousness of Mrs. Rosen; even when she is absent, her sentiments are deferred to by the other characters.[13] It is she who observes and interprets what goes on at the Templeton house next door, molding reader opinion, criticizing and defending the Templetons, helping to solve their problems, and then at the end slipping out of the narrative so as not to intrude on the family's awakening to the fact of Grandma's death. The opening sentence in the story establishes her function: "Mrs. David Rosen, cross-stitch in hand, sat looking out of the window across her own green lawn to the ragged sunburned back yard of her neighbours on the right" (p.

75). Though she disapproves of the Templetons' "ragged" yard and
some of their equally ragged ways, she worries over Grandma Harris, whom she believes is overworked and underappreciated by her
willful and attractive daughter Victoria. Mrs. Rosen may be
judgmental, but she is never unkind or small. She may disapprove of
the way Mrs. Templeton rears her children (or scarcely rears them,
that is the trouble) and dislike the clutter of the Templeton yard and
house, but she finds that she rather likes the Templetons in spite of
herself. Tolerant even of Vickie who is so oddly absorbed in books
and herself, Mrs. Rosen finds an occasional spark of charm in the
girl who comes to lounge quietly in her parlor and look through the
Rosen bookshelves.

Although the story sometimes moves into the consciousness of
both Mrs. Harris and Victoria, point of view is most often with Mrs.
Rosen. She watches over the activities next door like a loyal, if not
always approving, aunt. Mr. and Mrs. Rosen have made their home
a repository of culture in the midst of a somewhat coarse Colorado
town; and by establishing Mrs. Rosen as her principal observer,
Cather is able to show not only the clash between South and West,
but the clash between North and South and even between North and
West as well. The Rosens are clever enough not to assert themselves
in Skyline; they know how to merge inconspicuously. Because of her
education and flawless housekeeping, Mrs. Rosen holds a superior
position among the local women, but she never pushes her advantage. The Templetons are not so clever, however, and their southern
ways are sometimes an affront to more democratic northern and
western sensibilities.

Each of the Templetons is introduced first through Mrs. Rosen's
eyes. It is she who characterizes grandmother, daughter, and grand-
daughter, and she who perceives the conflicts that trouble each of
them. The story moves section by section treating various aspects of
the North (and West)-South conflict as perceived by Mrs. Rosen. Section I of the story describes Mrs. Rosen's surreptitious visit to
Grandma Harris with a "symmetrically plaited coffee-cake" (p. 76).
By design Mrs. Rosen arrives at the Templeton kitchen just minutes
after Victoria leaves, noting with distaste the clutter of the adjoining room and Grandma Harris's weariness. Grandma starts "guiltily" at the sight of her neighbor, and all the time Mrs. Rosen is there,
Grandma looks "troubled,—at a loss" (p. 77). On previous occasions,
Mrs. Rosen has left coffee-cake for Grandma, but she has learned

that Victoria appropriates for herself any sweets that enter the house. Thus this once, Mrs. Rosen determines to outmaneuver Victoria and sit down with Mrs. Harris to make certain that the old woman actually eats the treat prepared for her. Mrs. Harris, however, is so uncomfortable that "Mrs. Rosen doubted if she tasted the cake as she swallowed it" (pp. 79–80). This entire scene is constructed largely as Mrs. Rosen perceives it, not only in the physical details of the house, which she notes meticulously, but also in the details about Grandma Harris and her daughter.

The relationship between Mrs. Rosen and Grandma Harris is an important one, for it is partly Mrs. Rosen's appreciative point of view that accords Grandma dignity and personal worth. Without Mrs. Rosen's veneration, Grandma Harris might appear simply a pitiful, suffering old woman, foolishly clinging to a set of empty, self-demeaning customs. Mrs. Rosen thinks Grandma ill-treated, and perhaps even foolish in her stubborn adherence to southern proprieties, but she nevertheless senses Grandma's quality and genuinely respects her. Mrs. Rosen wants very much to know Grandma better, "to get past the others to the real grandmother"; but "the real grandmother was on her guard, as always" (p. 83). Mrs. Rosen questions her, pressing the old woman to admit that she liked Tennessee better than Colorado, or that she regrets the sale of her large home there and Hillary Templeton's mismanagement of the money from the sale, or that the cat Blue Boy is hers; but Mrs. Harris loyally resists every temptation to complain. The interview ends when Albert and Adelbert, Victoria's ten-year-old twins, and six-year-old Ronald, courteous boys with "nice voices, nice faces" (p. 86), return from school. As Mrs. Rosen prepares to leave with her tray, Mrs. Harris urges her to stay, "But her tone let Mrs. Rosen know that Grandma really wished her to leave before Victoria returned" (p. 87).

Mrs. Rosen is not actually present in the central time frame of section II, but she is referred to several times and her attitudes and opinions are distinctly felt. This section is mainly a description of Grandma's evening activities and night thoughts. After reading to the children and enjoying a foot rub offered by Mandy, the "bound girl" who had come with the family from Tennessee, Grandma retires to her springless lounge with "only a thin cotton mattress between her and the wooden slats" (p. 94). Since her blanket offers too little warmth, she wakes somewhat chilled around 4 A.M. to don an old sweater Mrs. Rosen had given her, a sweater she kept hidden under her mattress and had never told Victoria about. "She knew Mrs. Rosen understood how it was; that Victoria couldn't bear to have anything come into the house that was not for her to dispose of" (p. 95). Point of view has subtly shifted to Grandma Harris, and as she waits for the dawn she considers her situation, pondering all she left in Tennessee to come west with the Templetons. It was expected that she follow Victoria, and she had come. And "though she would never admit it to Mrs. Rosen" (p. 96), she is sorry to have left Tennessee. Clearly, her southern upbringing dictated the decision. Old women had no voice in what they did or did not do: "They were tied to the chariot of young life, and had to go where it went, because they were needed." Grandma knows it is different for people like Mrs. Rosen whose manner had convinced Grandma that "Jewish people had an altogether different attitude toward their old folks." These differences in training and cultural expectations make "her friendship with this kind neighbour . . . almost as disturbing as it was pleasant" (p. 97).

The clash of cultures is continually apparent in Grandma's anxious concern for what Mrs. Rosen might think or what she might find out. Mrs. Harris knows too that "if Victoria once suspected Mrs. Rosen's indignation" (p. 97) over Grandma's situation, Mrs. Harris would be denied the pleasure of Mrs. Rosen's company. Mrs. Harris's position in the Templeton household is made painfully clear (to northerners, at least) in this section of the story. Not only did she have no voice in the move from Tennessee, and probably in the sale of her own house, but in the small, crowded house where the family now lives, "Mrs. Harris and her 'things' were almost required to be invisible" (p. 98). The section ends with a reference back to Mrs. Rosen who marvels to her husband that Mrs. Templeton, who "takes no more responsibility for her children than a cat takes for her kittens" (p. 101), could have such nice children, while Mrs. Rosen's own sister and sister-in-law, who have sacrificed themselves to give their children "every advantage" (p. 100), could have reared such cold and thankless offspring.

Mrs. Rosen is continually perplexed by this family who on occasion display remarkable sensibilities, whose "feelings were so much finer than their way of living" (p. 110). She prefers visiting their house above others in the town, perhaps largely because one feels there family loyalty, genuine hospitality, and "a pleasantness in the human relationships" (p. 111). Whatever it lacks, this family has something of greater value than tidiness and strict democracy. And at the heart of the family, Mrs. Rosen perceives, is an old woman who so much "liked the light-heartedness in others" that "she drudged, indeed, to keep it going" (p. 112).

The next section of the story, section III, shows Mrs. Rosen in relationship first with Vickie and then with Victoria. It is only in this section and one other that Vickie figures prominently, and here Mrs. Rosen's is still the controlling view. She gives Vickie a somewhat cool reception at her door, and then passes judgment on Vickie's response to a book and her determination to try hard for a scholarship. Critical, but at the same time not pinched and stern, Mrs. Rosen likes many things about Vickie—her active, interested mind, her sturdy physical vitality, and her habitual half-smile. Try as she might, Mrs. Rosen cannot shake the feeling that she is somehow responsible for Vickie. It irritates her to think that "God knew, no one else felt responsible" (p. 109).

If Mrs. Rosen's earlier observations about Victoria Templeton seem rather harsh, they are mollified in this section where Mrs. Rosen describes Victoria's unconscious generosity and winsomeness. She contrasts the Templetons favorably against the typically rigid and self-serving families in Skyline and decides that on the whole she prefers the Templetons, who "were not selfish or scheming" and who were sometimes ill-advantaged because of their naivete. "Victoria might eat all the cookies her neighbour sent in, but she would give away anything she had"; and it was Mr. Templeton's mild manner that made him no match for "the hard old money-grubbers on Main Street" (p. 112). Mrs. Rosen remembers her first meeting with Victoria, at a women's card party some distance away one winter afternoon. As they played, a terrible storm came up, and the two neighbors struggled home together through the blowing snow and drifts, Victoria laughing as she repeatedly slipped off the walk into deep powder. At the Templeton gate Victoria insisted that Mrs. Rosen come in to dry out and to warm herself with a hot drink. Mrs. Rosen was surprised to find the parlor satisfyingly civilized; moreover, she was filled with something akin to wonder as Victoria, having changed into more comfortable clothes, began to nurse the insistent little Hughie. Mrs. Rosen was struck by the beauty of the baby and the completeness of the madonna-like picture as the mother, in perfect ease, satisfied her child's hunger. The religious overtones are intentional and gratifying.

Though in section IV Mrs. Rosen does not dominate the action, she and her husband are strategically present to observe it. The northern consciousness frames the action as southern and western cultures clash. The Rosens arrive at the church ice cream social in time to see Victoria, gently but not condescendingly, invite the poor little Maude children into the festivities, give them money for treats, and establish them at a table with her own children. Ever the southern belle, Mrs. Templeton joins the Rosens, basking in the glow of Mr. Rosen's obvious admiration. But the evening is ruined when the spiteful Mrs. Jackson approaches and makes cutting comments about how nice it would be if all of the women in town had someone confined in their kitchens to bake cakes for them. (Grandma Harris sent the Templetons' cake contribution, but she remained at home.) Coming from a background where no one ever deliberately embarrasses another, no matter what the provocation, Victoria does not understand the insult at first. The Rosens try to distract her, but as the implications of the insult sink in, Victoria realizes that she is the subject of criticism, the one thing she cannot bear. She concludes that so long as townspeople have access to her mother, they will invariably side with the old woman and against her. Anything anyone tried to do for Mrs. Harris would therefore seem a reproach to Victoria. The moment Victoria arrives home, Mrs. Harris divines what has happened. The relationship between Mrs. Harris and Victoria suffers in this new environment which does not comprehend the assumptions and customs, generations old, which regulate life and govern interrelationships in the Templeton household, particularly between the old woman and her daughter.

Section V explains the relationship between Mrs. Harris and Victoria, a relationship awkwardly out of step in a western town. Mrs. Harris does not understand any more than Victoria does why their Skyline neighbors disapprove of the Templetons' domestic arrangements, for "back in Tennessee, her place in the family was not exceptional, but perfectly regular" (pp. 129–30). There it was agreed that since a girl was only young and foolish once, and since she would soon enough have to surrender her youth and foolishness to the demands of marriage and family, she should be indulged as long as possible. Nearly every young wife had the services of some older woman who had no other family and no other place. It was easy to live this way in Tennessee where there was an abundance of extra help and where an old woman created a kind of back room subcul-

ture in the family home. Such a system guaranteed her a domain of
her own where she ruled and entertained as she liked, and where
she was able to salvage no small measure of pride. Let the young
folks have the parlor and front porch; there was plenty of room in
the kitchen and pantry. But here in Colorado it was different. Skyline is "a snappy little Western democracy, where every man was as
good as his neighbour and out to prove it" (p. 133).

The whole system is baffling both to Mrs. Harris and to Victoria,
for in the South Victoria had been much admired, while here she is
much criticized. Grandma is angry with "these meddlesome 'Northerners'" who "said things that made Victoria suspicious and unlike
herself." Mrs. Harris prefers the southern attitude, where it is generally accepted "that somebody ought to be in the parlour, and somebody in the kitchen." For Victoria to have donned a housedress and
become a western-style housekeeper would, to Mrs. Harris, "have
meant real poverty, coming down in the world so far that one could
no longer keep up appearances" (p. 134). As she works such thoughts
over in her mind, Mrs. Harris is aware, too, that Mrs. Rosen is of a
still different breed, different from Victoria and far superior to these
western women. Unable to explain Mrs. Rosen's immaculate and
wonderfully productive kitchen, Grandma attributes it to her "foreignness." Grandma's ruminations also serve the technical purpose
of keeping Mrs. Rosen and what she represents constantly before the
reader, an ordering principle who operates even in absentia.

Although Mrs. Rosen is not mentioned in section VI, a short section which recounts the illness and death of Blue Boy, the cat, she
enters the scene again in section VII when at Victoria's suggestion,
the Templeton twins stage a circus to help them forget their sorrow
over Blue Boy. Conversation in the Templeton parlor after the performance turns to the subject of Vickie's upcoming examinations in
collegiate scholarship competition, and her intensive preparation
for them. Again cultural differences surface as Mrs. Rosen defends
scholastic pursuits and Victoria, whose people never went to college,
fails to understand Vickie's compulsion. Uncomfortable with this
kind of discussion, Grandma Harris disappears. When, in section
VIII, Vickie learns that she has won a scholarship, she takes her
news first to Mrs. Rosen. Vickie steps to the forefront in this section,
but as before, only under the watchful eye of Mrs. Rosen.

Vickie later learns that the scholarship will not pay all her ex-
penses, and that she will need another three hundred dollars.

Grandma Harris, in one of her few daring moments of self-assertion, approaches Mr. Templeton to plead Vickie's case. Uncomfortably evasive, he tells her that the money from the sale of her Tennessee home is "invested" and is not available. Desperate, and feeling ill and low-spirited, Mrs. Harris turns to Mrs. Rosen who is packing her trunk for a trip to Chicago to see a niece married. Mrs. Rosen determines to speak to her husband in Vickie's behalf, but it is clear that the favor is really for Mrs. Harris. The two women experience their tenderest moment; Grandma's eyes fill with tears, and Mrs. Rosen kisses the back of the aged hand in her grip. Even then, Grandma Harris is aware of the cultural differences between her and Mrs. Rosen: "Grandma sat looking down at her hand. How easy it was for these foreigners to say what they felt" (p. 170)!

In section XII Mrs. Rosen departs, signaling to Grandma by a wink and a nod that all has been arranged for Vickie. Although she had inquired after Grandma's health two days earlier, she apparently does not notice today that Grandma is ill, an oversight for which the old woman is grateful. With Vickie's trouble resolved happily, Grandma's thoughts turn again to the question of manners and culture, and she realizes that different though she and Mrs. Rosen are, she "got along nicely" with such as Mrs. Rosen. "It was only with the ill-bred and unclassified, like this Mrs. Jackson next door, that she had disagreeable experiences. Such folks, she told herself, had come out of nothing and knew no better" (p. 173). Mrs. Harris had spoiled her daughter, true, but could she be blamed for favoring such a lively, handsome child? To the end, Grandma retains her social and cultural awareness, finding the South somewhat more compatible with the North than with the West.[14]

Mandy is the first to notice Mrs. Harris's illness. Vickie dashes by the old woman, and an obviously preoccupied Victoria speaks accusingly to her mother about "another bilious spell" (p. 175) and the inconvenience that would be to the household. Only at this point does the narrative move inside Victoria's mind, revealing her unconsolable distress over the discovery that another baby will soon be demanding space in the already cramped Templeton house. The generational conflict edges forward as she almost resentfully asserts that "she could do a great deal more with freedom than ever Vickie could." And yet Vickie is the free one. Victoria wants no more babies, no more responsibilities that turn one old and ugly. She sobs helplessly into her pillow. Swallowed up in her own grief, Victoria thinks nothing of her mother's illness until Mandy finds the old woman unconscious the next morning. Vickie's only response when she learns of her grandmother's illness and her mother's indisposition is impatient anger: "Wasn't it just like them all to go and get sick, when she had now only two weeks to get ready for school, and no trunk and no clothes or anything? Nobody but Mr. Rosen seemed to take the least interest" (pp. 185–86). Full of youthful desire and anxiety, Vickie can think only of herself.

Point of view shifts once more to Grandma, whose main concern as she dies is that she not disrupt anything. She is grateful that Mr. Templeton left town (his accustomed response to the news of a pregnancy), for "appearances had to be kept up when there was a man in the house." She is grateful, too, that Mrs. Rosen is away, for "Mrs. Rosen would have been indignant, and that would have made Victoria cross" (p. 188). Besides, she does not have to see her friend again to remember how much they care for each other. The old woman's last thoughts are for Victoria, and she relaxes in the assurance that the children will always love their mother a great deal and treat her well. She remembers happily her own pleasure and pride in her daughter as "a dashing, high-spirited girl" (p. 188) being courted in the lilac arbor by Hillary Templeton. It seems fortunate that Grandma should drift out of consciousness during the night, in her own bed, fortunate that she is oblivious to the great fuss generated the next day when she is dressed in one of Victoria's gowns and installed in Victoria's bed. It is fortunate that she does not know that at the last she lies under the bold scrutiny of none other than Mrs. Jackson, the guardian of western custom. She, like the women who invade the Forrester home after the Captain's death in *A Lost Lady*, finally penetrates the barriers and establishes herself as head nurse in the Templeton household. And it seems particularly appropriate that Mrs. Harris would slip away now, when Victoria and Vickie most need to find their own sources of inner strength.

Mrs. Rosen leaves the story when her work there as observer and northern conscience is completed. Mrs. Rosen could not have taught Victoria and Vickie the difficult things they now must learn. Grandma does not realize it, but her death means a break with southern custom that will force Victoria and Vickie into a new kind of responsibility they will have to accept. The narrator concludes that as Victoria and Vickie grow old, they will close the gap of understanding that has separated them from each other and from Mrs. Harris. The

larger cultural conflict, verbally diminished by the departures of
Mrs. Rosen and Mrs. Harris, may never be resolved, but Victoria
and Vickie must now move beyond conflicts that hurt from the outside to deal with sometimes tumultuous personal relationships
within the family and sometimes soul-racking conflicts within
themselves. Cather is talking, in her conclusion, of historical cycles
and their function within the family. The young woman will never
really understand the old woman until she one day becomes that old
woman. Then she will have to face the heartlessness of what she has
been. Like Grandmother before them, mother and daughter will
"look into the eager, unseeing eyes of young people and feel themselves alone." The story concludes, "They will say to themselves: 'I
was heartless, because I was young and strong and wanted things so
much. But now I know'" (p. 190). The prospect for a new baby's birth
as the old woman dies underlines the cyclical design of the continuing patterns of life. Although the story speaks of youth and generations passing, there is no lament over lost youth. Like "Neighbour
Rosicky," "Old Mrs. Harris" seems to predict recovery from the mistakes of youth, and to urge the necessity for learning the lessons life
has to teach.

And even though "Old Mrs. Harris" is about cultural and generational conflicts, Cather carefully constructs positive relationships
that cross barriers of culture, age, and social class. She shows clearly
that in spite of the isolation that troubles all of us at times, there is
that in human relationship which makes our essential aloneness
bearable, and indeed makes life lovely. Old Mrs. Harris and Mrs. Rosen manage to build a rather marvelous friendship across a difficult
cultural chasm. The younger Templeton children, too, manage to
span gaps of culture and age through their unconsciously good manners and natural inclination to care about people. Albert makes a
significant statement when Mrs. Rosen suggests one day that he fill
in the big ditch in his yard by shoveling a pile of sand into it. "Oh,
no, ma'am," he responds, "we like to have the ditch to build bridges
over" (p. 119)! The children do indeed build bridges. They enjoy a
wonderful kind of unity among themselves, and they also have a
special life-giving relationship with their grandmother. Some morn-
ings the old woman feels dreary and low, but the minute she hears
the children on the back stairs she is rejuvenated: "Indeed, she
ceased to be an individual, an old woman with aching feet; she became part of a group, became a relationship. She was drunk up into
their freshness when they burst in upon her, telling her about their

dreams, explaining their troubles with buttons and shoelaces and underwear shrunk too small. The tired, solitary old woman Grandmother had been at daybreak vanished. . ." (pp. 136–37).

When Mrs. Harris is ill, it is Mandy and the twins who take notice and try to give comfort. Albert volunteers to sit with his grandmother, and his every thought is to do something nice for her. When Adelbert comes home, he joins the pair of them, dragging the rocking chair close to Grandma's bed and curling up in it. At that moment, in spite of her illness, "Grandmother was perfectly happy. She and the twins were about the same age; they had in common all the realest and truest things. The years between them and her, it seemed to Mrs. Harris, were full of trouble and unimportant" (p. 184). Cather also stresses the unity within the Templeton family by pointing out that they liked having their own private table together at the ice cream social, and by noting the pride the boys always felt in their mother because of her good looks.

Still another chasm is spanned in the story, the chasm of social class. Mrs. Harris and Mandy, relegated more or less to the bottom rung on the family social ladder, find a natural camaraderie in each other. In what may be the most moving scene in the story, another which carries religious overtones, Mandy simply and sweetly offers service to Mrs. Harris, and the ailing old woman accepts it. At the end of a long, arduous day for both of them, Mandy appears at the kitchen door and volunteers to rub Mrs. Harris's feet to make her more comfortable for the night. Having prepared a little tub of warm water, Mandy kneels before Mrs. Harris, gently removing her slippers and stockings. Deeply grateful, Mrs. Harris sits quietly while Mandy rubs her swollen feet and legs. Cather is never better than at this moment:

> She never asked for this greatest solace of the day; it was something that Mandy gave, who had nothing else to give. If there could be a comparison in absolutes, Mandy was the needier of the two,—but she was younger. The kitchen was quiet and full of shadow, with only the light from an old lantern. Neither spoke. Mrs. Harris dozed from comfort, and Mandy herself was half asleep as she performed one of the oldest rites of compassion. (P. 93)

It is incidents like these that mute any harsh tones in the story. Though conflict is present, the power of love is also present to cushion its shocks. And while Mrs. Rosen is an element of the conflict, representing the northern consciousness and perhaps the older generation as well, she is also a healer, one who builds bridges across differences.

"Old Mrs. Harris" is good enough to rank among the very best of Cather's work.[15] If she had chosen to publish it separately, as a novel, it might already have earned an impressive reputation. It is longer than *My Mortal Enemy*, and not much shorter than *Alexander's Bridge*, both of which Cather elected to publish as separate books. Possibly, she liked the cohesive unit it formed with "Neighbour Rosicky" and "Two Friends."

C. HAVING AND LOSING

The final story in *Obscure Destinies* is "Two Friends," a highly stylized memory piece that is linked thematically, geographically, and emotionally with both "Neighbour Rosicky" and "Old Mrs. Harris." Although the collection's title makes an allusion to Gray's "Elegy Written in a Country Churchyard," an allusion applicable to all three stories, the allusion is perhaps most germane to "Two Friends." The story itself is something of a prose elegy in which emotion is isolated and formalized;[16] the subject is loss and the mood is controlled sorrow. The narrator, a poetic rendering of the young Willa Cather, is like the poet in Gray's elegy "who mindful of the unhonored dead / Dost in these lines their artless tale relate." By adopting conventional elegiac formality, Cather is able to remove herself several degrees from her own personal feelings about the events she describes and yet still convey the emotion of those events. The storybook quality, the oral flavor of the story, is also deliberate technique—technique she had long since perfected but to which she had not returned in a short story for many years. The narrator's manner makes it clear that this story is an artistic production, carefully constructed and managed to produce rather formal feelings about certain kinds of change and loss. We are reminded of the Emily Dickinson poem that begins, "After great pain a formal feeling comes." Cather had seen her father die, and she had watched her mother dying; it is natural that she would begin to ponder other things lost. It is natural, too, that she would continue to try through art to impose some kind of order on those experiences.

Cather's narrator speaks in the opening lines of the story about the human need, even of children, for "unalterable realities, somewhere at the bottom of things," for "anchors," for "retreats" (pp. 193–94) that give one a hold on experience. Artistic form is just such an anchor in this story; another is the friendship of two men which the narrator had come to rely on; and still another is Nebraska itself. Over the years, so long as her parents were there, Cather covered the miles to Red Cloud countless times, feeling the pull of the country "where I had been a kid, where they still called me Willie Cather."[17] But with her father's passing and her mother's lingering illness, Cather must have sensed that things would never be the same again, that she was losing Nebraska, except as a memory. "Two Friends" might well have been titled "Elegy Written in a Country Town." The story becomes a literary farewell that allows Cather to objectify her emotions about Nebraska and deal with its loss.

Apparently written in Pasadena in 1931, "Two Friends" appeared in July 1932, in the *Woman's Home Companion,* just before *Obscure Destinies* was published in August. Cather makes reference to the story in at least two letters to Carrie Miner Sherwood, both of which suggest that she was trying to produce a picture effect, an impression, a memory, an idea as it took shape in the mind of a youngster, rather than true-to-life portraits of the two men who figure in the story.[18] The narrative proper begins, "Long ago, before the invention of the motorcar . . . in a little wooden town in a shallow Kansas river valley, there lived two friends" (p. 194). And thus the stage is set for a tale about two prominent men who lived in this town, different as two men could be—in appearance, in background, in disposition, in political persuasion—and yet somehow friends out of mutual respect and genuine appreciation. One was a banker and owner of the general store, a lean, fastidious, earnest man, and a lovely talker. The other was a cattleman, a heavy set, more loosely strung man of few words who liked a good game of poker and a broad margin to his life. Mr. J. H. Trueman's penchant for poker, and maybe even for women, was never discussed between them, for Mr. R. E. Dillon valued J. H. Trueman's friendship too much to risk broaching such subjects in his presence.

The two met nightly for conversation and, in the winter, checkers. In cold weather, they sat in a back room at Dillon's store until 10 P.M. closing time. In good weather, they sat in chairs outside the store. After their talk, Trueman would open his own offices for a nightly poker game, but he always spent the earlier part of the evening with

Dillon. The narrator, from her tenth through her thirteenth year, hung about the two men when they met and talked evenings, finding their lives and their conversation more interesting than any others in the town. By town standards, these men were giants— intelligent, traveled (at least to St. Joseph and Chicago), powerful, and rich. In the fashion of a storyteller, the narrator reconstructs the essence of their conversations, describing how one might begin and then how the other might respond, rather than repeating their statements word for word as if reporting an actual event. Mr. Dillon might tell of a visit he had paid that day to one of the Swedish farmers, "Or he might come out with something sharp," such as a comment on some farmer's mortgages. Cather's intent is not to reproduce specific events, but to recreate the mood of "those April nights, when the darkness itself tasted dusty" (p. 209).

Dillon was a Democrat and Trueman a Republican, but they lived good-naturedly with those differences until William Jennings Bryan electrified the convention in Chicago and won the Democratic nomination for president. Dillon was there, and he never recovered from the impact of Bryan's "cross of gold" speech.[19] He bought Bryan's free silver philosophy and began preaching it around Main Street, querulously needling Trueman with it. Trueman felt it was a dangerous philosophy for a banker to hold, and he stopped coming to Dillon's store in the evenings. Trueman watched and waited, but when he saw that Dillon had pledged a sizeable contribution to Bryan's campaign, he made his decision. He transferred his money from Dillon's bank to the rival bank in town. The narrator recalls sadly that Dillon's new activity in politics changed him, reduced him, "made him more like other people and took away from his special personal quality" (p. 223). In some ways he seemed to be goaded on by Trueman's initial disdain, and then by his unbending silence. The friendship was destroyed for the two men, and something wonderful was ruined for the youngster whose presence they had tolerated and occasionally acknowledged. The narrator reflects, "Mr. Dillon seemed like another man. . . . Mr. Trueman I seldom saw" (p. 225).

The destruction of that friendship was enough to throw the earth into a tailspin. It was men like this and friendships like this that held things together, that ordered and stabilized experience for a sensitive youngster. In spite of the fact that by worldly standards these men would not have been considered distinguished, the rupture of their relationship was for the narrator an upheaval of almost cosmic significance. With the friendship destroyed, "Things were out of true, the equilibrium was gone. Formerly, when they used to sit in their old places on the sidewalk, two black figures with patches of shadow below, they seemed like two bodies held steady by some law of balance, an unconscious relation like that between the earth and the moon." The "mathematical harmony which gave a third person pleasure" (p. 227) was lost forever. Then Dillon died unexpectedly, of pneumonia. The day Trueman heard that news, he packed his bag and went as far as the train would take him, all the way to San Francisco. He returned later only to sell his holdings and clear out of his offices. He had lost his friend for good; and the narrator, who had lost her heroes, lamented that "now only the common, everyday people would be left" (p. 228). It is both the conversation and the silence she will miss, "the strong, rich outflowing silence between two friends, that was as full and satisfying as the moonlight. I was never to know its like again" (p. 226).

For the narrator, certain images are forever associated with her memory of the two friends. One of those images is the "long, red brick wall, with no windows except high overhead," that formed the side of Dillon's store. Along it was a board sidewalk, "wider than any other piece of walk in town, smoother, better laid, kept in perfect repair; very good to walk on in a community where most things were flimsy." It was on this walk and against this wall that Dillon arranged two chairs after supper on summer nights. The narrator recalls, "I liked the store and the brick wall and the sidewalk because they were solid and well built, and possibly I admired Dillon and Trueman for much the same reason. They were secure and established" (p. 197). They gave stability to a youngster who needed just that.

Two other important images are the moonlight and the dusty road that ran in front of the sidewalk. The narrator's memories of the two men and of the evenings when she sat on the edge of the sidewalk and listened to their talk are informed by the union of these images. The narrator confesses, "I suppose there were moonless nights, and dark ones with but a silver shaving and pale stars in the sky, just as in the spring. But I remember them all as flooded by the rich indolence of a full moon, or a half-moon set in uncertain blue. Then Trueman and Dillon . . . were more largely and positively themselves." They seemed solid and sure; "their shadows made two dark masses on the white sidewalk." Behind them was the brick wall, "faded almost pink by the burning of successive summers," which "took on a carnelian hue at night. Across the street, which was merely a dusty road, lay an open space. . ." (pp. 210–11). The whole scene was transformed by moonlight, abandoned buildings across the way melting "together into a curious pile" to become "an immaterial structure of velvet-white and glossy blackness" (p. 211). And the dusty road "just in front of the sidewalk where I sat and played jacks, would be ankle-deep in dust, and seemed to drink up the moonlight like folds of velvet." That road had special qualities: "It drank up sound, too; muffled the wagon-wheels and hoof-beats; lay soft and meek like the last residuum of material things,—the soft bottom resting-place. Nothing in the world, not snow mountains or blue seas, is so beautiful in moonlight as the soft, dry summer roads in a farming country, roads where the white dust falls back from the slow wagon-wheel" (pp. 211–12).

The narrator is especially aware of the mystery inherent in the blend of dusty road and moonlight when she tells of the occultation of Venus mentioned earlier. She begins her account of the event as any oral storyteller would: "Wonderful things do happen even in the dullest places—in the cornfields and the wheat-fields" (p. 212). This particular night the two men seemed especially close together, and they admitted the youngster into their exclusive community. Though the growing rift between Venus and the moon was prophetic of the rift that would divide Dillon and Trueman, for this night, at least, they had something wondrous and good. And the youngster who shared that event with the two friends can never forget what they had. But sadly, the images that were once symbols of stability and unity and wonder become symbols of aching memory and reminders of loss:

> The breaking-up of that friendship between two men who scarcely noticed my existence was a real loss to me, and has ever since been a regret. More than once, in Southern countries where there is a smell of dust and dryness in the air and the nights are intense, I have come upon a stretch of dusty white road drinking up the moonlight beside a blind wall, and have felt a sudden sadness. Perhaps it was not until the next morning that I knew why, —and then only because I had dreamed of Mr. Dillon or Mr. Trueman in my sleep. (Pp. 229–30)

The tone of regret is strong, and would be almost unbearable were the emotion not transmuted into a formal artistic lament which concludes the story: "When that old scar is occasionally touched by chance, it rouses the old uneasiness; the feeling of something broken that could so easily have been mended; of something delightful that was senselessly wasted, of a truth that was accidentally distorted—one of the truths we want to keep" (p. 230).

Certainly, Nebraska was one of the truths that Willa Cather wanted to keep, and she found a way to do that, through her art. The story is at once an elegaic farewell to Nebraska and an artistic realization of memory. It is as if Cather were saying, I may have lost the Nebraska of childhood, but I have retained the Nebraska of memory and art. In Nebraska were the beginnings of art, the first conscious sensitivities to the rhythms of language. It was language, in fact, that attracted the narrator to a post within earshot of the two men night after night. The verbally gifted Dillon did most of the talking, but occasionally Trueman, who preferred to listen, would put forth a long story. Dillon's conversation was enlivened by such a rich variousness that even a reprimand from him was almost a pleasure. "Every sentence he uttered was alive, never languid, perfunctory, slovenly, unaccented. When he made a remark, it not only meant something, but sounded like something—sounded like the thing he meant" (p. 206).

The narrator speaks at great length about Dillon's gift for language, describing the variations and subtle nuances of his voice and manner as he spoke with different clients and customers. She compares the talk of young men about town with that of Dillon and Trueman, asserting that the young men's talk was "scarcely speech, but noises, snorts, giggles, yawns, sneezes, with a few abbreviated words and slang expressions which stood for a hundred things" (pp. 207–8). The narrator's concern with language and expression is demonstrated repeatedly through the story. She recalls how the two men's discussion of a play that they had seen in the city created a living stage in her mind. And these were "business men who used none of the language in which such things are usually discussed." Their talk somehow created a "transference of experience" so that the actual "lives of those two men came across" to the listening youngster "as they talked, the strong, bracing reality of successful, large-minded men" (p. 218).

Significantly, it was at least partly an argument over language style that precipitated the final rupture between the two friends. Dillon returned from the Chicago convention praising Bryan as a great orator, and Trueman responded with a mutter, "Great wind-

bag" (p. 220). On that occasion, although Trueman sat down on his
usual chair, the narrator noticed that he did not cross his legs as was
his custom. The debate went on, with Dillon speaking more and
more to the gathering group around him and less and less to Trueman. Dillon, brightly and fluently, and ever more sharply and angri-
ly, extolled Bryan's eloquence, to be met only by increasingly bitter
comments from Trueman. Finally, Trueman "rose and walked away"
(p. 221), and he never returned. Thus, language has the power to disrupt and alienate as well as the power to heal and unify. It was language that brought the three together, it was language that split
them apart, and it was language that enabled the narrator to order
her emotions and deal with the loss.

Cather was not to write another short story until 1936, and that
one, "The Old Beauty," she set in France in the 1890s. Though she
looked to Nebraska for parts of *Lucy Gayheart* (1935), it was only in
"The Best Years," written near the end of her life, that she evoked
again the kind of total Nebraska flavor so distinctly present in *Obscure Destinies*. All three stories in this collection evince warmth
and breadth and wholeness. They project a positive view of human
potential for fineness, and stress the importance of human relationships. But at the same time they convey a sense of the mutability of
life, of the tenuousness of its ostensible certainties. They acknowledge that some of the most valuable and seemingly stable things are
subject to the most inexplicable fragility, the most surprising kind of
loss. Persons of relatively obscure destinies may not shake the larger world with their passing, but they shake a world nevertheless.
And all paths, glorious or not, lead, as Gray says, to the grave.

II. A REGRET AND A SUMMING UP

A. UNPARDONABLE WASTE

Although apparently written in 1936, "The Old Beauty" was not
published until it appeared posthumously in *The Old Beauty and
Others* (1948) along with "The Best Years" and "Before Breakfast."[20] According to Cather's biographers, Cather submitted the
story to the *Woman's Home Companion* which had previously published the serialized *Lucy Gayheart* and several shorter Cather pieces. The editor, Gertrude Lane, agreed to print it, but indicated to
Cather that she was not particularly enthusiastic about the story,
probably because she recognized that it was weak in comparison to

Cather's other mature work. Cather, too, must have felt somewhat dissatisfied with it, for she asked Lane to return the manuscript. She then put it aside, thinking possibly to bring it out later in a collection, but she never did. Just prior to this she had been working with her publisher, Alfred A. Knopf, to pull together a group of essays under the title *Not Under Forty* (1936). Her prefatory note to *Not Under Forty* has received perhaps more attention than the essays themselves, and one sentence from it may have been quoted more than any other line Cather ever wrote. After warning potential readers that "the book will have little interest for people under forty years of age," Cather explains, "The world broke in two in 1922 or thereabouts, and the persons and prejudices recalled in these sketches slid back into yesterday's seven thousand years." She concludes, "It is for the backward, and by one of their number, that these sketches were written."[21] When Cather prepared the Library Edition of her selected works, published through Houghton Mifflin in 1937–38, she wisely changed the title from *Not Under Forty* to *Literary Encounters* and dropped the preface.

Undoubtedly Cather saw much to condemn in the present and much to praise in the past, but one need only remember her exposure of the foolish worshipers of the past in some of her stories to realize that Cather would not condone a willful self-immersion in the past. Rosicky's attitude toward the past is the one Cather espouses. "The Old Beauty," even though set in the crucial year 1922, is not, as some have assumed, a shameful nostalgia trip. It is, in fact, just the opposite. Cather makes it clear, within the story and by implication in other writing she was working with at the time, that to hate the present and love only the past as Gabrielle Longstreet does, is to be guilty of unforgivable waste. In this story, as in others, Cather insists that the past must not be detached from the ongoing process of life. Thus, in some respects "The Old Beauty" is a reaffirmation of Marian Forrester's decision to have life at all costs, to live in the present rather than the past.

The story is told mainly through the consciousness of Henry Seabury, one of the few youthful men so fortunate as to have earned Gabrielle's favor in the days when she was the darling of the old men in London society. At age fifty-five Seabury arrives in Aix-les-Bains, at the very hotel where the Old Beauty is staying. Like Gabrielle, he has come to Aix seeking refuge against the changes that have overtaken much of the world. He does not recognize her at first because, whatever it was she had, "now it was all gone" (p. 24), and his gaze perceives only "a stern, gaunt-cheeked old woman with a yellowing complexion" (p. 9). She soon remembers him as the excellent young man whose timely arrival at her home had once saved her from the crude advances of her lecherous financial advisor.

One of the story's critical problems lies in accurately interpreting Cather's attitude toward Gabrielle Longstreet, an attitude which seems both sympathetic and mocking. Gabrielle is pale and lifeless beside most of Cather's heroines, for she is a woman hopelessly alienated in a present that, for all its imperfections, is better than she is. At least Marian Forrester learned to adapt and survive. Gabrielle is also pale beside her optimistic companion, the cheery, beaming Cherry Beamish. She is paler still beside the three women, all aging like herself, who figure prominently in the essays which Cather was then preparing for inclusion in *Not Under Forty:* Madame Franklin Grout, the niece of Flaubert whom Cather met during the summer of 1930 in Aix-les-Bains; Mrs. James T. (Annie) Fields, who entertained the most distinguished literary figures of her day in her gracious drawing room; and Sarah Orne Jewett, a New England writer who was a decided influence on Cather's own career, a friend and frequent guest of Mrs. Fields. These women provide remarkable contrasts for Gabrielle Longstreet.

The story itself makes it plain that although Gabrielle appears to have been a person of some distinction, she never showed the verve that was so attractive in Marian Forrester. She is not, and never has been, an extraordinary human being; she was only at one time extraordinarily beautiful. The descriptions of Lady Longstreet as a young woman, though not reprehensible or even indifferent, scrupulously avoid endowing her with much life or personality: "She was not witty or especially clever,—had no accomplishments beyond speaking French as naturally as English. She said nothing memorable in either language. She was beautiful, that was all. And she was fresh." The young Lady Longstreet "showed no great zest" and had "no glitter about her, no sparkle" (pp. 17–18). Trying "to remember her face just as it was," Seabury thinks, "Perhaps it was her eyes he remembered best; no glint in them, no sparkle, no drive" (p. 24).

Even then, when she was very young, the present was not so attractive to her as the past. She continually urged her doting old men "to tell her about events and personages already in the past; things she had come too late to see" (p. 19). But in a curiously mocking fashion Cather makes a little joke with regard to Gabrielle's throng of male loyalists. It is deliberately hinted that the attraction at Gabrielle's home was not so much her personal charm as it was her newly installed central heating system, a luxury most Londoners could not afford. What is not a joke, however, is that the old woman now carries about with her a multitude of ancient photographs of those ancient admirers. Seabury, who also has eyes only for the past, rejoices that the photographs can restore for the moment "the woman he used to know" (p. 34).

In various ways throughout the story Cather shows impatience with, if not outright disdain for, the attitudes and values exhibited by Gabrielle and Seabury. She makes them look absurdly old-fashioned and act pettily superior, and she has them express opinions about modernism and youth that are stupidly intolerant. For example, they cannot abide the modern style of dancing and must put all the young dancers at the Maison des Fleurs tea room to shame by swirling magnificently into a waltz, Hollywood style. On that occasion Gabrielle makes a particularly disturbing, even base, comment about the young people who she says are not dancing at all but are only "wriggling . . . like lizards dancing—or reptiles coupling" (p. 58).

The most important incident in the story reveals how truly narrow and intolerant the Old Beauty is, and exposes both Gabrielle and Seabury as singularly foolish. He is given a chance to "save" her again, but this time he has more gallantry to offer than the occasion demands. Thinking to bring Gabrielle a bit of cheer, he arranges a motor trip for her and Cherry to a magnificent old monastery high in the mountains, the Grande-Chartreuse. The return trip down a steep corkscrew road is spoiled when their driver is forced to ram the cliff to avoid sending a carelessly driven car and its occupants off the precipice. The occupants happen to be indecorous, sporty, loud young American women in dirty white knickers who address each other indelicately by nicknames. Gabrielle survives the accident, but not the encounter with modernity. She has to be carried from the auto to her bed, and she dies before morning. Seabury's heroics consist of springing over the running board on command and chasing the two young things away. His reward is a verbal biscuit: "How ever did you manage to dispose of them so quickly" (p. 68)? Gabrielle's reaction to the young women is as nasty as her reaction to the dancers. She agrees bitterly that Seabury's driver had no choice but to ram

the side of the cliff, and then adds with a sneer, "They happened to
be worth nobody's consideration, but that doesn't alter the code"
(p. 68).

Though Cather may feel sorry for Gabrielle, and admire some
things about her—her fine carriage, for example—she does not like
her. The person in the story Cather does like is Cherry, a woman of
what Seabury assumes is the "old manner" (p. 8), but a woman very
much alive and delighted in the present.[22] Cherry, a former comedi-
enne of music hall fame who played mainly boys' parts, is reminiscent of "Jimmy" Broadwood, the level-headed, witty, and unostenta-
tious actress in "Flavia and Her Artists." Cather uses the plump,
good-natured Cherry as a healthy antithesis to the slender, morose
Lady Longstreet, emphasizing Cherry's zest for living and her frank
enjoyment of people and the world. Unlike Gabrielle, who values
only the past, Cherry thinks the present "really very interesting"
and people "novel and amusing" (pp. 29–32). Cherry's generous nature, her willingness to ease Gabrielle through the last years of her
life, is also a lesson in compassion. She who accepts life so gladly,
who does not suffer over change, who has many friends, who finds
young people quite wonderful, is willing to humor and serve
Gabrielle until the Old Beauty can return in death to her "own
kind" (p. 71). Cherry never quits trying to alter Gabrielle's peevish
perceptions, but she never blames or belittles her.

Reinforcing the story's ample evidence that Gabrielle Longstreet
is not the kind of woman Cather could greatly admire, or offer as a
voice for herself, are Cather's essays of the same period. Her genuine admiration for the women she portrays in *Not Under Forty*—
the book that was supposedly her grandest gesture to the past—
suggests that her preference for lively, self-possessed women of
youthful outlook had not changed over the years.[23] The women described in *Not Under Forty* were of the "drawing room" type and
might have been expected to resemble Gabrielle Longstreet in numerous ways—that they do not is telling. The first of these women is
Madame Franklin Grout, mentioned earlier as Flaubert's niece with
whom Cather became acquainted in the old woman's eighty-fifth
year. In an essay titled "A Chance Meeting," Cather recounts her
"chance meeting" and subsequent meetings with Madame Grout in
the summer of 1930 in Aix-les-Bains—the same setting she selected
for "The Old Beauty." Several details in the essay are repeated in
the story, suggesting that Cather's experience with Madame Grout

was playing in her mind when she composed the story. As Cather created Gabrielle, and as she recreated Madame Grout, she must have been keenly aware of the striking contrast presented by the two women—one alive and vital in the present, even at age eighty-four, the other caught hopelessly in the past.

Madame Grout's pluck and zest, her insatiable appetite for experience, her physical and mental toughness, along with her love for music of both the past and present, contrast markedly with Gabrielle's physical and emotional weakness and her distaste for the modern. Madame Grout was a person of distinguished bearing, but she was not simply an ancient, self-satisfied figurehead: "No one could fail to recognize her distinction and authority; it was in the carriage of her head, in her fine hands, in her voice, in every word she uttered in any language, in her brilliant, very piercing eyes."[24] With her there was no studied passivity and no waning of the fire. Like Gabrielle, Madame Grout had been married twice and did not discuss her husbands, but unlike her, Madame Grout "was not an idealist," nor was she in "the least visionary and sentimental" (p. 40).

On one other point it is instructive to compare the essay with the story. In the story it is the careless insensitivity, even stupidity, of youth that precipitates Gabrielle's death. But in the essay, Cather defends as natural and therefore necessary the very things in young people that make them such a trial to adults. As has been noted, Cather had always felt a special affection for youth, an affection she reaffirms in *Lucy Gayheart,* also of this period, and in the other two stories in *The Old Beauty and Others.* It is significant, then, that the essay criticizes Flaubert's *L'Education Sentimentale* for being "a story of youth" that lacks "the voracious appetite which drives young people through silly and vulgar experiences" (p. 19). One of the blessed things about youth, Cather insists, is that one can be silly and vulgar without permanently damaging one's character. Read in connection with "The Old Beauty," the passage just noted sounds almost like an apology for the two young women who by their vulgarity send Gabrielle Longstreet into the emotional paroxysm that kills her.

Thus, it is possible to read "A Chance Meeting" as a gloss on "The Old Beauty." Further insights into the story are available as well in the essays titled "148 Charles Street" and "Miss Jewett," also published in *Not Under Forty.*[25] Cather introduces both Jewett and Mrs. Fields in the Charles Street essay, sitting at tea in Mrs. Fields's "long drawing-room" (p. 53). If ever a setting were designed to lend credence to the genteel world Gabrielle Longstreet yearned to recapture, this is it. Here Mrs. Fields had created an atmosphere in which "the past lived on" in a "protected and cherished . . . sanctuary from the noisy push of the present" (p. 61). Then too, Cather comments bitterly in the essay on the garage that now stands at the address where Mrs. Fields once graciously entertained great and noble talents from the past. This essay helps explain Cather's inclination toward sympathy for Gabrielle, but it also further substantiates her impatience with the Old Beauty who had given up on life many years before it actually ended.

The aged and fragile Mrs. Fields, like Madame Grout, would have put Gabrielle to shame, and so would Miss Jewett. When Cather entered the Fields drawing room for the first time, late in 1908, she noted the "great play of animation" in Mrs. Fields's face and the youthful look about her guest, Miss Jewett. Over and over again Cather stresses that Mrs. Fields "did not seem old to me. Frail, diminished in force, yes; but, emphatically, *not* old. . . . I had seldom heard so young, so merry, so musical a laugh; a laugh with countless shades of relish and appreciation and kindness in it" (pp. 57–58). How different she was from Lady Longstreet who looked old and gaunt and who never laughed unless ruefully.

The really remarkable thing about Mrs. Fields was the way in which she related to both past and present. "On the one hand," Cather remarks, Mrs. Fields was "distinctly young"; on the other she "seemed to me to reach back to Waterloo" (p. 60). Endowed with a marvelous sense of humor, Cather observes, "She had the very genius of survival. She was not, as she once laughingly told me, 'to escape anything, not even free verse or the Cubists.'" Cather adds approvingly that "she was not in the least dashed by either" (p. 67). Unlike Gabrielle Longstreet, "At eighty she could still entertain new people, new ideas, new forms of art. And she brought to her greeting of the new all the richness of her rich past. . ." (p. 71).

Cather's essay on Sarah Orne Jewett deals mainly with Jewett as a writer, but Cather does interject some comments that show Jewett to be another figure who approached life and change with a courage Gabrielle preferred not to muster. Like Cherry Beamish and Madame Grout and Mrs. Fields, Sarah Orne Jewett did not let her healthy respect for the past interfere with her appreciation of the new. Noting that Jewett was reading a new volume of Conrad the night she suffered the cerebral hemorrhage which eventually killed her, Cather says that "she had the most reverent and rejoicing admiration" (p. 90) for contemporary writers who showed real ability.

"The Old Beauty" is a very important indicator of Cather's attitudes as she grew older, and Cather's image has suffered as a result of misinterpretation of this story. Anyone tempted to assume that Cather's views of the past are represented by the Old Beauty should remember that Gabrielle created her past largely from events twice removed from real experience—the exploits of youth recollected in the minds of old men. Her own youthful past on Martinique, which could have had immense value for her, is never mentioned or remembered. Gabrielle has ignored that very real past in favor of a past she gathered secondhand from others. To suggest that Cather would condone a rejection of the present in favor of the past, especially a past severed from its roots and constructed on the remotest sorts of derived memories, is to deny the very essence of her life's work and to ignore her admiration for the women whose lives she juxtaposed against Gabrielle's—the three women of the essays and Cherry Beamish.

B. The Goodness at Last

The last two pieces of fiction Willa Cather completed were collected with "The Old Beauty" and published in 1948, the year after she died. Although "The Best Years" appears ahead of "Before Breakfast" in the collection, it is believed to have been completed a year later than that story, in 1945. In spite of nagging health problems, Cather was also working on another story, a *nouvelle* set in fourteenth-century Avignon; but the manuscript and notes for that work were probably destroyed in accordance with her request.[26]

In spite of the disappointing loss of the Avignon manuscript, nothing could have been more fitting than for Willa Cather to have finished her writing career with "Before Breakfast" and "The Best Years." In "Before Breakfast" the artist tries to answer in simple terms a few of the large perplexing questions about human experience that had been stirring through her fiction for half a century. In "The Best Years" the artist who is also sister and daughter fashions a loving tribute to her own family and the never-to-be-forgotten and never-to-be-recovered years of her childhood in Red Cloud. In these two stories, as in "Neighbour Rosicky," we sense Cather's abiding concern with unity, in systems both large and small—in nature, in the human family, and in the personal family unit. Here at the last, regardless of what doubts have plagued her along the way, and still rankle at times, Cather is affirming the goodness of life and love, "the goodness of planting and tending and harvesting at last."[27] She is insisting on the everlasting wholeness of things, asserting finally that regardless of what has changed, regardless of what seems to have been destroyed or lost forever, some things do not change; some things endure. They may not last 136 million years, like Henry Grenfell's island in "Before Breakfast," or aeons more than that, like Venus, but they last. The reality of love is immutable; human relationship and caring are immutable. So too is nature in its relationships with human beings. And though youth passes for each of us, it is a continuing miracle, generation after generation. Individuals may suffer wrenching changes, loved ones may die, bodies may grow old, trees may fall, crops may fail, or two people may drift apart; but there will always be people who care for each other, there will always be love somewhere, there will always be youth somewhere, there will always be trees and islands and the sea, there will always be another growing season, there will always be home somewhere for someone. That is what this life means, permanence in spite of impermanence, design in spite of chaos.

The three stories in this collection can be described as a search for that which endures. Gabrielle's search in "The Old Beauty" is doomed because all she wants is to petrify her own little secondhand past into eternity. She has mistaken the trappings of the past, which change, for the *fact* of the past, which does not change. Henry Grenfell in "Before Breakfast" very nearly makes a similar mistake, assuming that because some things have been recast in his individual life, or because he may have spent his life in pursuit of transitory things, nothing closer than a remote planet is fixed. But he learns that nature endures, as does his relationship with it, and that humanity is part of a larger design. In "The Best Years" a beloved sister and daughter is lost, but the story avows that her relationship with her family remains. Even though the family members will never have her again in their midst, the love they shared was a fact; and the fact of it endures. It is in that sense, and only that sense, that we can retain the past. We cannot relive it, but it is ours, nevertheless.

The mood of "The Old Beauty" is very different from that of the other two stories in the collection. While "The Old Beauty" shows a mature artist's understanding of a personality that has chosen to wrap itself in the remnants of an impoverished past, it does not present a final perspective of any sort. By contrast, the last two stories do. In "Before Breakfast" Grenfell is conscious that he is doing a "revaluation" (p. 149), making a self "audit" (p. 158) that is in many respects very painful. But in the end, he has caught a vision of the grand design of human existence and is, for the moment at least, totally reconciled. And while the story is replete with his temporary anger, he never succumbs to the temptation of lasting despair.

As has been suggested, Cather is dealing with two kinds of relationships in this story, the relationships of human beings with nature and with each other. She is exploring again, in both cosmic and personal terms, the problem of isolation, the need for solitude, and the counterurge for relationship. Cursed with a "hair-trigger stomach" (p. 156), Grenfell can scarcely enjoy the rewards of his worldly success. His rise from messenger boy at Western Union to senior partner in a brokerage firm is attributable both to his personal drive (which has ruined his stomach) and his fortuitous marriage into a prominent family. His way of getting even with his frail organs and escaping from his family is to "live rough" hunting big game in the wilderness. His favorite retreat, to which he has returned after a two-year absence, is a small crude cabin, his own, on a somewhat inaccessible island off the coast of Nova Scotia.[28] His feelings about the island are highly personal, and so when a geologist whom he meets on the boat begins rattling off scientific data about the island, Grenfell grows unreasonably angry. He sleeps badly his first night there, and the next morning his mind is full of unhappy thoughts about his family—a creditable wife and three sons, two of them brilliant and successful, though "cold as ice" (p. 152).

Whenever Grenfell leaves his family this way he never tells them "how long he would be away or where he was going" (p. 153). The island is a secret which he keeps hidden from them. He blames his family for their lack of warmth, scorning his sons' icy brilliance, and yet he has willfully held them at arm's length for years. Clearly, Grenfell is partly to blame for his estrangement: "He resented any intrusion on his private, personal, non-family life." Furthermore, "Grenfell never bothered his family with his personal diversions, and he never intruded upon theirs. Harrison and his mother were a team—a close corporation! Grenfell respected it absolutely. No questions, no explanations demanded by him." But it is obvious that he resents the "corporation" that shuts him out, and he admits that "there were times when he got back at the corporation just a little." His even-tempered wife will not let him make a quarrel, however, and by "being faultlessly polite" she rescues him whenever he swipes at "the domestic line-up" (pp. 153–56).

Off by himself, Grenfell passes through a crisis, a crisis spawned over days and years but climaxing when the geologist unwittingly reduces Grenfell's island to a set of figures. Grenfell rebels, then admits, "The bitter truth was that his worst enemy was closer even than the wife of his bosom—was his bosom itself" (p. 156)! A dyspeptic stomach is only symptomatic (or symbolic) of the larger festering inside him, the same conflict that tears Godfrey St. Peter in halves. Part of him insists on the value of humanness and desires human relationship (and resents his family's aloofness); and part of him wants to be totally alone, to have nothing to do with other human beings, to have a relationship only with nature. Like St. Peter, Grenfell talks about the need for humanness and prefers to read books that he regards as "human" (see pp. 147–48, and 153), but it has been largely humanity in the abstract that he has valued, humanity free from annoying human characteristics and the inclination to interrupt his solitude. Significantly, Grenfell's reconciliation is happier than St. Peter's. He accepts humanity in the end while St. Peter only grudgingly gives up his mesa dream and resigns himself to a life without joy among imperfect human beings.

After his sleepless night Grenfell feels especially alienated, from nature as well as humanity. He is disposed to think of himself as "poor Grenfell," an insignificant little germ in a vast universe. The planet Venus, the same symbol Cather had used in "Two Friends," corroborates his pessimistic views. Whereas in the earlier story the distant planet had seemed to suggest at least the possibility for human convergence as well as separation, to a grumpy Grenfell it represents "serene, impersonal splendour. Merciless perfection, ageless sovereignty" (p. 144). Our feeble lives and achievements set against that kind of ageless, untouchable magnificence seem stupid indeed —especially our self-satisfied assumptions about the geology of an island. The first sign of Grenfell's recovery from the effects of the geologist's battery of facts comes when he involuntarily glances a second time at Venus and sees it still "serene, terrible and splendid, looking at him" in its "immortal beauty"; but this time he cries out defiantly, ". . . yes, but only when somebody *saw* it" (p. 158)! What is a star, after all, without a human eye and heart to wonder at it?

Still out of sorts, Grenfell plunges out into the morning and into the miracle that is his island. Once among the familiar natural surroundings, he experiences a revelatory transformation. He decides that although bright Venus might offer a fixed point of stability, without beginning or end, it is too remote to bring comfort. What is close enough to bring comfort is his island. He realizes, happily, that all about him lie stable things, things that in his lifetime, at least, do not change substantially. Grenfell concludes that it matters not at all that the island may be as old as the geologist claims. What has that "to do with the green surface where men lived and trees lived" (p. 161) and flowers abound? He sees more and more of the things he has always loved and concludes, "Nothing had changed. Everything was the same, and he, Henry Grenfell, was the same: the relationship was unchanged" (p. 162). The essential relationship, his relationship with this bit of nature, has indeed remained unchanged. In fact, here are the same old trees, still clutching at the earth against the tug of the sea winds.

His newfound contentment is interrupted, however, for from the headland he sees the geologist's daughter picking her way through the rocks below him toward the water's edge. His first reaction is anger: she is disrupting his revery, and likely he will be required to rescue her from the rough sea. But then he allows himself to perceive that she too feels an intuitive harmony with his little strip of coastline, she too is really no stranger there. When she opens her robe, she looks like a clam opening its shell—he cannot get over the resemblance. And she pays nature's price, by swimming the rough tides. Watching her screw up her courage and plunge into the frosty water, he thinks, "There was no one watching her, she didn't have to keep face—except to herself. That she had to do and no fuss about it. She hadn't dodged. She had gone out, and she had come back. She would have a happy day. He knew just how she felt" (pp. 165–66). He finds himself chuckling with delight. Grenfell's quarrel with science, and even with human beings, stems from his desire to retain a sense of wonder about life and the universe. Science, he thinks, is trying to dispel the mystery. He had thought human relationships threatened it too. But as he watches the girl, he no longer resents her or regards her as an intruder. His new realization of oneness with her, another human creature, is in harmony with his newly restored sense of joy in his island.

And in the girl's youth he discovers still another source of pleasure, a revelation that youth, like age, is an eternal fact. Cather has come full circle, and she ends the story with Grenfell's heartfelt tribute to youth and his fable of endurance and permanence. Survival, in spite of great odds, is what we learn from the first amphibious frog who, having found his pond dry, hopped across land until he found another. Genuinely happy to admit that "plucky youth is more bracing than enduring age" (p. 166), Grenfell goes to breakfast a new man. The story hardly reads like the last groan of an aging writer turned bitter with despair. It is, rather, an impressive corrective to the philosophy of the Old Beauty.[29]

Both "Before Breakfast" and "The Best Years" stress the importance of place, of having a place to return to, a place of one's own. For Grenfell, it is a place of solitude, primarily, and of relationship with nature, where his "family" are a timid hare, a grandfather tree, and a youngster who is not even aware of his having adopted her. For Lesley Ferguesson in "The Best Years" it is a place of family togetherness where people are the essential ingredients for happiness. In Grenfell's darkest moment, in his anger over "inhuman" scientific facts that seem to rob mortals of even what "little hour" (p. 148) is allotted to them, his chief concern is that a human being might seem "accidental, unrelated to anything" (p. 149). What he insists upon is the necessity to belong. That same necessity informs "The Best Years," but on the level of family intimacies rather than natural affinities. In some respects, however, Grenfell's cabin is not really so different from the rustic, private attic loft where Lesley and her brothers spent so many lovely nights tucked away by themselves, together and yet separate.[30]

Cather's biographers believe that "The Best Years," with its wonderful recollections of childhood closeness between sister and younger brothers, was prompted by a very happy reunion between Cather and her brother Roscoe in 1941. She visited him in California, and the two spent many glorious hours together. Perhaps the story was indeed for Roscoe, who died shortly after it was finished. The Cather family is certainly suggested here, as it was in "Old Mrs. Harris," but it is much mellowed. The harmony is never disturbed; Mrs. Ferguesson has little of Victoria Templeton's spoiled selfishness, Lesley none of Vickie's impatient drive. In some ways the story recalls "Neighbour Rosicky," with its similar emphasis on family love and lasting values. In other ways, since it also portrays the anguish of loss, it resembles "Two Friends." The physical home in the story is, of course, the Cather home in Red Cloud, and hence the Kronborg home in *The Song of the Lark* as well as the Templeton home in "Old Mrs. Harris." But unlike Thea Kronborg and Vickie Templeton, Lesley feels no compulsion to leave home to seek new experiences in the larger world. Further, what Cather had said about the strain of family life in her essay on Katherine Mansfield, and intimated in both *The Song of the Lark* and "Old Mrs. Harris," apparently does not obtain here. The years seem to have mellowed Cather's memories of her childhood, or given her an increased desire to pay tribute to its loveliest aspects. In the essay Cather notes that Mansfield was especially skilled at portraying the dynamics of personal relationships within "everyday 'happy'" families. She says that in a Mansfield fictional family, even without "crises or shocks or bewildering complications,"

> ... every individual ... (even the children) is clinging passionately to his individual soul, is in terror of losing it in the general family flavour. As in most families, the mere struggle to have anything of one's own, to be one's self at all, creates an element of strain which keeps everybody almost at the breaking point.
>
> One realizes that even in harmonious families there is this double life: the group life, which is the one we can observe in our neighbour's household, and, underneath, another—secret and passionate and intense—which is the real life that stamps the faces and gives character to the voices of our friends. Always in his mind each member of these social units is escaping, running away, trying to break the net which circumstances and his own affections have woven about him.[31]

Perhaps partly because it has no plot in the usual sense, and because it acknowledges almost none of the tensions between individual and group lives that Cather describes in the Mansfield essay, "The Best Years" at times seems more like a collection of artistically rendered memories and feelings about a place and its people than like a short story. Cather herself might have preferred to call it a "narrative," as she did *Death Comes for the Archbishop*.[32] What gives the story a strong sense of design, yet at the same time maintains its quality of spontaneous memory, is Cather's control of tone through point of view. Given the story's abundant emotional content, the closeness of Cather to her materials, and her mood when she wrote it, "The Best Years" could easily have become highly sentimental. That it does not is a tribute to Cather's skill. Her omniscient narrator is in total control of tone, framing the entire piece with the kindly, yet stoical outlook of Evangeline Knightly, the county school superintendent for whom Lesley at age fifteen is teaching. Point of view alternately moves into the heart of the family through Lesley's unabashedly tender responses and recollections and then steps back into an authorial stance to balance Lesley's sentiment with rather objective observations about Mr. and Mrs. Ferguesson and Hector.

Miss Knightly, like the narrator, is a steadying force in the story, a solid, wise ballast in a sea of tender and, in the end, bitter emotion. At the beginning she quietly facilitates a visit home for a very homesick Lesley; and at the end, some twenty years later, she listens as a disheartened Mrs. Ferguesson calls up Lesley's memory and longs for a return to "the best years." Miss Knightly thus serves to counterbalance Lesley's ardent enthusiasm and to cushion Mrs. Ferguesson's complaint. When, in the aftermath of a terrible blizzard that traps Lesley and her "scholars" in the schoolhouse for several hours, the young teacher catches pneumonia and dies, Miss Knightly is stunned but not angry. She knows that there is no justice in what has happened to her little friend, but she has learned to accept whatever comes. Mrs. Ferguesson, on the other hand, even after twenty years, is unable to accept life's disappointments and injustices. Change is always painful to her.

Details of home, and especially of the children's attic room, are presented lovingly through Lesley's consciousness. In her eyes the home is a symbol of family love, unity, and safety, and her feelings are given full play while she is there. Even solitude is sweet to her so long as she is in the place where loved ones dwell. The things that call up the beloved are almost as dear to Lesley as the persons themselves. In her own place at last, she gratefully gives "herself up to the feeling of being at home. It went all through her, that feeling, like getting into a warm bath when one is tired. She was safe from everything, was where she ought to be" (p. 96). Mrs. Ferguesson understands this sense of unity too, knows that "her children were bound to her, and to that house, by the deepest, the most solemn loyalty. They never spoke that covenant to each other, never even formulated it in their own minds—never. It was a consciousness they shared, and it gave them a family complexion" (pp. 104–5). As Lesley sits on the porch floor that Saturday morning, she sinks "into idleness and safety and perfect love," realizing that "the boys were much the dearest things in the world to her. To love them so much was just . . . happiness" (p. 112).

Lesley knows that the source of her joy is the oneness she feels with her brothers. For her, Grenfell's cosmic unity, or even a unity with tangible nature, might have been too much to contemplate. The great thing into which she wants to be dissolved is simply her family, the love of her brothers. The attic room in the old house was the children's "place," a place where no outsider intruded, and it was with some reluctance that Lesley agreed to her mother's insistence that now, in deference to her teaching position, a little section of the attic must be partitioned off just for her. The attic was spacious, but the beds stood all in a row because "the children liked to be close enough together to share experiences" (p. 108). Only once does Cather indicate that the children guarded their individual lives. She says that each person did indeed have his private self as well as his group self, though she mentions no conflict between the two roles. In fact, every person's acceptance of the other's "right to his own" (p. 109) dream, his own love, enhanced the harmony of the attic.

Cather elected to describe the home and Lesley's feelings about it and her family from the inside—sincerely, tenderly, openly—with no attempt at objectivity. But for the account of Lesley's death, she moves as far from the event, emotionally, as possible. She informs the reader of the girl's death through a minor character's report of it to Miss Knightly, some days after it occurs. A railroad conductor mentions it, almost as an afterthought, in connection with other incidents pertinent to the fateful blizzard. To have depicted the death, or the family's reaction to it, firsthand would have been to shift tone from sweetness to sorrow too abruptly, and to have run the very real risk of blatant sentimentality. Cather keeps tight control on tone, however, by showing only Miss Knightly's reaction to the delayed news, a guarantee that feelings will be held in check. Only after twenty years have passed does Cather venture to show a direct family response, when Miss Knightly—now Mrs. Ralph Thorndike—returns to MacAlpin to find a more prosperous but less happy Mrs. Ferguesson. The still-bereaved mother insists that the family feels Lesley's death "as if it had happened yesterday" (p. 134). The former superintendent hears out Mrs. Ferguesson's lament over changes that have occurred in the town and in her family, but she gently refuses to indulge the older woman in her grievances.

It was probably not solely to achieve emotional distance that Cather handled Lesley's death the way she did. She may also have wished to mute the theme of death and loss so as not to let it overshadow her central theme of family love and harmony. Still, the dark current introduced into the narrative through Lesley's death cannot be dismissed. The story's very title, recalling as it does Jim Burden's remembered passage from Virgil, "The best days are the first to flee," keeps that theme ever present.[33] Nevertheless, Cather treats Lesley's death somewhat differently than she does the tragic deaths of her favored young people in the novels and earlier stories. Perhaps deliberately breaking form in this story, Cather brings forward no grieving survivor of her young character to make the expected gesture of reconciliation toward death. Even with the heart-shattering murders of Emil Bergson and Marie Shabata, for example, there is the recognition that death is, in some respects, a charitable release from what could have been a lifetime of unremitting agony. Alexandra is, in fact, able to sympathize with their hapless killer, and to visit him in prison. Similarly, Mrs. Wheeler expresses sorrowful gratitude that Claude will not have to suffer the postwar disillusionment so prevalent among young men who return from war. Professor St. Peter, too, acknowledges that Tom Outland is probably better off having died in Europe than he would have been returning to a greedy, shallow postwar world. And finally, Margaret is gratified that Nelly Deane lives on in her children, while Harry Gordon comes to at least a tentative reconciliation with Lucy Gayheart's death by avowing that even though she missed two-thirds of her life, she had had the best third. A statement such as this is conspicuous by its absence in "The Best Years."

Thus, while "The Best Years" is an affirmation of all the positive values of home and familial love, it is also a recognition of the reality of change and loss—sometimes beyond reason or explanation. In this story, Cather takes no care to justify young Lesley's death, or to moralize about it. Death, she seems to say, is just something that happens, and there is sometimes nothing to redeem the loss. Even though in its portrait of family unity "The Best Years" resembles "Neighbour Rosicky," the almost praising acceptance of death in that work is missing in the later story; in its place is Miss Knightly's gentle brand of stoicism.

Despite the story's dark motif, however, and Miss Knightly's studied acceptance of what she cannot change, "The Best Years" strikes the reader as being, in the main, highly positive and life-affirming. Contributing to that spirit is Cather's still lively capacity for humor, which in this story has a character all its own, mature and deftly timed. It comes from the narrative voice rather than from the char-

acters, and adds another note of objectivity to a story long on sentiment. To be sure, Cather generates smiles through juxtaposing
young Lesley's naivete against her skill in handling certain embar-
rassing situations in her classroom, but the story's most obvious
comedy lies in the characterization of James Ferguesson, Lesley's father. The humor he engenders makes the family more human and
endearing, and at the same time acts as another deterrent to what
could have been excessive sentiment in the story. This is how Cather
introduces him: "James Grahame Ferguesson was a farmer. He
spent most of his time on what he called an 'experimental farm.'
(The neighbours had other names for it—some of them amusing.)"
Cather earns one chuckle with "The neighbours had other names for
it," and another one with "some of them amusing." She indicates
that "his neighbours, both in town and in the country where he
farmed, liked him because he gave them so much to talk about." His
workday consists mainly in going to the farm, eating his lunch, rest-
ing and thinking, tending his horses, and then returning home for
supper. He hangs a sign on the farm whose most "important crop . . .
was an idea" that reads "Wide Awake Farm"; the neighbors quickly
convert it to "Hush-a-bye Farm." People warm to "Old Ferg" because
he has given them something to laugh about, and he never suspects
the reason for his increased popularity. Rather, "He ascribed it to
the power of his oratory" (pp. 100–3).

It is appropriate that in her last two completed stories Cather
could contemplate problems of the cosmos and of "Hush-a-bye Farm"
with equal ease. One story seeks answers to the sometimes terrifying perplexities of human life; the other seems to suggest that the
answers lie in the exercise of human love. But both Henry Grenfell
and Lesley Ferguesson are aware of some unifying scheme behind
mortal experience. Finally, it is Miss Knightly whom Cather desig-
nates to tie her last group of stories and, in a sense, the entirety of
her work together. As Miss Knightly perceives while driving her
slow mare across the Nebraska landscape, "The horizon was like a
perfect circle, a great embrace, and within it lay the cornfields, still
green, and the yellow wheat stubble . . . and the pasture lands. . ."
(p. 78). Within such a "great embrace" lie the stories of Willa Cather, and, indeed, the novels and poems and prose nonfiction too. She
perceived the wholeness of things, and she made her work a means
for imposing unity on experience.

NOTES

1. Woodress (*Willa Cather: Her Life and Art*, p. 226), citing a 1941 letter from Cather to Zoë Akins as evidence, says the first attack occurred in August; Brown (*Willa Cather: A Critical Biography*, p. 274) describes the ailment specifically as angina, and says it occurred at Christmastime; Lewis (*Willa Cather Living*, p. 152) also calls the heart problem angina, and sets the time vaguely as late fall or Christmas.

2. Cather also visited Quebec during this period, and the seeds for *Shadows on the Rock* began to germinate as well. "Neighbour Rosicky" was the first story she had set in the West since "The Bohemian Girl," which dates back to the year of her first novel, 1912.

3. Letters to friends in Nebraska after this time reveal that Cather often expressed a wish to visit them, but with the pull of family gone, and health problems, and the pressures of work seeming always to increase, she never made it.

4. Lewis, *Willa Cather Living*, p. 157.

5. See Stouck (*Willa Cather's Imagination*, p. 208) and his note of attribution, p. 239. Though Cather may set her prairie stories in Colorado or Kansas, the real settings are Nebraska, the town of Red Cloud and the countryside around it. The buildings, streets, and homes described are all recognizable in Red Cloud. This is particularly true of *The Song of the Lark* earlier, and now of "Old Mrs. Harris," "Two Friends," and "The Best Years."

6. Cather, *Obscure Destinies*, p. 213. Citations from the three stories in this volume are from this edition (page numbers are in parentheses in the text).

7. Giannone, *Music in Willa Cather's Fiction*, p. 207.

8. Brown, *Willa Cather: A Critical Biography*, p. 275. The story is dated 1928 in the collection, but Woodress (*Willa Cather: Her Life and Art*, p. 227) describes the year 1928 as "almost totally unproductive for Cather." The story was first published in the *Woman's Home Companion*, in April and May, 1930.

9. Woodress (*Willa Cather: Her Life and Art*, p. 226) describes Cather's reaction to her father's death in a way that seems to explain her mood of acceptance when she wrote "Neighbour Rosicky." When her father suffered his first attack in August, Cather sped from Wyoming, where she was vacationing, to Red Cloud. She returned to Red Cloud again at Christmastime to see him, staying through most of February. On 3 March he suffered a fatal attack and she rushed home again. She arrived at about 3 A.M. and went to his room without waking the family. According to Woodress, "She spent several unforgettable hours with him before anyone else in the house awoke. When the red dawn broke, it flushed his face with the rosy color which he always had, and he looked entirely himself and happy." Carrie

Miner Sherwood, however, indicated to Mildred R. Bennett that Cather was very upset and angry over the death of her father. (Bennett, address at Cather National Seminar, 18 June 1983.)

10. The story of his despair and rescue is in the tradition of folk literature, one of those Christmas stories of marvelous chance in which the deserving poverty-stricken lad is discovered by large-hearted persons willing and able to give him new life and new hope. An early Cather story, "The Burglar's Christmas," is one of this type.

11. Most of the deaths described or contemplated in Cather's work, however, are anything but serene like Rosicky's. The short stories are full of bitter or violent deaths—Peter Sadelack, Serge Povolitchky, Sum Loo's child, Jack-a-Boy, Hugh Treffinger, Harvey Merrick, Paul, Alexandra Ebbling, Nelly Deane, Caesarino, Kier Cavenaugh, Paul Wanning, Katharine Gaylord, Valentine Ramsay. The same is true for the novels—Bartley Alexander, Emil Bergson, Papa Shimerda, Claude Wheeler, Myra Henshawe, Lucy Gayheart, Sapphira Colbert. The list is much longer if we include minor characters and characters who figure in numerous tales and anecdotes. Nevertheless, we can assume with Carl Linstrum in *O Pioneers!* that death for Alexandra Bergson will be serene, as will death for a person like Ántonia. The character who knows oneness with the land in life will not find death disturbing.

12. Vickie could be regarded as one of the "three women," but since Cather typically calls her "the girl" in the story, such a reading would seem to distort the story by underplaying Mrs. Rosen's role.

13. Mrs. Rosen has still another cultural background, European. Cather seems to blend that with her northern city background, and for purposes of discussion Mrs. Rosen's "foreignness" will be considered a part of that northern blend.

14. Strong as her attachment was to Red Cloud, Cather seems never to have stopped smarting over what she regarded as its sometimes narrow attitudes. Her letters to Carrie Miner Sherwood over the years make repeated references to Cather's feeling that she was forever at the mercy of Red Cloud opinion, that her successes and her financial contributions to local causes would only generate disdain among certain of the townspeople. (Letters at Willa Cather archives in Red Cloud.)

15. "Old Mrs. Harris" was obviously one of Cather's favorites. She apparently sent a copy of *Obscure Destinies* to a Mrs. Mellen (identified only as Dick's mother) and attached a note which explains that it was not her custom to make gifts of her own books. She says that in this instance, however, she is making an exception because the second story in the collection is a particularly satisfying one to her. Speaking further of "Old Mrs. Harris," she says that it is often hardest to do the simplest things. One has to be patient and slip up on it unawares. (Letter at University of Virginia Library, Charlottesville.) In another undated letter, this one to George Seibel, she

also expresses her satisfaction with "Old Mrs. Harris," stating that she came closer to achieving her purposes with that story than she usually does. She goes on to say that working on a new story still brings her much pleasure, perhaps even more than it used to. (Letter at Willa Cather archives in Red Cloud.)

16. Cather does even better here what she had attempted in "Coming, Aphrodite!" There, in formalizing emotion, she made the story seem somewhat cold and remote. Here she retains the necessary distance from her subject and characters without sacrificing warmth and humanness.

17. Quoted from an interview by Eva Mahoney reported in the Omaha *Sunday World-Herald,* 27 November 1926. See Bennett, *World of Willa Cather,* p. 138.

18. The first of these letters to Carrie Miner Sherwood is dated 4 July [1932], the second, 27 January 1934. The Mr. Dillon of the story is drawn from Cather's memories of Carrie's father. (Letters at Willa Cather archives in Red Cloud.)

19. Under the pseudonym, "Henry Nicklemann," Cather wrote a piece for the *Library* called "The Personal Side of William Jennings Bryan." It was published 14 July 1900, after Bryan had been nominated a second time for the U.S. presidency. Though Nicklemann claims to have been present for the "cross of gold" speech in 1896, Cather's biographers agree that she probably was not. As a candidate for Congress from the First Congressional District of Nebraska, Bryan may well have crossed paths with Cather in her student days, however. In 1896 she had written about Mrs. Bryan in what she called a scoop on the wives of the candidates for the *Home Monthly.* A letter to Mrs. Gere of Lincoln, dated 13 October, asks for any information Mrs. Gere might be able to send Cather on Mrs. Bryan. (Letter at Nebraska State Historical Society in Lincoln.)

20. Cather, *The Old Beauty and Others.* All citations from the three stories are from this edition (page numbers are in parentheses in the text).

21. *Not Under Forty,* p. v. All citations are from this edition (page numbers are in parentheses in the text). Sergeant (*Willa Cather: A Memoir,* p. 159) calls this statement of Cather's "paradoxical," for in 1922 "Willa was full of creative ardor, very well, very productive, and steadily gaining in literary reputation." Bernice Slote, in "An Appointment with the Future," p. 45, quotes Moers ("The Survivors: Into the Twentieth Century," p. 9), and agrees with her that "Cather should have said . . . that 'the world broke in two, but I did not.'" Slote says, in fact, that instead of turning to the past, Cather "in one way . . . went strongly into the future." Slote also sees a relationship between "The Old Beauty" and *Not Under Forty,* and suggests that the story is a "fictional comment on the idea stated" in the preface to *Not Under Forty* (p. 43). A major issue in Slote's essay is concerned with Cather as a writer of and for the future, particularly during the 1920s, rather than a writer of and for the past, as some have assumed. For a discussion of

Cather's ambiguous attitude toward the past, see my article, "Willa Cather's Nostalgia: A Study in Ambivalence," pp. 23–34.

22. Woodress (*Willa Cather: Her Life and Art,* p. 257) does acknowledge, in spite of what he regards as profuse nostalgia in the story, that Cherry's "attitude more generally reflects Willa Cather's views than that of Gabrielle, who is an extreme case."

23. The delicate porcelain doll who languished her way through life had never appealed to Cather. For example, in a *Journal* column, 2 May 1897, she openly shows her impatience with Maude Adams' performance in *Rosemary:* "Oh, she is so abominably sweet; such a china kitten, you want to drop her to see if she will break. . . . The pose of a drooping Gibson lover is a pretty one, but in this case it is a reflection on your taste." See Curtin, *World and the Parish,* pp. 437–38. We are also reminded of Cather's comparison between the hired girls and the town girls in *My Ántonia.* The lifeless, limp-jointed town girls were no match for the ruddy, vigorous girls from the country. The same attitude prevails in Cather's newspaper descriptions of her first trip to Europe. As Kates notes repeatedly in his commentary, Cather's abiding interest lay not in the high and refined, but in the common people of character and hard experience. See his *Willa Cather in Europe.* Though she had an eye and a deep appreciation for fineness, Cather was no snob.

24. P. 14. Compare the passages in "The Old Beauty" cited earlier which indicate that although Gabrielle spoke both French and English, she "said nothing memorable in either language," nor did her eyes "glint" or "sparkle."

25. The Charles Street essay, except for the addition of some introductory pages, is essentially the review Cather wrote for Mark A. De Wolfe Howe's collection of extracts from the diaries of Mrs. James T. Fields, long-widowed wife of the eminent publisher. It was published in the *Literary Review* of the New York *Evening Post,* 4 November 1922, and titled "The House on Charles Street." Part I of "Miss Jewett," Cather explains in a footnote, was in large part "originally written as a preface to a two-volume collection of Miss Jewett's stories published by Houghton Mifflin in 1925" (*Not Under Forty,* p. 76).

26. See Lewis's account reported by Kates in "Willa Cather's Unfinished Avignon Story," an essay published in Cather, *Five Stories.*

27. Cather, *My Ántonia,* p. 229.

28. This story is the only one that Cather set on the North Atlantic coast, an area where she spent a great deal of time and where she did much of her later writing.

29. In *Kingdom of Art,* p. 92, Slote describes "Before Breakfast" as "one of the most remarkable things Cather wrote: at the end, a re-affirmation of the beginning." It is also useful to compare the attitudes toward youth expressed here with those expressed by the Old Beauty. Clearly, Cather never lost her appreciation for the young.

30. The attic loft described in this story is the loft of Cather's youth in Red Cloud where the children in her family slept. In a very real sense, this story is a final homecoming for Cather, a return to her own family memories.

31. "Katherine Mansfield," in Cather's *Not Under Forty*, pp. 135–36.

32. See her comment in a letter to the editor of the *Commonweal*, in *Willa Cather On Writing*, p. 12.

33. See Cather, *My Ántonia*, p. 171.

A Selected Bibliography

WORKS BY WILLA CATHER

NOVELS

Alexander's Bridge. New York: Bantam Books, 1962. Originally published by Houghton Mifflin in 1912. Now available in a Bison Book edition from the University of Nebraska Press, Lincoln. Introduction by Bernice Slote.

Death Comes for the Archbishop. New York: Alfred A. Knopf, 1927.

A Lost Lady. New York: Alfred A. Knopf, 1923.

Lucy Gayheart. New York: Alfred A. Knopf, 1935.

My Ántonia. Boston: Houghton Mifflin Sentry Edition, 1961. Originally published in 1918.

My Mortal Enemy. New York: Alfred A. Knopf, 1926.

One of Ours. New York: Alfred A. Knopf, 1922.

O Pioneers! Boston: Houghton Mifflin Sentry Edition, 1962. Originally published in 1913.

The Professor's House. New York: Alfred A. Knopf, 1925.

Sapphira and the Slave Girl. New York: Alfred A. Knopf, 1940.

Shadows on the Rock. New York: Alfred A. Knopf, 1931.

The Song of the Lark. Boston: Houghton Mifflin Sentry Edition, 1963. Originally published in 1915.

SHORT STORIES

Early Stories of Willa Cather. Edited with commentary by Mildred R. Bennett. New York: Dodd, Mead & Co., 1957.

Five Stories: Willa Cather. Ed. George N. Kates. New York: Vintage Books, 1956.

Obscure Destinies. New York: Alfred A. Knopf, 1932.

The Old Beauty and Others. New York: Alfred A. Knopf, 1948.

Uncle Valentine and Other Stories: Willa Cather's Uncollected Short Fiction, 1915-1929. Edited with an introduction by Bernice Slote. Lincoln: University of Nebraska Press, 1973.

Willa Cather's Collected Short Fiction, 1892-1912. Ed. Virginia Faulkner. Introduction by Mildred R. Bennett. (Includes *The Troll Garden,* first published in 1905 by McClure, Phillips & Co.) Lincoln: University of Nebraska Press, 1965. Rev. ed. 1970.

Youth and the Bright Medusa. New York: Alfred A. Knopf, 1920.

PROSE NONFICTION

Not Under Forty. New York: Alfred A. Knopf, 1936.

The Kingdom of Art: Willa Cather's First Principles and Critical Statements, 1893-1896. Edited with essays and commentary by Bernice Slote. Lincoln: University of Nebraska Press, 1970.

Willa Cather in Europe: Her Own Story of the First Journey. Edited with commentary by George N. Kates. New York: Alfred A. Knopf, 1956.

Willa Cather on Writing. New York: Alfred A. Knopf, 1940.

The World and the Parish: Willa Cather's Articles and Reviews, 1893-1902. Edited with commentary by William M. Curtin. 2 vols. Lincoln: University of Nebraska Press, 1970.

POETRY

April Twilights. Boston: Richard Badger, 1903.

April Twilights and Other Poems. New York: Alfred A. Knopf, 1923.

April Twilights (1903). Edited with an introduction by Bernice Slote. Lincoln: University of Nebraska Press, 1962. Rev. ed. 1968. Variorum edition edited by James Woodress soon to be available from University of Nebraska Press, Lincoln.

WILLA CATHER LETTER COLLECTIONS

I have consulted the Willa Cather letter collections at the following archives and libraries, and read many letters housed in smaller numbers at a wide variety of academic and public libraries:

Beinecke Rare Book and Manuscript Library, Yale University, New Haven, Connecticut

Columbia University, New York, New York

Guy Bailey Memorial Library, University of Vermont, Burlington, Vermont

Houghton Library, Harvard University, Cambridge, Massachusetts

Huntington Library, San Marino, California

Nebraska State Historical Society, Lincoln, Nebraska

New York Public Library, New York, New York

Newberry Library, Chicago, Illinois

Pierpont Morgan Library, New York, New York

University of Nebraska Library, Lincoln, Nebraska

University of Virginia Library, Charlottesville, Virginia

Willa Cather archives of the Nebraska State Historical Society, housed in Red Cloud, Nebraska, in association with the Willa Cather Pioneer Memorial and Educational Foundation

Willa Cather's will prohibits quoting from her letters.

BOOKS ABOUT WILLA CATHER

Bennett, Mildred R. *The World of Willa Cather*. Lincoln: University of Nebraska Press, 1961. Originally published in 1951.

Bloom, Edward A., and Lillian D. Bloom. *Willa Cather's Gift of Sympathy*. Carbondale: Southern Illinois University Press, 1962.

Brown, E. K. *Willa Cather: A Critical Biography*. Completed by Leon Edel. New York: Alfred A. Knopf, 1953.

Byrne, Kathleen D., and Richard C. Snyder. *Chrysalis: Willa Cather in Pittsburgh, 1896-1906*. Pittsburgh: Historical Society of Western Pennsylvania, 1980.

Crane, Joan. *Willa Cather: A Bibliography*. Lincoln: University of Nebraska Press, 1982.

Daiches, David. *Willa Cather: A Critical Introduction*. Ithaca, N.Y.: Cornell University Press, 1951.

Edel, Leon. *The Paradox of Success*. Washington: Library of Congress, 1950.

Gerber, Philip L. *Willa Cather*. New York: Twayne Publishers, 1975.

Giannone, Richard. *Music in Willa Cather's Fiction*. Lincoln: University of Nebraska Press, 1968.

Lathrop, Joanna, comp. *Willa Cather: A Checklist of Her Published Writing*. Lincoln: University of Nebraska Press, 1975.

Lewis, Edith. *Willa Cather Living: A Personal Record*. New York: Alfred A. Knopf, 1953.

Randall, John H. III. *The Landscape and the Looking Glass: Willa Cather's Search for Value*. Minneapolis: University of Minnesota Press, 1964.

Schroeter, James, ed. *Willa Cather and Her Critics*. Ithaca: Cornell University Press, 1967.

Sergeant, Elizabeth Shepley. *Willa Cather: A Memoir*. Lincoln: University of Nebraska Press, 1963.

Shively, James R. *Writings from Willa Cather's Campus Years*. Lincoln: University of Nebraska Press, 1950.

Slote, Bernice, and Virginia Faulkner, eds. *The Art of Willa Cather.* Lincoln: University of Nebraska Press, 1974.

Stouck, David. *Willa Cather's Imagination.* Lincoln: University of Nebraska Press, 1975.

Woodress, James C. *Willa Cather: Her Life and Art.* New York: Pegasus, 1970. Bison Book edition, Lincoln: University of Nebraska Press, 1975.

ARTICLES ABOUT WILLA CATHER

Albertini, Virgil. "Willa Cather's Early Short Stories: A Link to the Agrarian Realists." *Markham Review* 8 (Summer 1979): 69–72.

Andes, Cynthia J. "The Bohemian Folk Practice in 'Neighbour Rosicky.'" *Western American Literature* 7 (Spring 1972): 63–64.

Arnold, Marilyn. "The Function of Structure in Cather's *The Professor's House.*" *Colby Literary Quarterly* 11 (September 1975): 169–78.

_____. "Willa Cather's Nostalgia: A Study in Ambivalence." *Research Studies* 49 (March 1981): 23–24.

Baker, Bruce. "Nebraska Regionalism in Selected Works of Willa Cather." *Western American Literature* 3 (Spring 1968): 19–35.

Bennett, Mildred R. "A Note on . . . The White Bear Stories." *Newsletter* of the Willa Cather Pioneer Memorial and Educational Foundation, Red Cloud, Nebraska, 17 (Summer 1973): 4.

_____. "Willa Cather in Pittsburgh." *Prairie Schooner* 33 (Spring 1959): 64–76.

_____. "Willa Cather's Bodies for Ghosts." *Western American Literature* 17 (Spring 1982): 39–52.

Bohlke, Brent L. "Beginnings: Willa Cather and 'The Clemency of the Court.'" *Prairie Schooner* 48 (Summer 1974): 134–44.

Bradford, Curtis. "Willa Cather's Uncollected Short Stories." *American Literature* 26 (January 1955): 537–51.

Bush, Sargent, Jr. "'The Best Years': Willa Cather's Last Story and Its Relation to Her Canon." *Studies in Short Fiction* 5 (Spring 1968): 269–74.

Cary, Richard. "The Sculptor and the Spinster: Jewett's 'Influence' on Cather." *Colby Literary Quarterly* 10 (September 1973): 168–78.

Comeau, Paul. "The Fool Figure in Willa Cather's Fiction." *Western American Literature* 15 (Winter 1981): 265–78.

Ferguson, J. M., Jr. "'Vague Outlines': Willa Cather's Enchanted Bluffs." *Western Review: A Journal of the Humanities* 7 (Spring 1970): 61–64.

Gerber, Philip L. "Willa Cather and the Big Red Rock." *College English* 19 (January 1958): 152–57.

Hinz, John P. "Willa Cather in Pittsburgh." *New Colophon* 3 (1950): 190–207.

Moers, Ellen. "The Survivors: Into the Twentieth Century." *Twentieth Century Literature* 20 (January 1974): 1–10.

Piacentino, Edward J. "The Agrarian Mode in Cather's 'Neighbour Rosicky.'" *Markham Review* 8 (Summer 1979): 52–54.

Schneider, Sister Lucy. "Land Relevance in 'Neighbour Rosicky.'" *Kansas Quarterly* 1 (Winter 1968): 105–10.

_____. "Willa Cather's 'The Best Years': The Essence of Her 'Land-Philosophy.'" *Midwest Quarterly* 15 (October 1973): 61–69.

Seibel, George. "Miss Cather from Nebraska." *New Colophon* 2 (September 1949): 195–208.

Slote, Bernice. "An Appointment with the Future: Willa Cather." In Warren French, ed. *The Twenties: Fiction, Poetry, Drama*. Deland, Florida: Everett-Edwards, 1975, pp. 39–49.

_____. Introductions to "Wee Winkie's Wanderings" and an untitled sketch. *Newsletter* of the Willa Cather Pioneer Memorial and Educational Foundation, Red Cloud, Nebraska, 17 (Summer 1973): 2–3.

_____. "Willa Cather as a Regional Writer." *Kansas Quarterly* 2 (Spring 1970): 7–15.

_____. "Willa Cather: The Secret Web." *Five Essays on Willa Cather: The Merrimack Symposium*. Edited by John J. Murphy. North Andover, Mass.: Merrimack College, 1974, pp. 1–19.

Sullivan, Patrick J. "Willa Cather's Southwest." *Western American Literature* 7 (Spring 1972): 25–37.

OTHER SOURCES CITED

Mahoney, Eva. "Interview with Willa Cather." *Omaha Sunday World Herald*. 27 November 1926.

Putt, S. Gorley. *Henry James: A Reader's Guide*. Ithaca: Cornell University Press, 1967.

INDEX

BOOKS

BIOGRAPHY

CATHER STORIES AND ESSAYS

CHARACTERS IN CATHER WRITINGS